HEART OF THE
HIGHLANDER: MACKENZIE

BOOK FIVE

HIGHLAND CHIEFS

KATE ROBBINS

HEART OF THE HIGHLANDER
The Highland Chiefs Series
2nd Edition
Kate Robbins

Author Copyright 2024 Kate Robbins
Covert Art: Wicked Smart Designs
Editor: Christine MacPherson
Proofreader: Sharon Pickerel
ISBN: 978-1-990739-09-5

To Barb; a real life heroine writing her own happy ending. You're an inspiration to us all.

CHAPTER ONE

unrobin Castle, Scotland 1435

Toes curling over the outer window-ledge, Muren Grey gripped the shutters tight as she stared into the murky depths below. Her mind raced with images of the torment she would soon face if she did not find a way out of the situation in which her brother, Ronan, had placed her. She raised her head to the sky. Perhaps God would send one of his fastest angels down to carry her away from this mess. A light drizzle kissed her face and, yet again, her silent plea went unanswered.

Her demise was surely predestined.

Muren turned back toward her chamber and stepped off the ledge back onto the cold stone floor. She wrapped her arms around herself for comfort, but nothing would help. In less than an hour she would meet, and be betrothed to, one of the cruellest men in all of Scotland, and no amount of prayer or pleading could prevent it.

No matter how hard she tried, she could not find sense in Ronan's decision. He had always been kind to her, ever since childhood. But to break her betrothal to Rorie MacKenzie, whom she had come to love, and then promise her to the Black Douglas, who was surely Satan's spawn, brought Ronan's motives and his sanity into question.

A loud knock sounded at the door causing her to her jump. Her heavy crimson and gold brocade gown lay on the bed. She had not the stomach to don it, and so now stood in the middle of her chamber with her hair unkempt wearing only her shift. How would the Douglas feel if he saw her in such a state? Perhaps he might cancel the entire arrangement if he was not pleased with her. Muren would not credit the man with empathy for she had heard of all the atrocities bestowed upon new brides at the hands of his clan. She swallowed hard.

Her hand shook as she reached for the door's latch. Lifting it slowly, she whispered, "Who is there?"

"Someone who will give her life to protect you."

Muren swung the door open and let her breath out slowly when her brother's wife, Freya, came into view. Her frown shattered any hope Muren possessed for good news.

Freya stepped into the chamber and closed the door behind her. Pulling Muren into an embrace, she said, "He has arrived."

Icicles of dread clawed at Muren's insides until she was certain she would lose her wits and her consciousness. "Why is he doing this, Freya? What have I done to vex him so that he must punish me like this?"

"Would you believe me if I told you that it has nothing to do with you?"

Muren pulled back so she could see her sister-in-law's eyes. "No. Considering my life is the coveted prize in these barterings of his. Does he not realize who this man is?"

"I am on your side in this, Muren. You must believe me when I say that I have ranted and raved at him for days since he told me of this madness."

2

"And what did he tell you?"

"He said only that he is caught in a position which does not afford him any other option but to comply with this demand."

"Demand from whom?"

"From King James."

"But why?" Muren raised her arms in the air. "How did I manage to become ensnarled in the king's business? Who am I to him?"

Freya shook her head. "Like so many of us, unfortunately, we are too often used as barter to increase the position of the men around us."

"But you changed your fate, Freya. I recall it was originally you who were to marry my Rorie."

"Aye, but mine and Ronan's need for the other could not be denied. Marrying another surely would have killed me."

A lump formed in Muren's throat and she swallowed hard. "That is how I feel."

Freya frowned. "You're right. How can I expect you to accept that which I could not?" Freya's brows knit. "I am certain there must be a logical way out of this."

"Freya, if there was, do you not think we would have found it by now? I must either present myself to the Douglas or leave, and considering the fact that he is already here, it would not be easy for that to happen, would it?"

Shouts from outside drew Muren's attention to the window. "Do you think Ronan has refused him entry after all?"

"I do not know, but from the sound of it, someone is vexed."

From her chamber at the back of the third floor of Dunrobin, Muren could only see the ocean. But the din of men shouting from another side of the castle was unmistakable. "Should we go below to see what passes?"

Freya went to Muren's chest and pulled out a plain grey woollen gown Muren had not worn since coming to Dunrobin years earlier. Freya threw it at her and then pulled out her old black cloak. "Put these on, and we will use the passageways to get as close as we can."

Muren slipped the gown over her head and while Freya fastened the ties, straightened up her long braid. Her heart beat wildly in her chest as the shouting from outside grew louder and was now accompanied by the clang of metal on metal. Was Ronan fighting the Douglas? If so, Freya was right. They needed to find out exactly what was going on and the last place she should be was in her chamber. If the Douglas won, she did not want to be anywhere he could find her.

Freya went to the door and pressed her ear against it. "All quiet," she whispered.

She then opened it a crack and peeked out. "This way," she whispered.

The hallways were empty, and so they crossed and slipped into an alcove doubling as a hidden entrance to a series of secret passageways running all through the castle.

Muren's eyes adjusted quickly to the dark. She was familiar with this passage in particular and could feel her way along quite easily toward the great hall and a secret guard's chamber. She and Rorie had met in there many times over the last couple of years upon his visits, to enjoy stolen moments.

There were twenty-four steps down to the first landing and then a turn, and then twelve more. The hallway at the end of the second flight of steps veered off into three different directions, but the way to the great hall was in the middle.

"Muren, wait for me!" Freya whispered. "How exactly do you know where you are going with no light to guide you?"

"If I tell you, will you promise not to tell my brother?"

Freya chuckled. "He is my husband, and I love him more than my own life, but I do not tell him everything."

"Very well. Rorie and I met in here a few times when he visited. You all watched us so closely that sometimes we just wanted a moment or two to ourselves."

"I knew it!"

"Hush!"

"I knew it," Freya whispered. "I sensed there was more going on between you than you let on. Oh, Muren, I will not let you marry anyone but Rorie. I do not know how but we will find a way, I promise you that."

"Thank you, Freya. But you have your bairns to worry about. Now we are here. Let me check the chamber first to see if 'tis occupied."

Entering this chamber was not as easy as slipping around a corner. A heavy stone door lay between them and either the means to learning what was happening or being caught.

Muren felt along the wall for the release stone. Finding it, she tugged and released the door's inner lock as slowly as she could. The door popped open a crack; enough for her to peek inside to find it empty.

Letting out a deep breath, Muren pulled the door wide and ushered Freya through. Once inside, she secured the door again. The chamber was only large enough for four men. It was designed for guards to scan for danger while the chief held gatherings in the hall. Muren peeked through an arrow slit. She gasped and then placed her hand over her mouth so as to not give her presence away.

Her entire body shook with the sight before her. Not only was her brother in attendance; Freya's brother was, too, along with her Rorie. By the looks of him, he was ready to tear every man apart.

One man stood to the side of the argument with his arms

folded and a smirk upon his face. His hair was as black as night, and his eyes gleamed. The more Rorie and the others quarrelled, the more satisfied he appeared. The man had the gall to pull up a chair, clasp his hands behind his head, and stretch his legs out and cross them. His grin increased as the mayhem grew around him. A chill ran down her spine at the sight of him, and somehow she knew exactly who this man was.

Her heart constricted, and a tear slipped down her cheek. She would give anything at that moment to have Rorie wrap his strong arms around her. She turned from the slit and squeezed her eyes tight and focused on just that.

Slowly, all the noise in the hall quieted. Muren opened her eyes and peered into the great hall again. She gasped when Rorie's soft brown eyes met hers as he stared at the arrow slit at the exact position where she stood.

≈

*R*orie MacKenzie clenched his fists to keep them from flying. At this point, he didn't care who'd be on the receiving end either. Ronan had caved too easily to the king's demand and the Douglas needed the smirk wiped from his face.

"For the final time, MacKenzie, I had no choice. King James has blocked me at every turn, leaving me with no way to refuse him."

"Since when did you back down from the king or anyone else when it came to those you are sworn to protect?" Rorie asked, stepping toe-to-toe with Ronan. "We had an agreement, and you broke it. Wars have started with less provocation, Sutherland!"

"Do you dare threaten me?" Ronan said. "My sister will come to no harm, and I have the Douglas's assurance of that.

6

It's unfortunate that our agreement has dissolved, but the king assures me you will be compensated."

"Muren is the only compensation I want."

Ronan took a step back and scrubbed his hand down over his face. "I'm sorry, Rorie. There's nothing I can do."

Rorie shook his head. He would get nowhere trying to reason with this madness.

Resting one hand on the pommel of his long sword, he pointed at Ronan with his free hand. "We are not done with this, Sutherland." He then turned to the Douglas. "If you leave here with her, know that every MacKenzie and MacKay will be waiting to retrieve her."

Rorie glanced once more at the arrow slit, praying that what he thought he sensed was not true. Hopefully, Muren knew better than to risk revealing herself. He prayed further that she would find a way out of the castle and away from the clutches of these men. There was nothing he could do for her while she remained here.

"You are not daft enough to side with the MacKenzie in this business, are you, Fergus?" Ronan asked him.

Fergus was a man not to be challenged on the best of days; Ronan flirted with madness to poke that bear.

Fergus stepped forward and looked down at Ronan with a teeth-bared grin. "We've enjoyed peace in the last few years since you married my sister, but know this, Sutherland: I will side with MacKenzie a thousand times over before I stand by and watch you bend over and take it from the king, and then hand your own flesh and blood over to a Lowlander. Rorie has a right to be angry. Whatever course of action he decides on, we will support it."

Ronan leaned toward Fergus. "You do what your conscience tells you, and I'll do the same."

Rorie stepped between the two men. Cooler heads must prevail. Bloodshed would solve nothing at this point, only land them in the king's dungeon at Edinburgh Castle. "Come, Fergus. We will leave this traitor to his decision and his conscience."

With that, Rorie left the great hall of Dunrobin castle empty-handed. He swore he would not do so, but what choice did he have? He had not been able to raise enough men to challenge Sutherland, so he must retreat and find a more reasonable solution. And find one he would. He would die before he allowed Douglas to lay one finger on his beloved Muren. He mounted his horse and tore off outside the bailey toward the road leading west to his clan's seat at Eilean Donan Castle.

"What the hell do you think you're doing?" Fergus asked, riding up behind him.

Rorie slowed to a trot. "What does it look like I'm doing? I'm leaving before one of us gets killed, and where would that leave Muren? She needs my head to remain firmly planted on my shoulders to save her, and your Nessia needs the same of you." Rorie shook his head. "I don't understand what's at play here any more than you do, so the best course of action is to leave while we can and think through our options."

"Do you have any ideas?"

"Nothing comes to mind. Ronan assured me the only thing that would happen here today is a betrothal ceremony, so she's safe for now. A good warrior knows when to retreat, Fergus. You taught me that."

Fergus's grimace lessened. The fact that he said nothing in reply indicated concession to Rorie's point. Fergus's face was still drawn into a frown, mirroring Rorie's feelings to the letter. Staying put and arguing it out would provide no reasonable solution. Rorie had no choice but to retreat and formulate a plan.

Just as he was about to kick his horse into a trot, pressure formed around his heart—a familiar sensation he'd experienced every single time Muren was near. He looked over his shoulder and scanned the balcony on which she often stood after his past visits as they parted. Today it was empty. Perhaps it was just familiarity from the many times he had turned for one last look at this point on the road. Either way, he could not stay, and she could not come with him. Not today. But soon.

CHAPTER TWO

Feeling her way along, Muren hurried back to her chamber, her eyes filled with tears. Rorie had left her to her fate! Her heart ached as she tried to reason out whether to go through with the betrothal now and then escape, or leave straight away. Before she could decide either way, a familiar tingling began at the base of her neck and spread up the back of her skull until an invisible band pressed inward.

"No, not now," she said in a whimper, as she clutched her skull and crossed the chamber threshold.

"Sweet Brigit Muren! Is it happening again?" Freya said from somewhere behind
her.

Muren couldn't tell where Freya was and lacked the strength to focus on anything but the pain in her head. Doubling over the bed, she prayed to God that it would pass quickly this time.

The sensation of her legs lifting from the floor barely registered as she held her head and squeezed her eyes shut. If she stayed perfectly still for the next few minutes, she had a chance of riding this out quickly, but if she fought it, she was in for a long night.

"I will draw the curtains," Freya whispered. "And I'll have some cool water and cloths sent up."

Somewhere in her mind, Freya's words registered as a whisper, but in the throes of her affliction, she could have been on a battlefield commanding an army.

The latch on her door clicked, and it would have been just as well Freya had taken a maul to her. "Please," she whispered, not knowing if she could hear her or not.

"Ronan, you must leave. It's happening again."

"Can't you do anything about it? The Douglas wants to meet her." "Hush, come outside," Freya whispered.

The door opened, and the latch clicked so loud Muren was certain it and the voices would steal her consciousness.

"There's nothing I can do about it!" Her brother's voice pierced the heavy chamber door, pinning her to the bed as though he'd launched an arrow in her direction.

Muren tried to steady her breathing to help her relax, but the pain was too intense. Blackness inched toward her, tugging her downward to a place she had been before; a place she did not belong, but was beckoned time and again. A loud noise she could not discern was her breaking point. She fell backwards into the abyss.

Muren blinked her eyes open as the contents of her belly turned over and spewed from her lips. Kneeling up, she waited until the last waves of her sickness passed. All sound was muffled, like that time she fell into the loch and could not make out what her mother screamed at her, though she could see her plain enough from the stony bottom.

The next time she woke, she was on her back underneath the quilts with a cool cloth on her forehead. She slowly opened her eyes and was relieved that Freya sat beside her.

"How long was I out this time?"

"Hours. You thrashed around more this time than I've ever seen you, and I don't even want to talk about what you vomited." Freya pressed a cup to her lips and bade her drink.

Muren sipped the mead-based drink called metheglin. It likely contained valeria to help her relax and dull the ache in her head. It also likely tasted like horse dung. Not that she knew what that tasted like, but she could imagine.

Muren tried to smile, but her whole body was tender. "Is the hour late or have you drawn the drapes?"

"'Tis nearing the midnight hour."

Muren sensed hesitation in Freya's voice. "What is it?"

Freya shook her head as she reached for Muren's hand. "Muren. You spoke words this time. As though you were speaking another language. I shudder to think what some might assume if they had overheard."

Muren tried to sit up, but her body refused to comply. This was a conversation she was not prepared to have with anyone right now…maybe not ever. The things she saw when the pain came to her were not anything that could be discussed. As she lay back down, flashes of scenes from the great hall earlier reminded her of her situation.

"Is the Douglas still here?"

"Aye, that he is, and none too pleased to be kept waiting. I tell you, the only thing that kept my spirits up was the look on your brother's face when the Douglas toppled a table in his anger."

"Was Ronan displeased?"

"That's one way to put it. I think it finally dawned on him just how serious this situation really is."

"But he is still here."

"Aye."

"Freya, I cannot stay here. I cannot go with him. What if this happens on the road to his home?"

"My thoughts exactly. I have an idea that might just work,

but we would have to move you this night. Do you think you could walk with my help?"

"Aye, I believe so."

Freya helped her sit up. She brought Muren's leather-soled shoes over and slipped them on her feet, then pulled her to a standing position. "Can you manage while I get your cloak?"

Muren wobbled a little but steadied herself. If she were going to escape this madness, she would have to pull strength from the very depths of her soul. Taking a deep breath, she planted her feet as the room spun a little less.

Freya returned from the wardrobe and wrapped Muren in her cloak. "If we leave now, even with your slowed gait, we should make it before dawn."

"To where?" Muren asked.

"Do you recall another time we became invisible in this castle?"

Muren did. Some years ago, the threat to Freya had been very real from Ronan's uncle; not hers, thankfully. She thanked God every day she and her brother only shared a mother. Were it not for aid from the Bishop of Caithness, they may have never survived the carnage Alexander Sutherland had intended.

"To Dornoch then? Do you think the bishop will be able to help us this time?" He'd already extended his influence once in order to help Ronan and Freya, but this situation was different. In order for the bishop to help, he would have to defy the king and Ronan.

"I do not know, but I cannot turn my mind to any alternative. He had said he'd served the Sutherlands once and, since Ronan became earl and secured your lady's title from the king, Bishop de Strathbrook seems like the only logical choice."

"Freya, you do not need to come with me. I know the way

very well. You have responsibilities here that require you more than I."

"I will not let you go alone. Not recovering as you are."

"Freya, I will be much less likely discovered if I go alone. Ronan has guards posted everywhere these days, and I have no intention of being spotted, but it is more likely if there are two of us. You know I am right."

"Aye, I do, but I wish it were not. What if you have another attack?"

"Then I will find a place to hide until it passes. I have been afflicted thusly all my life, Freya. I can do this." Her mother called it a magryme; Muren called it hellfire in her head.

She had no choice. Though the after-effects of her affliction sometimes felt the same as if she had drunk ten tankards of ale, she would find her way to Dornoch.

Freya's expression grew grim. "Very well, but you must find a way to get word to me as soon as you have been received. I shall not share what I know with anyone for as long as I can."

"Thank you, Freya. Make sure it looks like I'm still covered under those quilts, and I will get word to you as soon as I can."

On wobbly legs, Muren walked to the door and listened for signs of movement outside. When she was sure no one was about, she lifted the latch and pulled the door open. Turning once to nod at Freya, Muren slipped out into the darkness of the hallway and crossed it quickly so as to find her way to the hidden entrance before her chamber door closed and consumed the only available light.

Once outside, Muren stood perfectly still so her eyes could adjust to her surroundings. She'd come this way a few times before when running late for mass, so she knew the path to the chapel like the back of her hand.

Only once or twice did she need to pause so that a guard may pass by without detecting her. Soon she was on the road leading south to Dornoch and the bishop. Muren did not like the dark normally, it reminded her too much of the images left with her after her magrymes, but the lack of moon and cloud cover this night aided her in her plight.

Still weak from earlier, Muren stopped to rest regularly, but still made good time.

As the first streaks of dawn crossed the sky, she lightly tapped on the priest's entrance to the chapel.

If God was kind, she would be granted sanctuary.

~

*A*pproaching Eilean Donan Castle, Rorie slowed to a trot. While Kinellen was well located when he and his clansmen went hunting, Eilean Donan was where all important clan business was held. And at this moment, he needed his best people around him to sort this mess out. Upon crossing the arched bridge, Rorie looked out to where three sea lochs met and kissed the shores of Eilean Donan.

While not overly large, this was his home and provided a strategic position should his enemies get it in their heads they wanted to attack. God knew, he'd known plenty of those.

Rorie entered the keep and made his way to the great hall. "Where is my brother?" he asked his steward, Iverson.

"In the armoury, m'lord."

"Tell him he's needed. Now."

"Aye, m'lord."

Rorie filled a goblet with ale and paced. Since his father's passing six months ago, it seemed he'd had nothing but trouble to contend with. Though there was no contest in him assuming his rightful place as clan chief, it seemed many of the decisions his father had made in his last year were a reflection of his failing health, both in body and mind. Rorie had settled more tenant disputes and squabbles over cattle than he thought possible. Unfortunately, he'd never realized just how taxing the chief's position really was until it was too late to tell his father so.

"Who's doing what to whose sheep now?" Ewen MacKenzie asked, leaning against the doorway.

His younger brother by two summers was just about the best war chief he could have imagined, though the man did have an odd sense of humour now and again.

"I wish it were that simple," Rorie said.

"Are you telling me you returned without Muren?"

Rorie took a long draught of his ale. "Aye, that's what I'm telling you. The Douglas was there, and Sutherland would not relent."

Ewen's head had turned the moment Heather, the voluptuous kitchen maid, entered the room to place a large pitcher on the table. When focused, he was a brilliant strategist, but put a beautiful woman in the room with him and the walls could fall down around them.

"And then Sutherland sprouted dragon's wings and flew about Dunrobin until we shot him down with a golden arrow tipped with a bright blue diamond."

Ewen turned back to him once Heather left the hall. "Well, that's that then. What is your plan?"

"Have you heard anything I've said?"

"Aye, I heard it all; Sutherland won't relent and something about a dragon," Ewen said with a grin.

"Ewen, I need your focus here with me."

Ewen smiled. "My head is always in the game, Rorie. You've no need to worry about that. Tell me about this Douglas."

Rorie pulled out a chair as Heather and another of the kitchen maids entered, this time with two trenchers filled with meat, bread, and cheese. He waited until they finished their task and noted they both glanced at Ewen and smiled once they caught his eye. Ewen's hand, midway to his mouth, stopped in mid-air as the lasses smiled at him. The scene got Rorie thinking. Perhaps what they needed was a diversion; something to draw Douglas's attention away from Muren so he could get her safely away.

Ewen turned to him when they were alone again. "So. You were telling me about Douglas."

"Aye, I do not know much, only that he is wealthier than the Stewart King and considered one of the cruelest men in Scotland. He's funded a portion of the king's palace at Linlithgow, and as such, the king is in his debt."

Ewen's brows drew in tight. "Cruel? How?"

"There are those who would suggest that lasses are not well treated under his care and that his first wife went mad from his beatings. The poor lass died just last year from the red fever. Many say Douglas poisoned her to get rid of her so he could begin anew with another young lass."

Ewen cocked his head to the side. "Rorie, 'tis not like you to give credence to idle gossip. Many such rumours have abounded about people we know, and each and every time they've turned out to be falsehoods. Why do you believe the rumours this time?"

"Because this time they involve Muren. Her countenance is gentle, and I fear for her more than I have ever feared for anyone. We cannot let the Douglas take her to Lancashire."

"Put it this way, if you wanted to strike fear into your enemies, would it not behoove you to allow such rumours to exist? Think of all Douglas gains from us fearing him. And what about these lands the king offers as compensation? Will you accept them?"

"No, I will not. I have no interest in warring with MacDonald at a time when our forces are down. We've secured Fergus's aid, and now we just need to unravel this knot to find all the ends."

"'Twill not be an easy task, Rorie. We have no allies in the Lowlands."

"We have few here in the Highlands now as well. Sinclair and Ross have offered their support to Sutherland, clearly wanting to stay on the good side of the king. Whatever happened to the clans sticking together in our time of need?"

Rorie sat back and took in the tapestries around the great hall. The stories they told were of many past victories, including the force of five hundred MacKenzies who fought under chief Ian MacKenzie at Bannockburn. But his favourite by far was of their ships sailing out to sea from Loch Alsh. Rorie loved the ships creaking, the smell of the salt air, and the brisk north wind that would cut you through if you were not mindful. Aye, the sea commanded respect. She could take everything from you or give you bounty, as she pleased.

Rorie sat up straight. "What is it?"

"The Douglas' are Lowlanders."

"Aye, that they are."

"Not seafarers."

"Do you know this for certain?"

"I know every ship builder in the High and Lowlands. None have ever mentioned a commission for a Douglas."

"What are you thinking? We put Muren on a ship? To go where?"

"We don't need to put her on a ship. We just need Douglas to think so."

"And you don't think he'll just pay someone to go find her?"

"Who among those of us who own ships up here do you know who will accept money from a Lowlander in order to let him ravage a wee lass from the Highlands?"

"Good point. Now, how do we get her out of Dunrobin?"

"With a well-crafted diversion."

CHAPTER THREE

$\mathcal{T}$eeth chattering, Muren rapped a little louder on the abbey's rear entrance. She'd made good time, and thankfully, the fresh air and exercise had helped her recovery, though she did hope a bed would be available in the near future.

She'd had much time to ponder her predicament over the hours it took her to walk to Dornoch. More than anything, she could not fathom why Rorie had left. He had always promised her he would protect her. But instead, he'd left. Her eyes burned from the tears she had shed along the road, though they were washed away by the rain as fast as they dropped from her eyes.

She tried hard to push thoughts of him aside while she waited for someone to answer the door. Never in her life had she been more alone than at that moment. Who in this world could she possibly rely on now?

The door opened a crack, and a pale blue eye shrouded in heavy wrinkles peeped out.

"Who is there?"

"Bishop de Strathbrook? I am Lady Muren. Do you

remember me?"

The door opened a little wider, revealing a very plump, grey-haired Robert de Strathbrook. He'd gained much weight since Muren last saw him. Despite the weight, he appeared in much stronger countenance.

"Aye, lass. I remember you. Though I cannot fathom what would bring you to my door at this hour and away from the protection of your most noble brother."

"I seek sanctuary, Your Grace. I wish you to grant me entry and then I will explain everything."

The bishop's jaw slackened, and his eyes grew wide. And then they narrowed. "You request sanctuary here? From whom?"

"From my brother."

"But why?"

"If you will but allow me entry, I will explain it all. I have taken great pains to remain undetected. However I fear the longer I stand in the drizzle on your doorstep, the more likely I will be seen."

The bishop, as if only just realizing where they were, looked around quickly, then ushered Muren inside. He closed the door behind her then bolted it.

"This way, my child," he said, as he led her to an inner chamber housing a small bunk, table, and hearth. "I keep to myself in this chamber these days."

Muren dare not ask why. It was not her business what a bishop did, and she did not want to appear impertinent, especially considering she was asking an enormous service. However, it was most unusual for a bishop to live in such humble conditions.

Bishop de Strathbrook took a seat by the fire and pointed to one directly across from him. Muren rushed to it and stretched her arms out to the fire to warm her hands. She had not realized just how much dampness had seeped into her bones. She pulled her cloak off and let it fall behind her to dry. Her hair was wet, so she spread it out, hoping the heat would dry it before she caught a chill.

"You are frozen to the bone, my child," he said, as he got up to put some more wood on the fire. He then collected two silver goblets and a pitcher from the table. "Did you walk here from Dunrobin?"

"Aye, Your Grace," she said as she accepted the goblet. The crimson liquid was sweet with a tangy aftertaste. Wine. She'd heard of it but had never tried it before.

Ronan only served ale and mead at his table.

"Are you hungry?" he asked, moving back to the table to lift a cloth from a trencher. "I have some bread and cheese left from my evening meal. The lady from the village will not be here with the morning meal for a couple of hours yet."

Muren accepted some bread and chewed slowly while she thought about what to say to him. Only now did she realize the delicate situation in which she placed him.

There was no way she expected Freya to remain quiet forever regarding her whereabouts, so at some point, Ronan would come hammering on the bishop's door. What did she expect him to do? Her thoughts briefly returned to Rorie abandoning her, but she shut them down.

"I thank you, Your Grace. I am quite troubled and did not know where else to turn." She wrung her hands and gulped air as she tried to collect her thoughts.

"Take your time, Muren. You are safe here and have my protection. Whatever you tell me will remain between God and us."

Muren let out a sob of relief. If he had turned her away, she truly did not know what she would do. And he still might yet once he learned of her plight and the inherent danger to himself and his priests for harbouring her.

Drawing a deep breath, she sat up a little straighter

hoping she might find courage. "You may recall some time ago, I was betrothed to Rorie MacKenzie."

"Aye, I remember it well," he said and smiled. "He is a good man, and your marriage will do much to ensure peace among the Highland clans."

"I thought so, too," she said.

"Has something happened to MacKenzie? Has he broken the betrothal?"

"No, not him. My brother and the king."

The bishop sat back. "The king? But why would he do such a thing where there is so much to gain in the alliance?"

"That is a question I cannot answer, Your Grace. But the broken betrothal is not why I come asking for sanctuary."

"Go on, my child. Tell me the rest," he said, leaning forward and reaching his hands out to hers.

Muren let him hold her hands. His were large and warm, making hers feel small and frail. She despised the feeling.

"My brother and the king have broken my betrothal to Rorie MacKenzie so that I may become attached to…William Douglas."

The bishop blinked a couple of times then released her hands and stood. "William Douglas? From Lancashire?"

"The very same."

"Well, I can see why you are concerned. The man's reputation precedes him 'ere he travels."

"Do you know him in person, Your Grace?"

"Aye, I have had the misfortune to be in his company at court. The man aims to put the king in his pocket and will not rest until he possesses half or all of Scotland."

"'Tis not his ambition that worries me, Your Grace."

The bishop returned to his seat and reached for her hands again. "I have heard the stories as well, but I do not have any evidence to verify or dispute them. But I can attest to the man's greed and temper. This I have seen first-hand. Sweet child, you are much too gentle in temperament to take on a man of his ilk. What in heaven's name can your brother be thinking?"

"He will not say anything other than the king made it impossible for him to refuse."

"That's not the Ronan I know."

"Nor I, Your Grace. And 'tis my life hanging in the balance of these schemes between men with all the power, whereas I have none."

"And what of MacKenzie? What has he to say about all of this?"

"I have not spoken with him." She drew in a steadying breath. "He has visited twice, and twice left without me. I fear he will not press his interest." Muren lowered her gaze to her lap. She had not realized she'd been clenching her fists. What a gnarly turn of events.

"Then 'tis settled. Muren Sutherland, I grant you sanctuary. You may remain here as long as you wish, or I can have you escorted to a larger abbey to the south, even Holyrood Abbey if you choose, though I suspect you would not wish to be closer to the king or Douglas."

"Thank you, Your Grace. I wish to remain here in this abbey."

"I will make all the arrangements and inform your brother." Muren hadn't thought of that. "Does he really need to know?"

"Aye, it is my duty to inform the family of the whereabouts of those seeking sanctuary so that they may not worry needlessly."

"Does it make me a bad sister if I say I would not mind if he worried a little?"

Bishop de Strathbrook smiled. "It does not. Perhaps my missive could be delayed a day or two."

"I thank you from the bottom of my heart, Your Grace.

My time here will allow me to decide what it is I wish to do and how to make that happen."

"Very well. Now you stay here and warm yourself while I see to your sleeping arrangements. There is another chamber available for a priest in residence, though we have not had one of those in a long time. I suggest you remain unseen for the time being. No need to draw unwanted attention."

When he left, Muren leaned back in the chair. At least the immediate threat was over. Now she could turn her mind to prayer and meditation and what she could do from this point onward.

$\approx$

*R*aising his arms to the crowd seated around the table, Rorie waited until the din in the hall settled. He'd called on his war council to discuss their options for removing Muren from Dunrobin. He'd already decided he would hide her at Eilean Donan.

There were plenty of empty bedchambers and, considering the castle was on an island, Douglas would not step foot inside it.

"Are ye telling us we're going to war with Sutherland and the king, Rorie?" Hugh MacKenzie asked.

"Aye, if they insist on giving Muren to that monster, we are," Rorie said.

"But we don't have the men!" Connor said from the end of the table.

"We do when you add MacKay and MacDonald to the numbers."

"MacDonald has married the queen's cousin. There's no way he will stand against the man now," Hugh said.

Hugh had a point, but MacDonald had said he would aid, especially since Rorie would not take the man's land.

"We have MacDonald's support in this. He told me so himself. While he may not stand on the battlefield with us, he can help in other ways."

"Like what?"

"Like paying for ships and supplies," Rorie said.

"Are we sailing somewhere then?" Hugh asked.

"Aye," Rorie replied. "We're going to Dunrobin, then we'll hide the ships in the bay on the western side of Rona."

"But that's no place to keep a lady."

"She won't be there. I'll cross to Kinellen and then to Eilean Donan with her on horseback. We'll keep to the old roads and sleep on the ground if we have to."

"So, you mean for us to create a diversion then?" Hugh said with a grin.

"Aye, that I do. And the more bluster you can make while you're at it, the better," Rorie said.

The scheme was elaborate, and much could fail, but with MacKay's men and MacDonald's coin, they just might be able to pull it off.

After the men settled into their appraisal of the plot, Ewen placed their sea map on the table. Pointing to their starting point at Loch Alsh and then tracing his finger around the north of Scotland and back down the north-eastern side, he said, "This is no easy sail, Rorie."

"Aye, but we did it before and for that bastard, Ronan, if you remember."

"I do. How many ships do you suggest we take?"

"All of them? We want him to think we're attacking from the sea. What he won't know is that you and I will go ashore north of Golspie and wait for our opportunity to enter the castle and rescue her. We will head west with her just as he sees our ships in the bay."

"It sounds good in theory, Rorie," Ewen said. "It will take

us a week to sail around to Golspie. Are you sure you wouldn't rather ride across land with the men instead?"

"No. This is a diversion. Ronan knows we do not have the numbers to attack him on land. If he sees our ships, he will think we mean to attack from the beach and so will divert his men in that direction away from us."

"I have to admit, brother, you're getting better at this strategy business."

Rorie smiled for the first time in weeks. He supposed he had the right kind of motivation this time around. "So, now that you know the guts of my plan, it's your job to tell me what I've missed."

"Aye," Ewen said. "Very well, we have nineteen ships, each requiring twenty-four men to sail. That's less than five hundred men and not much of a threat to a man who has an army of two thousand that can be amassed in a matter of days."

"Ahhh, but you forget, we don't need to engage him. We just need him to believe Muren is on the ship," Rorie pointed out.

"And how do you propose we do that?"

"You shall use that charm of yours on one of the maids and have her share an important piece of information at an opportune moment."

Ewen grinned. "I hear Sutherland lassies are not so easily charmed."

"I'm certain you will have a grand time finding out."

With that, Rorie left his brother to work out the details of which men to sail in which boat. Sailors were a hearty lot, but not all were of the same temperament, so it was important to select the crews carefully. This was where Ewen excelled, on the finer points of the plan. Together they worked well, and there was no doubt Rorie trusted no one more.

Much of the respect he'd inherited came without question, but there was always an element of contention when the chiefship passed from one to another. Ewen had been key in aiding Rorie to work out the sort of chief he wanted to be. And they'd succeeded. The men did not say they would not follow him, but they would not go blindly off to battle either. He respected that. It meant his men were used to thinking and having a voice, something he would honour.

CHAPTER FOUR

*M*uren paced in her chamber. The bishop had been true to his word. She'd been afforded the utmost in comfort as could be found in an abbey, with a chamber, clothes, more food than she could eat, and a warm bed. What more could one wish for? Well, as far as the basic comforts went. Muren spent her days in silent prayer in the sanctuary. Truth be told, sometimes she found herself swept away by the ornate beauty of the stained-glass windows and intricate carvings of the stations of the cross on the inside pillars. She had not felt this much at peace since living with her mother at Strathnaver. Thankfully, she'd not experienced another magryme since leaving Dunrobin.

There was no doubt her affliction was intensified at any time in her life when she was troubled. But something else had washed over her during her time at the abbey. For the first time in her life, no one was telling her what she must do. Her mother had coddled her, especially when the pains in her head overtook her, which was understandable, but Muren had never been given the opportunity to stand on her own two feet. And Ronan had just proved he was not capable of protecting her; Rorie was gone. Who did that leave?

No one except herself.

Well, by God, she would prove to herself and everyone else that she was not frail and did not need nor want their interference. Never again. Muren drew in a deep, steadying breath.

Peace was a fleeting commodity in these times. Word had come the day before from her brother, in response to the bishop's missive about her location. To say he was furious was a mild understatement. The words in his reply were of no use to Muren, since she could not read, but the heat was there as the bishop read them, though he had tried to be kind.

She squared her shoulders and glanced at the door time and again. Ronan had said he would come and collect her before the noon hour. What had taken her hours to walk would surely take him much less on his destrier. The road leading to Dornoch from Golspie was dry and flat. She expected him at any minute, considering it had been hours since the sun had risen.

A light tapping on the door made her jump. Her throat went dry, and the courage she had been working hard to muster melted away.

"Muren, 'tis me, Freya."

Muren rushed to the door and opened it wide. Upon seeing her sister-in-law's kind face, she flung herself into the woman's arms.

"Is Ronan here? Is he much vexed?"

Freya pulled out of her embrace. "Aye, Muren, he is here, and it took a lot of coaxing on my part to persuade him to let me come up here first. He does not know of my part in this, but I stand by you if you feel the need to be fully truthful in what has passed."

"I have no intention of telling him anything about your part in this. Were it not for you, I would be betrothed to Douglas by now. We may not have bought much time, but we have bought some, and we have the support of the bishop as well. Freya, he was mortified to learn to whom Ronan would give me."

"I am glad to hear it, but I am grieved to tell you that Ronan is more determined than ever to see this through."

"Muren!"

Ronan's voice boomed from the sanctuary. Muren jumped again and did her best to hold her composure. Cowering before him would get her nowhere. He'd always had a strong demeanour, but had so far protected her. So, there had never been a time when she felt it necessary to stand up to him. If she did not do so now, she would be right back to where she started a sennight ago, and what good would all of this have done?

Muren straightened her shoulders and set her jaw. Enough was enough. She was not marrying Douglas, and Ronan would not make her. She'd take nuns' vows this very moment if she had to, in order to prove her point.

"I am here," she said in the strongest clearest voice she could muster.

Freya's brows shot up. "Muren, what are you doing? He has his mind made up." "So do I," she said.

Muren marched out toward the sanctuary to where her brother and the bishop waited. She stopped just a few feet before them so she would not have to look up so far, and placed her hands on her hips.

"This is a house of God, Ronan. You disrespect it by shouting the place down looking for me."

Ronan's jaw slacked, as did the bishop's.

"What is it you want?" she asked, riding the brief victory she was awarded from their expressions.

Ronan recovered first. "You will return to Dunrobin at once, and do your duty as I have bid."

Muren almost laughed. Truly, she did not know what had come over her. Even an hour ago she would have done everything he told her to do. What had clicked in her to bring about this change she could not say, but she had not felt this determined in a long time.

"I will do no such thing."

Ronan blinked at her. "You will," he said, though a little less convincing than last time.

His tone fuelled Muren's confidence. "I will only return to Dunrobin on the condition that my betrothal to Douglas is broken immediately, and that I may choose the man I wish to marry when the time comes that I feel ready."

To this, Ronan's jaw slacked again.

"She has meditated on this much in the past few days, Ronan. I can assure you she has done little else besides eat, sleep, and pray."

Ronan turned to the bishop and frowned. "I can see that there has been a change in her. But I did not expect to find an absolute change in demeanour. Are you certain she has not become possessed?"

"Ronan!" Freya stood between Muren and her husband. "How dare you trivialize Muren's new-found courage. It is from the bull-headed decisions you have made that transformed her, not the kindness and compassion shown to her by His Grace. If you do not concede to Muren's demands, I may just take our bairns and move in here with her."

"So, what is this? A mutiny?"

"Aye," Muren said, stepping out from behind Freya. "Call it what you like, but I will not go willingly to the Douglas to endure God knows what horrors, and you are uncharacteristically cruel to expect it of me. What happened to the brother who always swore to protect me? How could he possibly agree to give me to a monster? Considering what our mother endured by your father, I cannot imagine you so heartless."

Muren did not regret her words, even when they appeared to hit Ronan like a blow. He slumped onto a bench and held his hands in his head. Freya rushed to him and placed her arms around him.

"Ronan, what is it? What did the king say to you to make you agree to this madness?"

Ronan took a deep breath and looked up at Muren with despair in his eyes. "Muren, I'm so sorry. King James assured me he would provide an honourable man for the match, and offer sufficient compensation for the MacKenzies, who we all know needed the money since the elder chief squandered away so much in the last year."

"But even when I flatly refused, you became even more determined."

"I agree with Muren, Ronan," Freya said. "This was not just an alternate arrangement you agreed to on a whim. You acted like there was much more at stake here."

"What was it, Ronan? What did the king say to you?"

"He said he would reverse the writ and allow the Earldom to revert back to the crown. He threatened to take it all and to force all the chiefs of the north to bend to his authority. Muren, I am sorry, I would have never agreed to this had I realized he would send a monster to you."

"He is a menace who needs to be reined in," the bishop said.

Muren could not have been more shocked if she tried. The church and the crown did not always concur. However, this particular bishop made it a point not to ruffle royal feathers.

"What are you saying, Your Grace?" Ronan asked. "Do you support me in defiance? Do you know what it will mean to the people up here if the king is allowed to rule from Edinburgh Castle?"

"What does it mean?" Muren asked.

Ronan turned to her with sadness in his eyes. "It means that the king's magistrates will be allowed to be judge and jury in his stead. Men from the south, who know nothing of our Highland ways, imposing laws that make no sense to our way of life."

Muren's belly coiled. So, she was to be sacrificed in order to preserve the way of life of thousands. But what a sacrifice it was! Could she survive it? Could she survive him?

"If I were to go with him now, how long would this peace last? I remember the king promising you that the chiefs could retain their power. How long before he changes his mind again, and then I'm stuck in the belly of the beast for all time?"

Muren clenched her fists. The king abused his right to make decisions for the greater good of the people in order to line his pockets.

"Is it true the Douglas has aided in the construction of Linlithgow Palace? Is that why the king is so eager to help him?"

"Aye, from what I understand."

"So, he pays off his debt with my life, and gains full control over the Highlands in the same deal!" Muren couldn't believe her own words. She had assumed the situation would be dire, and wished now that Ronan had explained this all to her earlier. Not that she had any further clarity on the situation, but at least now she knew all the pieces of the puzzle.

And what of Rorie? Twice he'd come, and twice he'd left. How would he react if he knew all of this? If only he had gotten word to her. At this point, she could not be certain if he had accepted Ronan's decision or not. Either way, Muren was determined to find another solution to satisfy all parties involved.

~

*F*eet splashing through the water, Rorie and Ewen made their way to shore while the rowboat returned to the birlinn anchored offshore. Once on land again, Rorie bent over to catch his breath.

"Come on, old man, we have no time to waste," Ewen said, running up the embankment away from the beach.

"Speak for yourself," Rorie said as he passed him. They'd been playing this game since they were wee lads. The only two boys in a family with eight children, they had often jested that they need stick together to avoid being overrun by the women in the family. All headstrong and brave, Rorie would not dare challenge any of them when they were determined to get their way.

Before long, they approached a heavily wooded area to the side of the castle. There were few ways inside, but Rorie understood from Fergus that the best way was a tunnel leading from the beach. With the best instructions, he followed it and entered the bowels of Dunrobin Castle undetected.

"Where to now?" Ewen asked.

"This way." Rorie pointed to a flight of stairs.

As they neared the top, many voices could be heard. Some men barking orders, but mostly just movement of people working.

"What are we doing here?" Ewen asked. "They'll know we don't belong here."

"Leave that to me," Rorie said and stepped into the larder. "You just find a pretty lass and remember what I told you."

"Who are you?" A grey-haired, stern-looking man asked, stepping toward them.

"We're here about the barley," Rorie said. "The king sent us."

"Aye. We have barley. What do you want to know about it?"

"We need to inspect it for root rot."

"But we grow our own and store it ourselves."

"Is that so? In any case, I need to see your barley and make sure it is dry. The king insists on checking all the castles on the occasion he may visit from time to time, and wants to be sure the ale is not sour."

Rorie could have laughed; the man looked positively perplexed and worried. He hadn't quite worked out what he would say and was surprised himself when he blurted out something about barley. In any case, the inspection would give Ewen plenty of time to put the second part of their plan into action.

An hour later, they were under cover of the copse of trees to the side of the castle, waiting to see if Muren would appear.

"You are sure she could get word to her?" Rorie asked Ewen.

"Aye, she said she is one of the maids who brings food to her chamber."

"Did she say if she fared well?"

"No, she did not, but she did say that she recognized you. Rorie, I fear this may have been too risky. What if someone else recognized you?"

"I cannot see how. I've not spent that much time at Dunrobin."

"Then you have lost your ability to count, along with your wits." Ewen ducked then. "Dammit."

Rorie looked at the edge of the castle. "What is it?"

"It's the lass I was talking to in the larder. I promised her a tryst but assumed we would be away from here by now."

"So, if she is here, then where is Muren?"

"I do not know, but I think we should make haste to the road. We do not have much time before the ships sail around the point."

Rorie was right, but the plan was completely foiled if Muren did not show. "Look! There she is!" Ewen whispered.

Rorie watched as Muren shooed the kitchen maid back into the castle. Ewen let out a deep breath beside him.

"Rorie, where are you?" Muren whispered, whilst scanning the embankment. "I'm up here, love," he said and stood up. He could not help but smile when he saw she was dressed in the emerald gown he loved on her the most; it showed off her flaming locks and delicious curves. By God, no other man would ever touch her.

When she didn't move toward him, he grew wary. "Muren, come up to me, love. We have a plan to get you out of here, but you must make haste."

"I cannot come with you, Rorie."

Christ's teeth, he was too late. Without care for who might see him, he scrambled down the embankment and held her face in his hands. "Muren, tell me I'm not too late. Tell me you have not married that beast."

Muren took his hands away from her face, her expression pained. "You are not too late, Rorie, I am not married to Douglas. But we are set to become betrothed this day."

"Then our timing is perfect," he said and grabbed her hand to lead her away. "We have but a few minutes before the ships arrive and, when they do, we must be on the other side of the castle."

"Rorie, you do not understand. I have agreed to the betrothal."

"To hell, you have," Rorie said and turned back to her. "If

you can look me in the eye and tell me you prefer that monster over me, I will let you go. And I will know if you lie."

Rorie watched as various expressions crossed her face. But try as she might, she could not mask her trembling as he drew her closer. She could not mask the heat in her eyes when he bent low to kiss her.

"Muren, you can come with me willingly, or I will carry you out of here over my shoulder. The choice is yours. You belong to me. I do not know what they have told you in order to coerce you into this business, but I can say without a doubt you will marry him over my dead body."

He watched as she warred with herself. Finally, after a couple of minutes, she tugged on her arm so that he would release it. When he did, she squared her shoulders and climbed up the embankment with no help from him. Not that she was incapable, but this change in her was notable, and not unwelcome. Rorie could not wait to find out what had brought it on.

Muren fell silent as they made their way to the road leading west. When they were well away from Dunrobin and on the road to Kinellen, he stopped her and lifted her chin so that she would look into his eyes.

"When we reach Eilean Donan, we will talk about what you've been put through, I promise you that. But for now, we need to make certain haste. I will not rest until you are safely behind the castle walls and away from this madness."

"Aye, Rorie, I will go with you, and then we will talk. And know this, I have a lot to say."

Reaching Kinellen was fairly easy. The roads were good and dry, and it was not difficult to hide by the roadside when riders approached. For Rorie's part, he could only assume the plan worked. His men had instructions to stay offshore until the alarm at Dunrobin was sounded upon discovering

38

Muren's absence. Only then were they to pull anchor and set sail for Rona.

Upon entering the keep, Rorie took Muren by the hand and led her to the stairs. Moments later, maids followed with trenchers and pitchers. He'd sent word ahead to have food prepared. They would stay here to pass the night and leave on horseback at dawn on the morrow for Eilean Donan. Rorie would hear Muren out, but he was determined to see this through, and if she were willing to go fully against her brother and the king, by this time tomorrow, they would be wed.

Inside the master chamber, the fire had already been lit, so the chill had been chased away. Rorie led Muren to a table and chairs near the fire and pulled out the one closest to the fire then placed a fur over her shoulders.

She promptly lifted it off her shoulders and placed it on the back of the chair. "Thank you, but I do not need the fur," she said to him.

"Will you take some ale and food, then?" Rorie asked. He'd never felt awkward around her before. Theirs had been a sweet, budding attraction up to this point, but this woman was almost new to him. She appeared to possess a new courage and strength about her that he'd never witnessed before. It was like getting to know her all over again, and he had to admit the thought excited him.

"Aye, ale and meat and bread would please me," she said.

Rorie chuckled. Muren never drank aught but mead. He could not help but wonder if she had been pushed to her limits by the events involving the Douglas. He would not wish harm upon her for a moment, but a part of him was excited by the prospect of this new determination she wore.

CHAPTER FIVE

*C*hewing her food, Muren collected her thoughts and what she wanted to say to Rorie. She would give him a chance to say his piece. Part of her was thrilled he had come for her again, and this time with a definite plan rather than to merely talk to her brother. But Rorie did not know half of the situation yet or what she was about to do in order to preserve the peace, if even for a little while. Had she actually made up her mind to follow through with the Douglas? Mayhap not, but she had certainly intended to talk through her terms with the Douglas before agreeing to anything— with the bishop's aide, of course. Apparently, he was quite open to putting things in the betrothal contract for her benefit as well. It was something Muren was sure never existed before now, though the bishop insisted the French had been using such contracts for centuries.

"You seem much changed," Rorie said.

Was she really that much changed? She had experienced that moment when she realized that no one could champion her cause better than herself, but was her determination really that visible to everyone else?

It was true, all her life having been plagued with her headaches, she'd leaned on others to help her through the weakness and supposed she became accustomed to doing what others expected of her. If only there was a way for her to take control of her headaches, now that would be truly something.

"Am I, Rorie? Or perhaps I am finally standing up for myself in matters that affect me so very directly." She had not tried to sound harsh, though she supposed she could not help it.

"Are you vexed with me for some reason?"

Was she? Logically, she had no reason to be. He had come for her three times, and this last time was successful in getting her away from Dunrobin. It didn't really matter that she had made significant strides by her own convictions. Not that marrying Douglas was wanted. Far from it. What she wanted was the man in front of her to love and cherish her as he had always done. But would her feelings for him survive now that she viewed her world a little clearer?

"I am not vexed with you, Rorie. You see, I have only just returned to Dunrobin, having spent a sennight at the abbey in Dornoch. Bishop de Strathbrook granted me sanctuary after I fled Dunrobin upon your leaving." Muren did not find pleasure in the resulting wince she received from that statement.

"You think I left because I did not want to fight for you?"

"I think the situation at the time was impossible, and so I managed to find a way to change the rules, so to speak. By remaining at the abbey, I was able to secure an audience with my brother away from Dunrobin and Douglas, to ferret out the truth of why he had allowed the king to break our betrothal in the first place."

"And did you discover the reason?"

"Aye, 'tis much more complex than I had imagined. You

see, the king owes Douglas quite a lot of money. In offering me to him as compensation, he was also able to bully Ronan by reversing his earlier commitment to reversing his writ of bastardy, and also of allowing all the chiefs to hold onto their authority. In short, Douglas gets me and my substantial dowry which equals the debt the king owes him, and the king gets all the power here in the north."

"No wonder the man looked like he'd been dragged through the nine levels of hell the last time I met with him."

"Aye, the situation has weighed heavily on him. My brother has aged much in the past two months."

"Why did he not seek council with the other chiefs? We would have all come to his—and your—aide and defence."

"I cannot answer that."

Rorie took her hands in his. The look he gave her was one she had seen many times before when the pain in her head overtook her. She didn't ever want to see that look again. Taking her hands back from his, her heart constricted when he frowned.

"Muren, I tried to help you—help us. I want us to get back to where we were before this, planning our life together. Don't you still want that?"

Did she still want that? Aye, she still loved this man. She gazed at his features, his soft brown eyes and dark-brown hair, his strong jaw and firm lips. He had always been able to make her insides flutter just by looking at her. But could she move forward at this time? Would he wait for her if she asked?

"So much has changed, Rorie—"

He sat back and released her hands. "Are you saying you do not want me anymore?"

"I'm not saying that, Rorie. I do love you, and I want to spend my life with you. But I have only just caught a piece of the strength I truly possess. How can I be sure of that which I

42

am capable if I run off and marry you without standing on my own two feet first?"

Rorie crossed his arms over his chest. It was obvious to her he did not understand. Well, if he wanted her love, then he would have to find a way to understand.

"And how do you propose to stand on your own two feet? If you return to Dunrobin, your brother will marry you off to a Lowlander. He has no choice, as you yourself have described. And if you stay here, I will insist you marry me."

She'd heard enough. Muren stood. "You will insist?"

Rorie stood, too. Stepping closer to her, she had to strain her neck to look up at him, and that fuelled her anger even more.

"Aye, I will insist," he said.

Muren had reached her breaking point with him. She pulled her chair over and stepped onto it so that she was now face-to-face with him. "Well, insist upon this. I will not be going to Eilean Donan with you, or anywhere else for that matter. Where I go and what I do will not be your problem any longer. I do not care who says what or what says who; I would not marry you now if you were to beg me on your hands and knees."

Muren seethed as she met his gaze head-on. His eyes were narrowed and his nostrils flared, his lips pressed into a hard line. "You will not leave this castle or my sight until your brother and I sort out this mess, do you understand?" His voice was too calm. Before today, this would have upset her, but not anymore.

"I ken your meaning quite clearly. Now, let me tell you something. If you had been reasonable, I was willing to let you court me to see if there was something still there between us, but you have proven that all you want is to get your own way without any consideration for what I need. And I will not have it."

43

"You are saying you will not have me now?"

Muren held her breath. Was that what she was saying? Words spoken in the heat of anger could not be unsaid. She needed to choose her next wisely or risk losing him forever, and that was not what she wanted. She only wanted time he did not seem prepared to give.

"Are you saying you will not wait for me to sort through my feelings?"

"If you do not know how you feel about me after all this time, then I do not know if there is any more to say."

Muren's heart squeezed hard in her chest. That in and of itself told her how she felt about this man, but by God, it was not right that he would rather have her a cowering, terrified flower, than a strong woman. As much as it pained her now and would for the rest of her life, she had to let him go.

"Rorie," she said in a whisper.

Before she could say another word, his lips pressed hard against hers. As if to swallow the next words they would both speak, he kissed her as though he would never get another chance. And Muren returned the kiss with every-thing in her very being. She kissed him for all those they had shared before and all those they would never share again. Tears streamed down her face as his tongue swept into her mouth and his arms encircled her. Muren's hands went to the back of his neck to pull him closer. Large arms picked her up and carried her to the bed. Before she could register what he was about, he laid her on the bed and pressed his body over hers. His pelvis pushing into the soft apex of her thighs sent a fire through her the like she had never felt before.

Deeper and deeper his kiss pulled her into him. Their breathing heavy, when he lifted his head to gaze into her eyes, she saw everything there. All the love and torment he felt was all revealed for her to see.

But it did not change a thing. Muren turned her head away and pressed hard against his chest until he rolled away from her.

⌒

*R*orie sat on the edge of the bed. He didn't dare to speak for fear of the rejection he saw in her eyes. Had he lost her so completely then?

"I do not want to lose you, Rorie," Muren said. "I just want us to begin anew."

"And the passion we obviously still share is not enough for you to be sure?"

"I do not know yet," she said in a quiet voice behind him.

Rorie's heart was heavy in his chest. He didn't know what to suggest. "Do you wish to go back to Dunrobin?"

"No," she said.

That one word gave him a sliver of hope. At least she didn't wish to return home. "Do you want to stay here?"

"No."

Rorie turned to her. Kneeling on the bed with her head hung low, she didn't appear to have as much confidence in her new self as she proclaimed, but he was not about to push her in any direction she would not wish to go.

"Eilean Donan?"

With that suggestion, her head came up. "You would let me come to your family home despite my uncertainty? But without a member of my family present, that would not be proper." Though she was in that exact position at the moment.

"If it is your wish, I will speak with Ronan and make the proper arrangements. I only want your happiness, Muren. If it is time you wish, time you shall have. I will court you anew if that is your wish. I will do anything you want."

She smiled at him then, and it warmed his heart. God, how he loved this woman.

Muren moved closer to him and placed her hand on his cheek. "I will return to my mother in Strathnaver."

Rorie's heart sank. He fought back his disappointment as he took her hand in his and kissed it. "I will take you wherever you wish to go, Muren. But do not fight me when I insist on leaving men to protect you. I know you believe this letter of yours would have protected you from the Douglas, but once he finds out you've gone, I trust he will come and claim you anyway."

Her head cocked to the side. "If you had not come for me, I would likely be bound to him right now. Thank you, Rorie."

"My heart is yours, Muren. It will be waiting for you when you are ready."

Tears welled in her eyes. Such a statement put more pressure on her, but she needed to know that his love for her would not change.

"Please take me home now, Rorie."

They travelled north to Strathnaver on horseback in silence. Rorie could not think of what to say to her. She'd made up her mind to do things her way, and he admired her all the more for it. Her mother, Morag, was on the doorstep as they rode up.

"Muren! Why are you here, love?"

Muren dismounted and embraced her mother. "I've left Ronan to his schemes, and asked Rorie to bring me here to you."

"But 'tis not safe for you here. Ronan was here yesterday and told me everything. I expect he will return any time with men to return you to Dunrobin."

"Ronan was here?" Rorie asked. "So, he did not take the bait."

"He said he would have the ships followed, but that if it

was him, he would have used the ships as a diversion. His theory in his mind was confirmed when you did not come ashore and offer terms. Muren, he really does mean to find you and bring you back to Dunrobin to see this business through with Douglas. You had agreed to it, and it is his honour now at stake."

"I will not return there, and I will not marry Douglas either."

Her mother looked at Rorie. He shrugged. What could he say? Even her mother could see the transformation in her.

"I am very glad to hear that, but you are not safe here. Have you two married then?"

"No, we are not married, or betrothed," Muren said.

When she did not offer any further explanation, Rorie realized she wanted time alone with her mother to talk, without him present. And there would be plenty of time for that. Like it or not, both women were coming with him to Eilean Donan now. She could have her space there, and at least he could be sure she would be safe.

"Pack lightly, Morag," Rorie said. "We ride hard to Eilean Donan. If we leave as soon as the horses are watered and rested, we can be there by dawn."

Muren turned to him. "I have not said I will go there."

"No, you have not, and I will give you all the space you desire, but I will not stand by and watch you fall back into a situation with no logical recourse. If your mother accompanies you, the issue of propriety is resolved, as is the matter of your safety."

"I agree with Rorie, Muren. We would be safe at Eilean Donan, and at this point, no one knows where you are. If Ronan goes there, Rorie can say he never saw her."

Muren passed a look between them both. Rorie could tell she was mulling it over. After several heartbeats, she said, "So be it."

CHAPTER SIX

a light drizzle fell sideways as dawn broke while they travelled south and west toward Loch Duich and Eilean Donan. Muren had never travelled this far west before and marvelled at the sharp crags and mountains of Glen Shiel. Out here in the wide-open expanse of this rugged and wild land, Muren thought almost anything was possible. Her mother had not probed her about her betrothal to Rorie, but she supposed that was because he was within earshot. She suspected the inquisition would begin once they were alone.

They trotted along the road leading to the castle much later in the morning than expected. As they rounded a turn and the castle came into view, Muren's heart squeezed tight. The castle was situated on a small island, which allowed for a perfect vantage point for preventing attack. The stone bridge leading from the shore to the castle had three arches, giving it an almost whimsical appearance, though she realized it was for structural integrity.

Rorie turned toward her with a smile. "I take it you approve?" he asked. "Aye, that I do. 'Tis a perfect size and perfectly situated."

He grinned at her, revealing his deep dimples. Something clicked within her. She was drawn to this place and to him.

"Come, let us get you two settled. I shall have a chamber set up for you both, and a bath and food sent up."

They crossed the bridge and entered the castle, climbing down several steps then up again. The first place they stopped was in the great hall. Muren took a deep breath. The stone walls were covered with tapestries depicting battles and victories. The fire in the large hearth raged and had two chairs on either side beckoning her to warm herself there. While Rorie gave orders for her and her mother's comfort, Muren took the time to explore the hall.

Heavy chairs with cushioned seats flanked a long wooden table. Atop was a large silver candle holder holding at least a dozen candles. She moved from the table to the tapestries and marvelled at the intricate stitching, especially the ones of their birlinns at sea. She'd never been on a ship, and looking at these images now, wondered if she would have gotten a chance had she agreed to marry Rorie.

But was she refusing? She could find no sensible reason to refuse coming here when her safety was most definitely at stake. But did that mean she would accept him now? She was still uncertain of how she felt, and in fairness to him wanted to be certain of her own self first. Thankfully, he seemed to be willing to wait. For that, she was truly grateful.

"This way, ladies," Rorie said. "Your chambers are just up these stairs."

They followed him to the second level. More tapestries covered the narrow hallways giving the castle a cozy feeling, which she never felt at Dunrobin. That castle was much larger by comparison and always felt cold to her.

"This first chamber is for you, Muren." She entered the room and felt immediately at home, as though she belonged there. With a large four-poster bed and a side chamber housing a wooden tub, Muren smiled as she envisioned herself enveloped in it later.

Turning to the corner of the chamber, she spied a staircase leading up.

Curiously, she moved toward it and looked up.

"It leads to the tower. There's only one other way up there, and that's from the master chamber."

"May I see?" she asked.

"Aye," he said, and led the way up.

Once at the top, Muren's breath caught from the view. Three sea lochs met at the point where the castle stood. All around her was sea and mountains. She drew in a deep breath as the wind lifted her tresses. Surely there was nowhere else with such perfection. She turned to Rorie who was watching her. Only then did she realize her mother had not followed them up.

"You are so lovely, Muren."

Truly, she wanted nothing more than to wrap her arms around him and stay there forever. Instead, she turned her back to him and looked out over the loch.

"Do you sail often?" she asked him.

"Aye, I used to all the time before my father's passing. Now, it seems I have more responsibilities than I know what to do with."

Muren turned back to him. There was a sadness in his expression now. Without thinking, she moved to him and pulled him close. His arms went around her waist, and he buried his face in her hair. His warm breath on her neck sent tingles down her back. God, how she wanted him.

"Rorie!" a man's voice called from below the stairs. "Up here, Ewen."

"I see you persuaded the lass to return here with you," the man said, as he reached the top. "I am Rorie's much younger brother, Ewen," he said as he bowed to her and grinned.

He looked younger and more mischievous than his older brother, and Muren could not help but smile at his jest.

"You are but two summers younger than me," Rorie said with a glare.

Muren could understand the weight Rorie carried, and in truth, he did appear aged since they had first met. The chiefship had added much pressure on him.

"As much as I would like to debate the true difference in age between us, we have bigger troubles."

"What has happened?"

"A scout from Glenelg just brought a message that a large party rides hard toward Eilean Donan. Their banners were undoubtedly Sutherland and another he didn't recognize, bearing a blue lion."

"Any word from our ships?"

"Aye, they are amassed at Rona as you requested, awaiting word from you."

"Send a pigeon. Get them to sail for here immediately."

With that, Ewen tore off down the stairs again.

Rorie took Muren's arm and led her toward the stairs. "We must get you safely in your chamber. I do not want you or your mother to come out unless myself or Ewen comes for you, is that clear?"

Halfway down the stairs, he showed her a door she had not seen on the way up. "If you need to hide, you can do so in here. I will have your mother brought to your chamber so you may stay together."

"Rorie, do you think the Douglas is with my brother?"

"Aye, I do." He stopped when they were back in her chamber, and held her shoulders. "Muren, I know you want to take your time and decide what is right for you. Believe me, I accept that, and I would never suggest what I'm about to if you were not in danger. You know I would wait for you forever."

"Rorie, what are you saying?"

"I am saying that if you thought you could be happy with me, now would be a very good time to decide."

"Would it be fair to you if I were to accept you now to save myself?"

"I know you loved me once. I believe you do still, and I know we could make one another happy."

"If you will have me just to save me knowing I may never love you as I once did, then aye, Rorie, I will accept your offer. But I have terms."

His smile made her insides flutter. How he could disarm her, and she was certain there was no safer place for her but with him.

"I will accept any term you put forth. But we need to formalize this before your brother arrives."

"Do you have a priest in residence?"

"Not often, but I do today."

She smiled. "That confident, were you?"

"Not even a little bit."

"You still have not heard my terms."

"I will when time is not a concern."

Muren had no choice but to be satisfied with that. "Will you tell me all that passes?"

"Aye, Muren. I will tell your brother you are not here, and if he accepts that, then it should be a short visit. If he does not accept it, we will likely be holed up here for a long time."

"Thank you, Rorie, for keeping my mother and me safe."

Rorie cupped her face in his hands and then pressed his lips to hers. His scent enveloped her. She wished they had time to enjoy one another, but it seemed there was always an obstacle in their way. Rorie placed his forehead against hers. "I love you, Muren Grey."

With that, he left the chamber.

Just as the first tingling crept up the back of her neck,

Muren sat on the bed, holding onto the post, closed her eyes and drew in deep breaths. When she opened her eyes, her vision was filled with dancing black and white shapes. Her mother entered the chamber and locked the door behind her then raced to Muren.

"Oh, love, is it happening again?" her mother whispered.

Muren could only nod. She crawled up onto the bed and covered her face with her arms to block the light. Darkness held little relief this time. Sharp pain pierced her skull, more severe than any other time. Within minutes, the sickening blackness enveloped her.

When Muren opened her eyes, she was in a thick wood clinging to a standing stone. It was the place she always saw during these magryme, and she had often wondered if this was, in fact, another realm or simply the conjuring of her unconscious imagination. Either way, her body tensed, and waves of sickness threatened to claim her.

"You have returned to us, my child," a voice said. It was like something very sharp scraping across stone. Muren shuddered.

"I do not wish to be here. Please send me back."

"It is not I who summon you here, Muren. You are drawn to this place, and come here of your own free will."

"Please do not make me look," she said and closed her eyes. The crone with her spindly hair and long fingers had first come to her like this when she was but four summers. Muren had screamed and screamed, but no one came to help her. The crone tried to show her things she did not want to see, and now would be no different.

Bony fingers picked at her gown, urging her forward. Muren knew better than to resist. The one time she had, the crone picked her up and carried her to the pool.

She could still feel the sensation of cold bones digging into her flesh.

Muren knelt by the pool with her eyes shut tight. "Look."

"I do not want to see."

"But you must."

A bony hand pushed Muren's head forward. When she opened her eyes, she was directly over the pool and staring at her own reflection.

The crone touched the water, and the resulting ripple drew new images to the surface. Muren's stomach tightened, and her body trembled. She wanted to turn away, but the crone held her shoulders so that she could not move.

Muren let out a sob as Rorie's face appeared moments before a sword was shoved through his middle. Muren broke free from the crone's grasp, the image of Rorie falling to the ground and clutching his bloody wound burning in her mind.

∼

*R*orie stood at the lower tower and watched as Sutherland and his party approached Eilean Donan. He folded his arms across his chest and waited for Sutherland to speak first. He had no reason to welcome or banish them, and if he wanted to draw less attention to the fact that he harboured Muren and her mother, appearing defensive would not aid in his efforts.

Travelling with what Rorie estimated to be one hundred men, Sutherland and one other rider left them on the shore and crossed the bridge. When he was in the outer courtyard, he lifted his gaze to Rorie.

"Where is my sister?"

"I left her with you at Dunrobin."

"You know very well she is not there, MacKenzie."

"And exactly how would I know that?"

"Because you were spotted with her leaving Dunrobin."

"Really? By whom?"

"By the same young lass who has now been taken out of my service for aiding you in abducting my sister."

"I know not of what you speak," Rorie said. God, were they going to do this all day?

"You have defied a direct order from the king, and as such your actions leave me with no alternative but to declare you an enemy of the crown. I have the papers here signed by the bishop," Sutherland said as he held a parchment aloft.

"I care not for your orders, Sutherland. The king does not have the authority to interfere in a betrothal between two clans unless those clans agree to let him have it. I do not know where your sister is, and I suggest you take your friends and leave my lands."

"I do believe the king would strongly disagree with you, MacKenzie," the other man said as he dismounted and walked toward the keep. Douglas.

Sutherland followed closely behind him. "You will let us in to discuss your options, MacKenzie, or I will return with mine and the king's army to resolve this."

"Do as you see fit, Sutherland. Your sister is not here, and as you so graciously confirmed, I have no hold over her any longer. The king has spoken, and my betrothal to her is dissolved. She, and you, are no longer my concern."

With that, Sutherland and Douglas returned to their horses and mounted. Ewen leaned in close to Rorie. "Did they really think we'd let them in?"

"Say nothing, Ewen. We need them to leave, and then we can act. Did you send the pigeon to Rona?"

"Aye. This latest lot is much better trained than the last ones. I hope to have a returned message by the morrow."

"Good, we will need our ships. When Sutherland is out of sight, go below to the larder and instruct the cook to gather as much as he can spare to stock a ship. We will bring them to Rona and wait it out there."

"You do not think he will attack the castle anyway?"

"Aye, I do, but I plan to ensure Muren and her mother are far away from any of the fighting. We need to get word to Fergus and MacDonald, too. Draft a missive saying only that Sutherland and Douglas intend to attack. They will know what they promised."

As soon as Sutherland was out of sight, Ewen retreated to do as Rorie had asked. Rorie, in turn, went straight to Muren's chamber.

She was propped up in bed with her mother attending her. Her face was pale and dark circles rimmed her eyes. He hated that she had to endure these headaches, and most especially that there was nothing he could do to help her.

"Mother, I am well, I assure you." Then to Rorie, she asked, "What happened?"

"They believe you are here and intend to return with an army."

"So, what now?" Morag asked.

"Now we put you both somewhere safe until this all dies down."

"Where?" Muren asked.

"Rona. I have a hunting lodge there in a secluded harbour. We take one ship which can be easily hidden in a cove and not visible from the sea. The rest of the ships will stay here, so as to not draw attention."

"Will you come with us?"

"Aye, at first. But I cannot leave Eilean Donan unprotected, and if I am not here, it will only make your brother more determined to look for me in order to find you."

"How did this get so complicated?" Morag asked.

"Your son has been bullied by the king to break our betrothal and give her to a nobleman from Lancashire."

"A Lowlander? I cannot believe Ronan would agree to such a thing."

"Agree to it he did, Mother. If it were not for Freya assisting my escape to the bishop, and then Rorie's rescue, I would be betrothed to the Black Douglas by now."

"Dear God in heaven, what is he thinking?"

"The king threatened to claim the noble's power and instate his own magistrates to carry out his rule. Left to their own devices, it would be devastating for all who live here," Rorie said.

"I convinced Ronan, with the bishop's help, to insist upon a prenuptial arrangement."

"What sort of arrangement."

"The Black Douglas has a very ugly reputation for his mistreatment of women." With that, Morag was on her feet. "Then he'll not come near my daughter."

Muren smiled. "You don't have to worry about that now. Rorie will give us safe harbour until this all passes."

"And we are very grateful to you, Rorie. I know this cannot have been easy for you. Almost losing Muren to another, and when you both have grown so close. Thankfully, now you may marry in secret and then the king's eye will have to fall on some other poor unfortunate miss."

"There will be no wedding yet," Rorie said in a quiet voice. He did not want Muren to feel pressured by her mother either, and so hoped Morag would drop the subject.

"Are you saying you will not have her now?"

"Mother, 'tis I who have asked Rorie for some time."

"Whatever for, child? You love him, and he loves you. The wolf is at your doorstep, and this is the way to protect yourself."

"Aye, and I am very aware of how fortunate I am for Rorie."

"There's something different about you, love. I cannot put my finger on it."

Muren smiled. "Aye, I am changed. For the better, I hope. Rorie understands it, mayhap better than I, and has agreed to give me some time to better understand my feelings. I also understand the danger I am in and place him in by waiting. I assure you, I do not do so with a light heart."

"She speaks the truth, Morag. I will wait for her forever, but we will hasten a more permanent arrangement to protect her if the need arises."

"I think you are both forgetting the fact that an army will be here in a few short weeks."

"I assure you, the army can come, but they will not get near Muren, and they will not harm one hair on a MacKenzie's head." Rorie would tear them apart one by one.

CHAPTER SEVEN

*M*uren sat at the stern of the birlinn and watched Rorie as he stood at the bow with one foot on the side. Her body trembled with both excitement and fear. She'd longed to sail ever since she was a wee lass but never had the opportunity until now. In truth, she had always been drawn to, and frightened of, the sea. Her dreams usually contained water in some way or another. Oft times when the pain was too much for her to bear, she felt as though she was falling deep into the ocean with only shards of light above her.

Rorie's back was to her, affording her the opportunity to admire him. His wide shoulders were covered in his tunic and plaid to keep out the cold. His long brown hair was tied back with a single leather strap, and from time to time the wind allowed a few wisps of hair to escape. He was tall and broad and strong, and she loved the feeling of his muscular arms around her waist as he buried his face in her hair and kissed the back of her neck. Warmth spread through her as she recalled the trysts they'd shared. When he looked at her, it was as though he looked into her soul.

Though she could not see his soft brown eyes, she imagined them fixed on the end of the loch to where it widened and then poured into the sea.

There was no doubt she was attracted to, and loved, this man. She considered herself blessed to have found someone who would go to such pains to protect her. Aye, her heart was sound as far as Rorie was concerned. But she had much to resolve about herself. She envisioned a newborn eaglet breaking through its shell and spreading its tiny wings for the first time. How enormous and daunting was the world around it?

But eaglets grew into daunting beasts themselves. What would be her transformation?

Her mother's hand on hers drew Muren back to the situation at hand. "Does the sea still bother you, love?"

Muren looked around at the mountains on either side of Loch Alsh enjoying the lapping sound of the oars as they dipped into the water. Twenty-four men all keeping time, while one chanted to aid them in their effort until the wind in the large sail eased their work.

"No. Like this, I believe I could stay on the sea forever."

She chuckled, "You say that now whilst we remain on the loch, but you may not think so when we are out on the open sea. Though, Rorie says the weather points to a good crossing."

"Mother, I know there is much you would ask me. We do not need to discuss the weather."

"You know me better than I know myself sometimes," Morag said.

"Very well, love. Tell me what happened at the abbey that brought about such a change in you."

"It did not happen as abruptly as you might imagine. I was there for several days and was afforded the opportunity to meditate on many things, namely my constitution and the headaches I've always suffered."

Her mother smoothed a hair that had fallen out of place and frowned. "I used to weep with you when you were smaller."

"I remember," Muren said. "You would sing to me."

"Have the headaches gotten worse?"

"Aye, in the past year, they've gotten so bad that Freya has needed to attend me. Oft times now, I will fall into blackness, and sometimes…" Muren did not know if she could repeat the things she had experienced, but they were too frequent and identical, each and every time she fell into the black.

"Sometimes what?"

Drawing in a deep breath, she said, "I have a recurring dream or vision, I'm not quite sure what it is, but 'tis the exact same every time, and it frightens me."

Her mother's face went a little pale then. "What sort of visions?"

"A crone comes to me with spindly fingers, beckoning me to look into a pool."

Her mother gasped.

"What is it? Do you know anything about this?"

"I—it just seems very frightening."

Muren narrowed her eyes. If her mother knew anything about the horror she experienced, that would actually validate it; she didn't know what was worse, thinking she had slipped into madness or knowing it was real.

"Please tell me the rest. What happens when you look into the pool?"

"I see only my reflection at first, but then I see other people. Some I know, like Ronan and Rorie and you, but then I see other people. Mostly battles and fighting, and it scares me so."

Her mother wrapped her arms around her and squeezed tight. "Oh love, I did not want this for you."

"What are you saying? They're just dreams."

"Aye, just dreams," her mother said.

Muren sat up and pulled out of her mother's embrace. The old Muren would have dropped the subject and never asked about it again. But if she did not probe, then she might never know how to make them stop.

"You believe they are not just dreams."

She shook her head. "No, I do not believe it to be so."

"Why would you say that?"

"Because your grandmother had the sight, love. She had a horrible time of it, too, until I was born. My aunt told me all about it one time after Mother passed on. She would scream out names and later that person would fall ill, so they had to move. There was a real danger of my mother being labelled a witch, so they moved around a great deal. Eventually, once she had children, the sight and the headaches faded."

Muren did not know what to make of it. The old woman in her dreams was frightening to her, but perhaps it would not be so if she understood it better.

"Has anything you've seen ever come true?" her mother asked.

Was she ready to answer that question to anyone other than herself? The second she opened her mouth and let the words out, her life would change forever.

Instead of answering, Muren turned her head to watch the shore pass by. They were nearing the mouth of the loch and would soon be at sea.

Her mother smoothed her hair and held her hand; a silent affirmation that she would not press the question. Thankfully.

A moment later, Rorie walked down between the men to

pass furs to both Muren and her mother, breaking the tense silence.

"It will likely be much colder out here on the open water, so hunker down and cover up well. You're safer back here."

Rorie smiled at her, which warmed her heart. What would he think of her mother's words? He'd witnessed her headaches on more than one occasion and was always sympathetic and gentle with her. But would he be as under-standing if she shouted prophecy? She did not think she could place that kind of burden on him.

"What is it, Muren?" he asked.

He sometimes knew her better than she knew herself. "I am well, Rorie. Just a little wary of the sea."

He knelt and cupped her face with his large hands. "I would never let anything happen to you. Never forget that."

She believed him with every fibre of her being. Surely, no one loved her more. "I know that," she said, forcing a smile.

With that, he kissed her forehead and returned to the bow of the birlinn.

Just then, the wind picked up and blew the sail full out, its ropes straining against the large wooden mast. The ship creaked in protest as the men stroked and chanted. There was something ethereal about the scene as the mists drew near and a light drizzle kissed her face. She smiled as she envisioned them journeying off to another world where men did not barter people for personal gain.

⁓

The sea had always been home to him. As a young lad, his father had taken him out many times. The MacKenzies were a seafaring clan, his father had told him. A clan blessed by the old Norse goddess, Nehelennia herself, and was meant to rule over the waters and protect it from those who would rape her for their own profit.

As it was, his clan only ever took what they needed for themselves. When the Norse lived there, a sacrifice would be made back to her. Rorie had loved listening to his old grandfather tell tales of squid so large it could swallow a birlinn whole, and a whale the colour of the sky on a clear day and that was longer than two birlinns together.

The wind gusts increased out here in the open, away from the shelter of the loch, and from time to time the ship lurched and listed to one side from the swell. Rorie turned back to Muren at those times to see how she fared. Oddly enough, she appeared more at peace here than on land. Perhaps there was something more on her mind than nervousness from being on the water for the first time.

"Heave!"

Rorie loved the rhythm of the men rowing. "Ho!"

It always had a calming effect on him, and this time was no different, but added to that was the fact that Muren was with him. He would ensure her safety on Rona and focus on a way to protect Eilean Donan. While she was near, all he could think about was protecting her, but he was responsible for those whom he had sworn to protect. One way or another he needed to find a way to protect her. The best way to do that was to insist on a marriage. No man could lay claim to her then, and Ronan could not barter her again.

Would she accept it if he pushed his will on her? She had already said she would concede if he insisted there was no better way to secure her. But he didn't want her to concede. He wanted her to be as desperate for him as he was for her. They would make one another miserable if they began their marriage like that.

Rorie mulled it over and over while they sailed to Rona. Many did not inhabit this island on the northwest edge of

Scotland. Fierce and unforgiving, the best part of it was the secluded harbour. From time to time, Rorie had gone there to stay whilst fishing out farther. Instead of travelling back to Eilean Donan, it provided a safe place to lodge when they fished in the summer. There was a time some clansmen from the north had even brought sheep out here to graze for the summer, but that wasn't common anymore.

By the time the sun was just going down over the hills, they had sailed into Rona's best harbour and docked on the wooden stage built many years ago by Rorie's grandfather.

The men secured the ship while Rorie helped Muren and Morag onto the wharf.

He then led them up a narrow path toward the lodge.

Whilst the women looked around, he brought in some wood and lit a fire. Before long, the place was warm enough to get a pot going. Morag saw to the meat they had brought and began making a stew. Muren had been quiet ever since they arrived. Wrapped in a fur and sitting by the fire, she hardly looked at him. At first, he'd been too busy trying to get things in order for them to notice, but as the silence stretched, he began to wonder just what was troubling her.

"Will you walk with me a while, Muren?" he asked.

When she did not answer, he repeated his question a little louder this time. "Oh, aye, I would like that," she said.

"Supper will be ready in an hour," Morag said.

"We will not be long, I just want to show her the waterfall and berry bushes."

He guided her up the path, holding her hand. Still, she was quiet. Oft times before when they were together, she chattered like a little bird.

"Muren, do you trust me?" he asked.

She had been a couple of paces ahead and now turned to him, her brows furrowed.

"Aye, Rorie, you know that I do."

"Then you must tell me what troubles you so." She shook her head and frowned.

Rorie cupped her face in his hands and bent low to brush his lips across hers. "You can tell me anything, love. I will never judge you."

"'Tis only a conversation I had with my mother about my grandmother. Something I did not know before."

"And it matters that much to you?"

"Aye. It makes a lot of difference to me, but I do not yet know what it means."

"Perhaps if you talk about it, you would understand it better. I do not have to say anything. I promise I will just listen."

She smiled at him then. By God, she was lovely when she did.

"My grandmother used to suffer from the same affliction of the head as I."

"She did?"

"Aye, my mother's aunt told her all about it after her death. She said that the pain would be so bad that she would scream out names, and those people would soon fall ill."

An uncomfortable feeling entered the pit of Rorie's gut. Such a thing would be dangerous for any woman. Witch hunts were alive and well in all of Britain, but especially in Scotland.

"Does she think this is linked to your headaches?"

"Aye, she does."

"And what do you think?" He wanted to know, and he would stand by her no matter what she said, but he had to admit he was wary of her next words.

"I do not know what to believe. 'Tis true I have dreams when the blackness overtakes me. The fact that the dreams are exactly the same troubles me more."

"Muren, you can tell me. I will never tell another living soul. Do you have the sight?"

She dropped her gaze to the forest floor and wrung her hands. He'd seen her like this before, and on occasion, it happened just before she took the pain in her head.

"I think I do," she whispered. A moment later, she was on her hands and knees and bellowing in pain.

The sudden onset startled him for a moment, but then he gathered her up and walked swiftly back to the lodge. Kicking the door open with his foot, Rorie called to Morag.

Muren's body contorted as he carried her to the back bedchamber. No need for all hands to overhear her should she cry out.

Placing her on the bed, he smoothed her hair. The window shutters had not yet been opened, and there were not yet linens on the bed, but he managed to quickly locate the fur she had been wrapped up in earlier and draped it over her.

Her whimpering drove daggers through his heart. He would do anything to take this pain for her.

"We must secure her and then leave her in silence. I shall provide a pail in case she loses her belly," said Morag. "Come, Rorie, there's nothing you can do for her right now."

Once back out by the hearth, Rorie said, "Tell me everything you talked about on the crossing."

Morag's brows shot up. "She told you about that?"

"Only a little, before the pain took her. Morag, I cannot protect her unless I know exactly what it is that I'm up against. Does she have the sight?"

"Aye, I believe she does. 'Tis complicated and delicate, Rorie. Not something that's easily explained or easily understood."

"Try me."

"Very well. My mother had it too, and I believe she is

visiting Muren in her visions. She is led to a pool in which she is shown things that have not yet come to pass."

"Muren believes this to be true. Has she seen something to prove this?"

"Aye, I believe she has, but would not tell me about it."

"When she wakes, she must tell us what she saw. And you must tell no one of this. Ever. There are many Christians among us who would quickly label her, and then we would have even worse troubles on our doorsteps than we already do."

Morag nodded. Thankfully, the woman was strong and sensible. The last thing he needed was a fear-mongering, wailing woman on his hands when he felt like he'd just been dealt a deadly blow. When he made plans to bring Muren here, he had no idea in how much danger she really was. Now he was sure he did not want her to step foot back on the mainland until he had a full understanding of her affliction and time to process it, and perhaps consult with old Ada at Strathpeffer. A gifted healer, the woman would most definitely be able to help them figure out what exactly was going on and if there was any sort of remedy they could avail of for the pain.

Right on cue, Muren let out a mighty howl from the back chamber. Rorie rushed to her side. Her eyes were open and staring off into the distance, as though she focused hard on something.

"Muren, I am here, love," he said.

"Hush, Rorie," Morag said from behind him. "She does not hear you. All you can do now is hold her hand."

Rorie knelt by the bed and slipped her delicate hand into his, careful not to disturb her. Formless words tumbled from her lips as though she were praying under her breath. God's teeth, he had not seen her in this much pain before. If anyone ever witnessed this, he was certain she would be burned at the stake by sundown.

"Rorie?" Muren whispered. "I'm here, love."

"Mother?"

"Aye, Muren, I am here as well."

"Ronan?"

A sliver of unease crept into Rorie's stomach.

"I see the bishop, too, but what does it mean?" Muren asked.

She clearly did not even register that he and Morag were present. Rorie had never witnessed this part of her headaches before. She'd had such a violent reaction and without warning that he wondered how she'd managed to keep this so well hidden up until now.

Finally, after hours, and when the first streaks of grey crossed the sky, Muren's body relaxed. Her eyes closed and her head fell to one side. Rorie let out a sigh of relief.

"That was the worst I've ever seen her," Morag said.

Rorie looked up at her and noted the worry in her expression. If her affliction was getting worse, then he had to get help sooner rather than later. Even if he left this very moment, it would be days or a sennight before he could return to her. He prayed she would be well until then.

He stood, kissed her on the forehead, and made to leave the chamber. At the door, Morag caught up to him.

"You look determined," she said.

He opened the door and beckoned her to follow him. They walked down to the ship and, once there, he pulled out a purse.

"This may not do you a lot of good here, but I must leave you with something. There's plenty in there to ward off anyone who might happen by, though to my knowledge naught but a MacKenzie has ever landed on these shores for a long time."

"Where do you go?"

"I must consult with an elder. If there is anyone who can offer aid here, 'tis her."

"Oh Rorie, we have brought so much turmoil into your life."

"No, Morag, that wee lass in there has brought life to me. I will see her healed and protected."

He looked away when Morag's eyes filled with tears. Rorie left four men to guard the women and then ordered the rest to row hard to Eilean Donan. Please God, the wind would be in their favour this morn.

CHAPTER EIGHT

*B*linking her eyes open a crack, Muren took stock of her senses. The pounding in her head had subsided a while ago, but her body had ached so much all she could do was lay there with her eyes closed finding pleasure in pain-free moments.

She jumped when a cool cloth touched her forehead.

"Hush, my love, 'tis your mother," she said in a soothing voice.

"Where is Rorie?" Muren asked.

"No need to worry about him right now, love, you need your rest."

Muren opened her eyes fully and glanced around the chamber. "Has he left already?" She could not help the disappointment that had entered her heart and, no doubt, her voice.

Morag took her hand in hers. "This was the worst I've seen you, love, and Rorie stayed here until the worst had passed. It was torture watching you go through this, Muren. For both of us."

"So, why then did he leave?"

"He said he would go see an elder in Strathpeffer who may be able to help."

"An elder? But what could they do that a healer could not?"

"He did not explain but, Muren, I must tell you that you spoke this time. You cried out in pain, and then you spoke many things this time. Do you remember anything?"

She tried to focus, but her mind was foggy. Images floated across her mind of people she knew, but not in the way she normally saw them in her waking state. The pool. She'd looked into it this time without shutting her eyes, and had seen more than she could process.

"Bits and pieces, maybe. I looked this time. I mean, really looked."

"Muren, you must never speak of this outside of this chamber and tell no one besides myself or Rorie. Do you understand?"

Her mother's voice contained enough urgency for Muren to heed the warning well.

"You said I spoke. Could you make anything out?"

Her mother frowned. "Aye, love. Not a great deal, but still too much. You spoke names and mumbled prayers a great deal."

Muren struggled to sit up then. "I spoke names? Like your mother? Does that mean those people will fall ill, too?"

Muren wished now she had never heard the story. Was all of this real, or just dreams based on what was in her mind at the time her headaches started? She feared she may drive herself mad wondering. And who was this elder Rorie had gone to see? He'd known of her headaches for a long time now. What had changed to make him leave so abruptly?

"It does not mean anything, Muren," her mother said.

Though her frown and furrowed brow made her words less convincing than likely intended. "Now, I want you to lay back and cover up. I will bring you some broth and bread. You have not eaten since yestermorn, and I am sure you must feel terrible."

Aye, that she did. She was broken. Like the golden eaglet at Dunrobin who tried to fly for the first time but fell to the ground instead. Sliding back down underneath the fur, Muren closed her eyes again. A calm warmth spread through her. Though she was concerned about what she had seen this time, the relief she experienced once the pain subsided was always something that gave her comfort.

When she woke again, her mother was sitting by her side, and the light was brighter in the chamber. For a lodge, the chamber was larger than she would have expected. Clearly, Rorie's grandfather wanted this place to be comfortable from when they returned from the sea.

"Sit up now, love, you need something in your belly."

Muren struggled, but managed to sit, then accepted a bowl of steaming broth.

She took a sip and enjoyed the taste of the warm liquid. "What is this?" she asked.

"Broth from rabbit stew I made yesterday."

Once a little of the broth reached her belly, Muren's hunger reared its head with a vengeance. "May I have some more?"

"Aye, love. I will bring in some meat with the next bowl."

Muren, in fact, finished off three bowls of the stew and was much improved by the time she had completed the third. Having been in bed for hours, she wanted nothing more than to find Rorie and convince him to take her to the elder with him.

"Has the ship left the dock?"

"Aye, love. He is long gone; do not fret yourself over him now. We are safe here, and he promised he would return as quickly as possible."

Muren lay back on the bed and stared at the wooden ceiling. The place did seem very well built. Not that she had travelled much, but she had a reasonable idea where Rorie was headed. By her limited estimation, he would be gone the better part of a sennight at least. Until that time, she would go mad with idleness. She sat up and threw the fur off her bare legs. The early morning chill seeped into her bones, and so she quickly spread the fur back over her legs again as she sat at the edge of the bed.

"I pray we have lots of wood for fires," she said.

Morag grinned. "Aye, we have a whole forest full, and four MacKenzie clansmen who would chop it all down to please their chief's lady."

The comment gave her pause. Was that what she was? Had she fully agreed to the betrothal then? Muren shook her head. "No need for an entire forest, but enough kindling to build a fire to break the chill in here might be nice. How is it you are not cold?"

"I'll see to it," her mother said with a smile. "In the meantime, I've laid out a clean shift and gown for you over here," she said, pointing to the wooden chest they had brought with them.

Once the door was closed and Muren was alone, she quickly donned her shift and gown; its ties were accessible so that she could secure them herself. Her cloak was there as well, so she donned it and her soft leather slippers then left the chamber.

Out in the main hall, she was enveloped in the aroma of cooking food and a crackling fire. Her mother busied herself with arranging items into the larder. They had not brought a large amount of food; the men would fish or hunt for them whilst they were there. Since their party was small, Muren found before much time had passed that she was left with very little to do and so decided to explore the island a little.

"Take these strips of cloth and tie them to the trees along your path so that you may find your way back easily."

Muren took the cloth strips, tucked them inside her cloak, and headed out in the direction Rorie had walked with her the day before. He had said something about a small waterfall with a pool for swimming. She could pick out rushing water and so suspected it was not far.

As she walked along the path, she noted the peaty scent in the air. The tree covering was thick, blocking the sun. The ground was soggy, and she suspected the sun did not kiss it often.

A short way ahead, Muren came across a small clearing with a pool and a waterfall beyond. She stopped and took in the scene. Surrounded by a crag on one side and thick trees on another, it was perfectly secluded. The sun broke through the trees here, so the clearing was not soggy and mossy, rather carpeted with lush green grass.

The temptation was too much. Muren stepped to the water's edge and sat with the sun warming her back and started into the pool. Its blackness suggested it was quite deep.

Wind rustled the leaves in the trees, and the air grew thick with the scent of sweet wildflowers. Muren sat transfixed by the ripple on the water until the wind died down and the surface before her calmed, resembling smooth glass.

Something shifted beneath the surface. A fish, no doubt. Muren smiled. She would let the clansmen know so they could come and fetch them for supper. Better yet, mayhap they would teach her how so that she may return her and try herself. Who knows how long she would be here?

The thing in the pool swam closer to the surface now; its shape was odd for a fish.

Muren's breath caught in her throat as it drew closer. Grey, spindly hair surrounded a white wrinkly face. Her body froze in place; she could not move her arms or legs. Her heart pounded hard as the face came as close as possible without actually breaking the surface. Muren's stomach coiled into a knot.

Then it opened its eyes. Staring back at her, she recognized the face from her dreams. Did that mean she was dreaming now, too? Or had she completely slipped into insanity? Mayhap her body still lay at the lodge, and this was a very vivid dream. If God was kind, this was a dream, and she would wake now.

Its mouth moved over noiseless words. An unseen force drew her closer to that mouth in an attempt to discern the message. A faint mumble grew until three words registered.

Hide. Muren. Hide.

Branches cracked from somewhere behind her, drawing her attention away from the pool. Someone was coming. Muren jumped up and ran behind a large rock on the other side of the pool and waited. Before long, two men she did not recognize broke through the trees.

"Are you sure he said she came in this direction?"

"Aye, that's what he said."

"Well, unless she's turned into a fish, she's not here. Come on, let's get back to the ship. This is a waste of our time."

Muren's heart thudded in her chest. Not only did she not recognize the men, but also their plaid was common, with no distinct markings. They could be anyone from any clan. Ronan had enemies aplenty, as did Rorie. She was not fool enough to think that did not translate to her. She had no choice but to follow them and find out what she could.

Please, God, her mother had managed to find a chance to hide.

~

*R*orie knocked on the door to old Ada's cottage. Nothing. He rapped a little harder the second time, then peered in the window. Just as his eyes accustomed to the darkness inside, the door swung wide.

A tiny, frail-looking woman waved him in without saying a word. He prayed she could provide some advice, because there was certainly no way she would survive the trip to Rona to see Muren in person, and he would not risk exposing her.

"Please sit, my lord MacKenzie," she said in a surprisingly strong voice. "What ails you?"

"You know who I am?"

"Aye, my lord. I think there are few around here who do not know who you are." It was reasonable enough. Though he knew who she was and where to find her, Rorie had never needed to lay eyes on the woman in his life. Like his father, he'd been fortunate to have avoided the sickness that befell so many each winter.

"Do you know why I have come to see you then?"

The old woman tilted her head back and croaked out a laugh. "I am a healer, my lord, not a seer. If 'tis the future you want, I suggest you seek out the lass who was grey but now green."

Rorie tensed, his senses rising to full alert. "What do you know about her?" "I know much, my lord."

Rorie leaned in closer. He did not condone bullying tactics, and he would tear off his own arm before laying one finger on this woman, but she needed to stop talking in riddles and tell him what she knew.

77

"You will tell me everything you know. Now."

The woman's eyes widened slightly. "Aye, my lord. I hope I do not offend thee by saying so, but many have overheard her screams. 'Tis not something a wee lassie can hide as much as her mother and brother would like to think so. Servants overhear, and people talk. Some say some terrible things I do not wish to repeat."

"What things?"

"Nay, I fear it will anger your lordship, and I do not wish to poke at a wolf when he's in my den."

Rorie drew a deep breath and sat back. She was right; pressing her or using any forcefulness with her was not his way. He'd come seeking aid, and he needed to get back on track.

"Ada, I have come seeking your help for that very lass. It sounds to me like you already know of her affliction. Surely there is something I can do to ease her suffering."

"Aye, there is much. You must take me to her."

"'Tis a long journey to where she stays."

"And I am stronger than I look," she said and stood. Ada removed her cloak, and what had appeared to be an old, frail body now stood straight and tall as she removed a padded pillow from her shoulders.

"Clever lass."

"Come now, my lord. I may be strong, but I am still old. You will help me collect the things we will need."

Rorie was impressed. The woman moved about her cottage collecting vials and wrapping up dried herbs into cloth as though she had only seen twenty summers.

Her deception made sense to him, and he could not help but smile when she put her fake lump back on her shoulder and then donned her cloak over it. With just a slight shift, she was back to the hobbling old woman again. The transformation complete, he opened the door and waited for her to pass through.

"'Tis been many years since I've been on an adventure, my lord. I believe you may have breathed new life into me."

"If you can aid this, lass, I will give you anything your heart desires."

She stopped and looked at him. The lines around her eyes crinkled. "Be careful what you promise, my lord. You could not possibly know what I desire."

Rorie stepped over to a small carriage he had secured. He helped her step inside and saw to her comfort then mounted his horse.

Flipping the horseman a coin, he said, "Follow me as swiftly as the carriage can manage."

"Aye, my lord. Will she be safe in there?"

"Aye, she will be well, I assure you."

The road leading back toward Eilean Donan castle was straight and clear in very few places. While they could have covered much more terrain if they were all on horseback, there was no way Ada could have managed it. Spry or not, she was much better off in a bouncing carriage than atop a horse trying to hold on.

After a full day's ride, they rode over the bridge at Eilean Donan just as the sun was setting. Rorie saw to Ada's comfort then went to the great hall to seek out Ewen.

"What news of Sutherland?"

"Not much movement so far. Though rumours have spread that the king's army amasses at Stirling. Could be nothing but, knowing that lot, it's always something to watch."

"Aye, I agree."

"Why do you bring the healer here?"

"I bring her to Rona. Muren's headaches have gotten

worse. She may be in hiding for a long time, and I will not sit by and watch her suffer."

"She would not need to be in hiding if she would accept you and take the vows."

"Do not start with me, Ewen."

"I do not start anything. Merely stating a fact. She accepts your protection, yet will not accept that which you give freely and without any demands of her. Do you not see the potential for manipulation?"

Rorie grabbed Ewen by his tunic. The man was only smaller by a fraction, and they'd had many scraps in their youth. If Rorie were to take him on, there would be serious damage done to both of them. He did not wish to quarrel with his brother, but he would not hear Muren's good name sullied either.

"You will not say a foul word about her in my presence or otherwise. Do you understand?"

"Aye, I understand. And I pray to God every night I never let a woman get under my skin the way this lass has gotten under yours. She has you so wound up in her, you cannot see anything else around you."

"Like what?"

"Like the fact that we potentially have a large army heading our way, and you are more concerned about a minor affliction in a woman who refuses to marry you though you have every right to press the matter."

"I will not force her."

"Nay you will not, and I fear we will all burn in our beds once the army arrives."

"Are you afraid, Ewen?"

"No. But we all should be preparing for battle, not collecting dried herbs for metheglin."

Ewen made much sense, and Rorie had no intention of leaving Eilean Donan while under attack. But he needed to get Ada to Rona. With Muren out of harm's way and under her care, he could focus on whatever lay ahead with Sutherland and the king.

"Very well. What do you suggest?"

"Let some of the men bring Ada to Muren. Your place is here preparing for battle. Rorie, you know this to be true."

Aye, he did. Damn Sutherland and damn the king. Rorie looked out over the loch toward shore. There was only one way for an army to reach them and that was through the mountain pass. It would be slow going and, if they had not yet left Stirling, would take weeks to get here. He had time to prepare, so why was Ewen in such a panic to keep Rorie away from Muren?

"We have a few weeks before any army could possibly arrive here. I will accompany Ada to Rona on the morrow and be back the day after that."

Ewen shook his head. "We cannot afford that kind of time. Your place is here. You are needed here."

"Ewen, what are you not telling me? We have weeks before the king could possibly get here unless his horses have suddenly sprouted wings. I do not understand the problem that two days of my absence will cause."

Ewen drew a deep breath. "I did not want to tell you, as I did not want this to influence your decision."

"What is it?"

"Mairi has threatened to run off with MacLeod if you do not secure a betrothal." "What?"

"Aye, she is more determined than ever."

Dear God in heaven. His sister had only seen sixteen summers. MacLeod was twenty summers, and Rorie—though approving of the match—was not prepared to promise her until at least another year had passed.

His two older sisters had been married far too young by

his estimation, and he was determined not to make the same mistakes his father made.

"I will speak with Mairi upon my return."

"And if she runs off in the meantime?"

"Christ's teeth, Ewen. Lock her in her chamber if necessary."

He had enough to deal with right now, and the idle threats of his younger, headstrong sister was not a priority while Muren was in danger and with a battle hanging over his head.

CHAPTER NINE

*M*uren crept up to the back of the lodge. The shutters had been opened in the back chamber in which she had passed the previous night, providing an opportunity to discern any goings-on inside.

Shifting along the wall, she leaned in as close to the window as possible.

Nothing. That meant only one of two things, and she preferred to keep optimistic thoughts in her head. Perhaps she could climb into the window and take a closer look at the hall undetected.

Muren stepped out around the shutter just as a quilt was tossed outside. She grabbed it and held fast. There was no way they would take her like this. Tugging hard, she managed to wrap the heavy quilt over the person, who was quickly subdued.

"Let me go!" The voice was female and familiar. Oh no!

Muren lifted the blanket off her mother and helped her stand again.

"What are you doing?" she asked, her face flushed and her

eyes full of the scolding look Muren had received many times as a child.

"I thought you were one of the men," she whispered. "I saw them at the pool, and came back to make sure you were safe." Her heart was beating like a drum, her hands still clutching the quilt.

"Muren, love, you look positively terrified. What has happened?" "Did you not see the men?"

"There are no men, love. No one is here but us and the clansmen." Her mother took the quilt and placed it back on the bed. She returned to the window and took Muren's hand to guide her inside.

Muren sat on the window-ledge then swung her legs inside. "You are certain there is no one here? We should ask the men." They were real, she was certain of it. An uneasy feeling washed through her in waves. She reached out and closed the shutters, latching them from the inside.

"Muren, there is no one else here. Come out to the front, and we shall talk to the men together."

"They will need to do a search. Rorie should have left us more men."

Her mother took her by the hand and led her to the front room, where the men were eating. Muren's belly rumbled in approval, but her skin tingled as though a thousand needles all brushed against her at the same time.

"Muren says she's seen two other men up behind the lodge near the pool. Have you seen anyone?"

Hugh glanced up first. Thomas stood and moved to the door, quickly followed by Hamish, Connor, and Hugh.

"No, my lady, but we will search them out now," he said.

Hamish unsheathed his sword. "Stay here and away from the windows." They pushed the table against the door and placed the benches on top of it. "Do not open this for anyone."

Thomas unsheathed his sword and crept to the back chamber. "My lady, will you latch the shutters behind us?"

Muren followed her mother to the back chamber. The men slipped out and closed the shutters behind them.

"What now?" Muren asked.

Her mother took her hand. "There is nothing we can do right now but wait for them to search the area. You will come with me and eat something, then tell me exactly what happened and where you were."

Muren sat in the large chair by the fire staring into the flames. While she was very grateful for the clansmen, she would only feel truly safe if Rorie was there.

"Muren, tell me where you were when you saw the men."

"Just up behind there, along the path, is a clearing and a lovely pool. I think mayhap the men swim there when 'tis warm." She envisioned Rorie's thick muscular body gliding through the water, which sent warmth through her.

"They were at the pool or in it?"

She shook her head. "Neither. I was staring into the pool and saw…" Muren lowered her head. She was going mad. That was what was happening here.

Her mother knelt in front of her, looking up into her eyes, and placed her hands over hers. "I am here, love. You are free to say anything with me."

Muren took a deep breath. "I saw the old woman from my dreams." "In the water?"

"Aye, in the place where I usually see my face. Instead, I saw hers."

"Where did you see the men?"

"The woman mouthed for me to hide and I did, just as the men came into the clearing. I think they were looking for me."

"You hid well? They did not sense you were near?"

"No, I hid behind a large rock, and they left once they scanned the clearing."

Her mother sat back on her feet. "Muren, I have been working inside and outside the lodge all morning. I swear I neither saw, nor heard, anyone. If they were looking for you, they would have had to pass by the men and me in order to get to where you were."

"I know. It makes no sense. I am sorry about the quilt. I truly thought you were one of them."

Her mother smiled. "It may be something we laugh at some time, you throwing a blanket over my head to subdue me."

A part of Muren could already see the humour in it. But more prominently right now was the fact that she had seen some men no one else had.

"What if they had come ashore in another cove? Perhaps there are other paths here which allowed them to observe you."

"But that would mean they know what you look like. With my hair up, and bound like this, how would they know I am not you?"

She made a valid point. Her mother's frame was much like Muren's and, with her woollen gown and apron, they could pass as sisters; many had said it in the past.

"I did not recognize them."

Just then a pounding came on the back-chamber window. "My ladies, please let us in, we must make haste."

Muren and her mother dashed to the window and lifted the latch, allowing the men to enter. They bolted the shutters again and then quickly moved the benches and table in the front room. Placing them back where they belonged, they swung the door wide.

"A small row boat is about to make landfall. There are two

men inside we do not recognize. Grab your cloaks. We need to hide."

The two women did as bid. Muren's heart thudded hard in her chest as they raced along the path leading up behind the lodge. Her mother would not let go of her hand, which made running a little more difficult, but the physical contact helped her from feeling like she was about to break apart inch by inch.

After running for what felt like an hour, they came to another smaller cottage hidden behind the moss that had grown over it; it would be easy to miss if you did not know exactly where it was. But they did not go inside. Rather, they walked around to the back of it to find stone stairs leading up.

Once at the top of the small crag, a watchtower came into view. Hugh ushered them inside and bolted the door.

"Quickly now, climb those stairs."

Once the six of them were at the top, the men urged them to sit beside the wall, but Muren's curiosity was piqued. She sneaked a look back toward the cove just as the boat hit the shore. Two men exited the vessel and hauled the boat up onto the beach. From here, she could also see the pool and clearing, and the lodge. Though the watch tower was not large, its position awarded an incredible view. It was surrounded by trees, so where they stood was up at tree level and not visible from the path. The trees then sloped downward, which was why they could view so much.

"Sit back there, and don't say a word, my ladies, please," Hamish said.

She and her mother scooted to the wall opposite the ocean and sat close together so that they may share heat. The air was cool, though the sun would no doubt soon warm them. Her mother lifted her hood over her hair then did the same for Muren. How long they sat like that, she could not have guessed. But it wasn't until Thomas lifted his finger to his mouth that she became aware of the visitors' proximity.

"Looks like an old watch tower," a voice said from below. "Well, go on then, open it."

"I cannot. 'Tis stuck."

Sounds of a body slamming against the wooden door met her ears just as her mother squeezed her hand.

"Get out of the way."

"If I can't open it, surely you cannot."

Moments passed into minutes as the strangers tried in vain to open the door. "Walk around the perimeter. See if there's another way in."

"No, look, there's a keyhole, you daft idiot. And by the looks of it, for a pretty big lock."

"You could have noticed that before we spent half an hour trying to break it down."

"You did not notice it at all. Don't call me daft."

"Come on. She's not here, and I want to get out of here before the MacKenzie gets here."

Muren's heart leapt with joy. Rorie was coming? She looked over at her mother and smiled.

~

*R*orie was out of the ship as soon as he was close enough to the dock to jump.

Helping the men secure the vessel, he then lifted Ada and walked with her in his arms up the path leading to the lodge.

"I am perfectly capable of walking, my lord," she said when they had only gone a few steps.

"'Tis a steep incline up the path, are you sure?"

She pointed to the ground, "Aye. I've not been this high off the ground since I was a wee lass and seated on my father's shoulders. If you keep me up here much longer, I may really lose my stomach."

Rorie set her on her feet as easily as he could.

"I am not as delicate as I look, my lord. I thought you understood that."

"I would not see you harmed," he said. She had been a few shades of green on the voyage over to the island. He would not embarrass her by bringing it up, but she was his responsibility, and he intended to ensure she was looked after.

A warm rush flowed through him. The wind picked up just enough for a familiar scent to reach him. He smiled and turned just as Muren came into view, running down the path.

"Is this your wee lass, then?" Ada asked.

"Aye, that she is." He tried his best to keep the ache in his heart from seeping into his words, but he was never very good at hiding his feelings.

"She does not look ill."

Examining her closer as she drew nearer, he first noticed her beaming smile. His heart picked up a few beats. He was lost in that smile; by God, she was glorious. He never wanted to see aught but that smile on her face for the rest of her life.

"Rorie," she said, a little out of breath by the time she reached him. "I am so happy you've returned."

His body hummed with a need to take her in his arms and make her truly his once and for all. Damn Sutherland and the king. Mayhap they could board the ship right now and sail west. Let the king have it all if he wanted. The only thing Rorie wanted—nay, needed—was standing right in front of him.

Ada cleared her throat beside them, drawing Rorie back to the present. He blinked a few times then returned Muren's smile.

"Muren, this is Ada. She's a healer."

Ada took Muren's hand into both of hers and held them. Upon contact, she jerked slightly. The reaction was brief and would have been lost had he not been watching closely.

Muren frowned. "Have I hurt you, Ada?"

"Nay, lass. But I would sit by the fire with you. We have much to talk about."

Muren linked arms with Ada, and they strolled up the path together, their heads bent low. Rorie could not make out what they said, but he had a good idea Ada was asking her all the questions she'd asked him.

"We had visitors," Hugh said.

"Two, and they came in a skiff," Thomas said.

Christ's teeth! "When?"

"Yesterday."

"Tell me everything," Rorie said. Perhaps his secret hideout was not so secret after all. He'd told no one but his closest men and swore them to secrecy, not that he needed to. He'd trust any of them with his life.

They walked together to the lodge while the men described the skiff, the two men, and their encounter. Rorie's guts coiled at the thought of them happening across Muren. Clearly, they were not MacKenzies or any of his neighbours. With MacKay and MacDonald to the north and south as allies, that only left a few options. They'd quarrelled with MacLeod often enough over this island, and it had changed hands a few times, though in recent years, his father had made a pact with the elder MacLeod. Rorie had not sensed any dispute the last time he'd spoken with the current MacLeod chief. But what would MacLeod want with Muren?

"And you say they were definitely looking for Muren?"

"They said 'she's not here,' Rorie. We took that to mean the lass."

It was a safe assumption. The question now was, were they safe here? With Sutherland and the king likely on his doorstep at any time, Rorie needed to come up with a plan that would protect Eilean Donan *and* Muren. She could not stay there, but he was not so sure she could stay here anymore either.

"Put two men in the watch tower; one with good eyes and one with fast legs. There's another cottage further inland, but I don't think it's in very good shape. Follow the path, and you'll find it easily enough. 'Tis much older and made of stone, so it will need to be opened up and cleaned out in case some wee creatures have been living in there. Take Morag with you."

This whole business was getting ridiculous. If Muren would just marry him, much of this would be resolved. He understood and respected her need for certainty but, by God, people's safety was at risk now. His own people, and those who would be hers, too. If he were to press the issue, what would happen? Would he drive her away, or would it lead to the peace he desperately sought?

Stepping inside the lodge, he watched as Ada and Muren sat together. Muren's hands were palm up in her lap, and Ada stroked them and then studied them carefully.

They both looked up when he entered. "Your wee lass is very strong," Ada said.

"Aye, that she is. But can you help her when the pain comes to her head?"

"I may be able to help a little, but 'tis something she must overcome on her own."

"What does that mean? She has to heal herself? But how is that possible?"

"In her heart, she knows what must happen, don't you, lass?" Muren nodded.

Rorie was losing patience. Couldn't one of them speak plainly?

Ada stood and moved past Rorie with a smile on her face as she left them alone. "Will you sit with me?" Muren asked.

"Aye, but you must tell me what Ada said and what must happen. We also need to talk about this situation. I do not think you understand the full scope of it."

"What do you mean?"

"The king amasses an army at Stirling. 'Tis thought he will ride to Eilean Donan. In turn, I must gather my own forces and that of my neighbours. It will take weeks for the army to march north, but in the meantime, and in light of the visitors here yesterday, I fear you are not safe anywhere."

"Rorie, what are you saying?"

"I'm saying what I have been all along. I understand you need time to be sure, but all of this would go away if you would consent to marry me."

There, he'd put it out there. Her jaw dropped open a little, and her eyes went wide.

"Are you telling me that everyone is in danger of the king's wrath because of me? You're putting that on me? I did not agree for the betrothal to be broken. How can you possibly blame me for the ways in which men use women as barter for their own gain?"

"You are taking my words and twisting them. I am saying that much would be resolved if you would consent to marry me. Douglas would go harass someone else, the king would not bring his army north, and I would not need to hide you."

Muren's brows drew in tight, and her eyes narrowed. "Very well. Get the priest."

"You are vexed."

"I am well beyond vexed. If you believe that our marriage will ensure the safety of everyone, then so be it," she said and crossed her arms over her chest.

He wanted her more than anything, but not like this. Why

couldn't the woman see reason without turning it into some grand drama?

"I did not bring a priest with me."

"Well then, I guess we will have to think of another way to resolve this."

"Like what?"

"My mother and I can make our way west. Surely there is somewhere in Ireland we can live that will not put everyone at risk of being slain by the king, or kidnapped and raped by the Douglas, or hunted by whoever in Christ's teeth's name was here yesterday!"

"Muren, I have not brought this upon you. I have done everything in my power to protect you and allow you the time you need."

"Are you saying I owe you?"

He shook his head and scraped his hands down over his beard. She was driving him to madness. "Why do you twist my words? I offer to love and protect you, and you act as though I have orchestrated the madness around us to make it so."

She opened her mouth to speak but closed it again. He watched as her expression softened before she lowered her head.

Rorie reached for her hand. What used to be a delicate hold now contained strength. Aye, she had transformed, and he gloried in it. But she needed to trust him, not push him away.

"Muren, of all the people in your life, I have never lied to you, nor have I ever pushed you to do something you did not want."

"I know that."

"Then tell me why you won't have me."

She looked up into his eyes; the conflict there nearly broke his heart into a million pieces.

"Do you know what Ada told me?"

"No. But I would like to."

"She said I must bear a child in order for my affliction to cease."

It was what he wanted more than anything. But it appeared to him that she did not.

CHAPTER TEN

*I*n her heart, Muren wanted everything she was being offered. The man she loved more than her own life was sitting before her offering his hand, and with him, she would be happier than anything. But still she hesitated. Ada's words had affected her deeply. She'd said that Muren would need to bear a child in order for all her pain to end. Cold dread had crept into her belly at those words, at the possible meanings.

"Muren, we have talked about the many children we want. Why does this make you hold back? What are you afraid of?"

How could she tell him that Ada had suggested there was truth in her visions? Though he was supportive, it was likely he would try to convince her no one could see the future. Yet she was certain now that it was possible, for she had seen the men in the clearing hours before they had even arrived.

What then was she afraid of? Everything, but mostly her new self. She had never been more assertive in her life, and that may be a good thing, but not to her own or anyone else's detriment.

"I do not want to hurt you, but it seems I shall, whichever decision I make."

"How do you hurt me if you marry me? The way I see it, you will be giving me the greatest gift of my life."

Mayhap she could be happy for a while. God knew the only time in her life she was truly happy was when she was with Rorie. Mayhap the future was not set, and mayhap it didn't need to result in him being wounded. If she married him, he would not need to go to battle.

"Then I consent, Rorie. I do love you, and I do want to be yours."

The smile that spread across his face warmed her to her very core. God, how this man could affect her so.

"Do you truly mean it? No more hesitation?"

She could not help but smile at him when he was so filled with joy at the prospect of their joining. How she longed for peace between them and for those around them. Just for now, she could put her worries aside and enjoy the love they shared. Never did she feel as much alive as when she was with him.

"No more hesitation, I truly mean it. Do you think we will be safe at Eilean Donan?"

"We will be married here, and I will have word sent to your brother. What happens after that we will have to wait and see. While Eilean Donan is very well placed strategically at the moment, no one knows where you are, and I would like to keep it that way until I am certain this is settled."

"So, we will stay here for the summer?"

"You will, aye. I will travel back and forth, as I will need to see to some other family business."

"What do you mean?"

"My young sister wants a betrothal to the MacLeod and has threatened to run off with him if I do not. She is head-strong, but she is too young."

"I am sorry I am causing you added grief."

"No, love. I will do anything and everything to protect you and keep you safe. You are the other half of my heart, and to see it harmed would do great damage to me."

'Twas the same way with her own heart. Rorie's hand still held hers, only now his thumb stroked her skin, sending tingles up her arm. Her body's reaction to him caused her to squirm in her chair. Staring into his brown eyes, she noted how his lips parted, wanting to feel them on her mouth, her neck, her body. It had always been like this between them.

"I will send for a priest," he said with a smile. "I cannot wait to make you mine." His voice was so low that it almost resembled a growl.

Muren's nipples tightened, and her pulse picked up. She longed to discover what the rest of him could do to her, considering what his voice and stroking thumb could. "Aye, Rorie. I long to make you mine as well. Whatever may come, we will face it together." Her words caught in her throat. How she could bear losing him, she did not know.

Her mother entered the lodge then. "You wish to move us farther inland?"

Rorie grinned at Muren. "That may not be necessary now."

"I do not understand? Hamish said I was to accompany them to a cottage and help sort it for us."

"Do you think we will be safe here now?" Muren asked him. He obviously thought that her marrying him would provide a certain level of protection. But was it enough?

"We will need to be sure everyone knows, so they will not come looking."

She glanced at her mother with a grin. "Knows what?"

Muren looked into Rorie's eyes again. There was no uncertainty left. Though she was grateful for the time he'd allowed her, and she still had much to discover about herself, she would have him by her side to explore it together.

"Rorie and I will be wed as soon as we can find a priest."

With that, Morag spread her arms wide and approached. Muren stood and embraced her mother.

"Oh love, I am so pleased to hear it. You will not find a better man in all the Highlands."

Muren laughed. "Are you saying I might find a better man elsewhere?"

"Hey!" Rorie said.

"Well, I hear those Norsemen are quite the sight to behold."

"Enough of that," Rorie said, breaking the two apart. "She said yes, and she's not taking it back or looking at any other man."

"I may look."

Rorie tipped her chin up with his finger and leaned in close enough so that his breath fanned her face. He held her gaze and waited. She loved the way his right dimple was deeper than his left, even when he wasn't smiling. Excitement tingled along her belly as his lips brushed across hers.

"You may, but you will only see me," he said.

Muren blinked a couple of times to make sense of what he'd said. Then she remembered and smiled. He was right. No other man would hold her attention or her interest the way Rorie did.

"Where will you find a priest?" asked her mother. "Skye? Iona?"

Muren had never been to either. "Mayhap we can travel there together."

"'Tis too dangerous. By now, your brother will have scouts placed all along the Hebrides. We've been fortunate enough to escape notice, and I intend to keep it that way. I'll send my men to return with a priest. That should not take more than three days." He picked her up and swung her around. "If I can wait that long."

Holding onto him as he swung her, Muren could almost believe everything would be well. Perhaps it was just a dream, and there was no imminent danger to him or their future child. All she could say with absolute certainty right now was that it felt right and good to be in his arms.

≈

*R*orie walked along the path to the watchtower. If they were to stay here for any length of time, this structure would need to be sound and operational. As he passed the path leading to the pool, he grinned. The next warm day he fully intended to enjoy the deep cool pool with Muren. How he longed to explore her body and bury himself deep within her. He'd known her now for two years, and in that time, had grown to love her, but his passion for her had only intensified. Somehow, the prospect of losing her had fired his need for her even more.

For now, he was satisfied they were away from prying eyes, and that awarded him time to breathe and think of his next move. Hugh and Thomas had sailed with the men to collect their family priest, Father Iain. In fact, the man's counsel would be very much appreciated now. He was devout but possessed an uncommon understanding of the world and a perspective Rorie appreciated.

In addition to the priest, Rorie had called for Ewen as well. He'd left his brother to ensure Mairi did nothing foolish, but if he was to get married, he wanted the only person he trusted with his life—save Muren—to attend.

The only other thing he'd requested was a pair of pigeons. He'd need to build a rudimentary doocot for them, but he needed to communicate if he was to spend any time here and could not afford a three-day round trip each time. Ewen could keep him abreast of any advancement of the king's army much easier that way.

Standing at the base of the watchtower, Rorie noted the carvings in the wooden door. *Hold Fast.* 'Twas the motto of Clan MacLeod. They'd built this watchtower during his grandfather's time when both clans had battled over this land. He supposed technically it belonged to them, but he and the current chief, William the Long Sword, had met soon after his father's death and determined that the MacKenzies could come and go as they chose if they would forfeit their claim. That was a satisfactory deal as far as Rorie was concerned. And it came in handy now since most would not think to check this island as they would think it MacLeod land.

Which begged the question: who were the two men who had come looking for Muren, and why here? Though courtesy would dictate Rorie should send word to the MacLeod, he was not willing to risk discovery. Carrier pigeons were only so reliable and, unless highly trained over similar paths, could be easily intercepted. Or the damned things sometimes just flew off. As it was, he wasn't even sure if this distance was too much. The bird keeper, Bates, was gifted with them, for sure. If anyone could make it work, he could.

Rorie inspected the structure then entered the watch tower. It was only about thirty feet high and its top barely rose above the trees. In a few more years, the trees would need to be trimmed back or else it would afford a view of a random bird's nest.

The stairs on the inside were intact. Surprising for a structure some fifty-odd years old, and unused for much of it. He suspected being surrounded by the trees afforded it a certain amount of protection from the elements.

At the top, he scanned the island before him. He had a

great view of the pool and the cove. He could see the lodge, as well. It had been many years since he had stood in this very spot, and he'd forgotten just how perfect a vantage point it actually was. To the south, he could see Raasay and Skye farther beyond; to the east, he could see the mainland far off in the distance; and to the north and west, the sea.

Aye, he'd keep a man up here and another on the ground. Unless anyone came by darkness of night, or under a blanket of mist, there would be no reason for a surprise visit. That satisfied him enough, and he turned to retreat down the stairs when movement caught his eye near the pool.

Muren broke through the trees with Ada in tow. She guided the older lady to the pool and pointed to it. The old woman shook her head and tugged her hand away then turned to go back the way they had come. But Muren ran around in front of her. He could hear her voice raised but could not make out what she said.

Ada placed her hands on her hips and pointed at Muren's chest. Muren's head lowered and her shoulders slumped. Then Ada stepped out around her and walked slowly through the path's opening in the trees. Muren slumped to the ground and placed her head in her hands.

Rorie descended the stairs two at a time. He ran along the path to the pool.

When he got there, she was still on the ground and weeping. "Muren, what is it? Why do you quarrel with Ada?"

She looked up with tear-streaked cheeks. "'Tis nothing, Rorie. I just asked her to look in the pool and tell me if she saw the same thing I did, but she refused to go near it."

"Why?"

"She said that I need to forget those dreams and live in the here and now, but I can't ignore them, Rorie. They are so very real to me."

His heart squeezed at the sight of her distress. He had never had a dream affect him so. "Perhaps she is right."

Her head snapped up, and she jumped to her feet, nearly knocking him over in the process.

"How can you say that? I cannot just ignore what's in front of me." She marched over to the pool and pointed. "I saw a woman's face in that pool, and I was fully awake when I saw her."

Rorie walked over to her and peered into the depths. As lads, he and Ewen had swum down to try to find the bottom and nearly drowned in doing so. After diving about ten feet, a strong undercurrent had pulled them down, and it was only by the grace of God that the two of them had managed to surface. His father had told them to only swim on the surface and to never dive there again. He had suspected the pool connected to a tunnel leading to the sea.

"Muren, this pool is very deep. There is no way a woman could have been in there."

"I am not saying she was really there. I mean, she was there, but not a living, breathing person, like you and me."

Rorie shook his head. She was not making sense. "And you do not think you lay back and closed your eyes so that you may have dreamed it?"

"No! I've said it before, I was not dreaming." She placed her head in her hands again and sobbed. "I feel like I have lost my wits."

Rorie took her in his arms and tightly embraced her.

"You are not going mad. There has been much happening around you, and you just need some time to let everything settle. Muren, I want you to talk to me, and only me, about these dreams, do you understand?"

"Aye, but why?"

"Love, if you start talking about a woman in a pool who tells you things that have not yet happened, I fear the stakes will be raised before you can blink an eye. People do not want to hear of such things. It frightens them."

"Does it frighten you?"

"Aye, a little."

"Then imagine how I feel, and understand that I need answers."

"I do understand, love, and we will find them together."

She wrapped her arms around his torso and placed her head on his chest. Rorie returned the embrace and placed his chin on the top of her head. There was no doubt this was a messed-up situation. He longed for the day when they could sit by the hearth at Eilean Donan and enjoy a quiet evening, before taking her to his bed and pleasuring her all night. Just her nearness stirred him. But her vulnerability brought out his desperate need to keep her safe and away from a world that would have her on her knees and broken in a fortnight.

Stronger she was; aye, that was true. But there was still much to be cautious about concerning her headaches and these dreams. Or visions. Which they were, in truth he could not say. But the point was, they bothered her and that was cause enough for him to help find some kind of solution.

"Come, love, let us return to the lodge and speak with Ada. I am sure she can make up a concoction to help you relax."

"I do not want valeria or anything else that will dull my senses, but I would speak with her and offer an apology for my poor temper."

"I am sure she will understand. There is much more to that woman than meets the eye."

"That may be true, but she is wrong in telling me to ignore these visions, Rorie."

"You are too close to it to know that, Muren. I'm sure they feel very real to you, but look at it from where I stand, watching you suffer in pain, and then talking about visions and old women in a pool. It sounds—"

"Like what? Like I am mad? That's what I've been saying, Rorie. I feel like I am slipping into my own personal form of insanity and no one can see it, but me."

"You are not going mad. I won't allow it."

She laughed a little then. "And how do you propose to stop it?"

"I will drain this pool if I have to and haul the woman out by the hair of her head."

Muren laughed a little louder and longer. He loved the sound and wished he could hear more of it from her like he used to.

"And what if she gets stuck in my head?"

He pulled her close and cupped her bottom then squeezed, pressing her against his growing erection.

"Then I will have to find ways to ensure only I am in your head." Her expression softened, and her lips parted.

"Kiss me, Rorie. Make me not think."

He needed no further encouragement. Rorie dipped his head until his lips were almost upon hers. He hovered there while she closed her eyes and waited. How far would he take it? They were alone and to be wed in three days. He couldn't imagine anyone would chastise them for consummating their marriage a little early.

Mayhap she needed this place to hold a better memory. Rorie grinned as he claimed her mouth and set about the task of wiping her memory clean of anything but the intense passion they shared.

CHAPTER ELEVEN

*R*orie's mouth on her neck sent shivers down her body so intense she was certain she'd burst into flames. She did not care if anyone happened upon them. She needed him now like she had never needed anything in her life.

Tugging at the belt securing his tunic and his sword, Muren worked to get closer to the body she had longed for and now craved. His mouth found hers again as he undid the ties at the sides of her gown. Once the garment loosened, he grabbed a fistful of her skirt and pulled it upward.

Cool air caressed her thighs, making her tingle and ache in ways she never had.

Sure, they'd kissed before, but never with such a need and urgency. Muren pulled his plaid away from him and tugged his tunic up and over his head, forcing their kiss to break. She spread her hands wide across his muscular chest and upward to the back of his neck to pull him down again. Did she claim him or did he claim her? Did it even matter?

Rorie lifted the other side of her skirt, and in one swift

move pulled the garment off her entirely. Now completely bare, she hesitated.

He placed her gown on the ground and then lowered them both, covering her body with his. As soon as his warmth touched her body, all other thought fled. The weight of him pressed her into the soft grass beneath her. His knee slipped between her legs, and as soon as his thigh made contact with her most private area, she bucked in response.

"God, I want to be inside you now, Muren," he whispered, as though he were in pain.

Slipping his tongue inside her mouth at the same time he slipped a finger inside her, was enough to fire Muren to the point of no return. She writhed beneath him, tugging at his hair and lifting her body to meet his hand as he stroked in a rhythm, which brought about the most delicious and wicked sensations deep within her.

Rorie broke the kiss and then bent low to take her nipple into his mouth. Oft times before, a look or a kiss from him would harden her nipples, but that was nothing compared to the shot of pleasure she received the moment he sucked hard and then put his teeth together very lightly.

Muren's head tilted back as Rorie continued his sweet torture, bringing her to heights she had never imagined possible. He sucked and stroked until finally, her hips lifted just briefly, and she was sure he would have her now.

Instead, he shimmied his arms under her pelvis and buried his face into her womanhood. At the first stroke of his tongue, she cried out, and her hips shot upward. When he pinned her so that she could not move, Muren was sure she could not remain conscious much longer. Higher and higher the pleasure built. Rorie slipped two fingers inside her at the same time as he sucked hard on her bud.

Muren's whole body shook in response then went rigid,

and wave after wave of ecstasy coursed through her throbbing body.

Before the full effect had washed through her, Rorie positioned himself between her legs and thrust. Her breath caught in her throat. She had caught a glance of his enlarged manhood but had no idea just how large he was until he was buried deep within her. The intensity of her climax, coupled with this new sensation of being so completely impaled by him, made her breath catch in her throat.

Then he didn't move. Dear God, she hoped that wasn't it. She was not done.

She wanted more, so much more of him, but did not understand what she needed to do. Instinctively, she moved her hips, causing him to slide out of her a little, then moving again brought him back deep within. Oh God, it was glorious!

"I will not last if you keep doing that."

"I want you to do that. I like how that feels."

Rorie moved inside her. He kissed her deeply as he stroked in and out, building her pleasure again. She clung to his shoulders and tilted her head back, thrusting her breasts upward as he moved faster. His breath came in pants, and he slipped his hands underneath her shoulders and held on. His slow thrusts gained speed, and Muren matched his rhythm. The sound of his flesh pounding against hers, and his own intoxicating scent only heightened the sensations brought on by the maddening feeling of him inside her, thickening and hardening more with each passing second.

Muren's body ached and throbbed for more of him. As though he could not thrust deep enough or get close enough to her. She wrapped her legs around his waist and squeezed tight.

Rorie groaned and pushed deeper into her. She was at the tipping point and marvelled in the sensations racing through her veins. She knew what was to come and ached for it, but wanted to hold here on the brink just for a few more seconds. Then Rorie pulled almost all the way out. She held her breath, knowing that when he entered her again, she would shatter into a million pieces and likely float away on the wind.

Rorie's body tensed above her. "Open your eyes, Muren,"

She did and locked gazes with him just as he pushed back inside her. His stiff erection grew as he tensed above her, sending her over the edge into the pounding waves of her climax. Her body shook in time with his as his additional movements served to heighten her pleasure. Her body squeezed around his erection until there was no energy left in her. She let her legs fall to the ground and her arms fall wide.

Rorie moved to the side and lay flat as well. They both breathed heavy as a cloud passed overhead and a light mist began. Rorie rolled back to her side and wrapped his arm and leg around her. He nuzzled and kissed her neck. She was grateful he did not speak. For there were no words that could do justice to what they had shared. Now she was truly his and he hers.

~

*S*itting up, Rorie was careful not to wake her. She'd given herself to him with such abandon, he knew this was their way forward. They had not just shared passion; theirs was a joining of the souls. For as much as she was uncertain about her own true self, she could not deny what they had anymore.

Rorie donned his tunic and belt. He wrapped his plaid around her and turned toward the pool. It had been many years since he played here with Ewen. Though his father had instructed them to avoid it, 'twas no surprise that they dove from the highest rock nearby.

He sat by the pool, just as Muren had, and peered into its depths. With the clouds passing overhead and the sunlight shining through from time to time, it was fair enough to say one could imagine something in blackness changing.

Leaning in for a closer look, Rorie jumped when a hand touched his shoulder.

Delighted laughter met his ears, and he turned and swiftly grabbed Muren's waist, pulling her in front of him onto his lap.

"'Tis not wise to sneak up on a man whist he is intent on something else."

She smiled up at him as she brushed her fingers over his chest. "Is it not? And what will happen to a lass if she does just that?"

Rorie bent low and nuzzled her neck then kissed a path down to her breasts before sucking hard on her nipple through her shift. Her soft gasp made his loins tighten. He'd have her again before they left. The thought thrilled him.

"I think a lass might find delight in the ways in which she will be punished. Shall I show you how?"

Muren placed her hands on either side of his face and pulled him toward her for a kiss. Her mouth searched his, her tongue seeking, yearning for his touch. He returned it wholeheartedly. Rorie held her head as he laid her back on the soft grass and covered her body with his. He'd known only two women in his time, but neither experience could compare to what he and Muren had just shared.

Stroking his tongue across hers, he pressed his erection against her. He was not sure if she was ready or not so would hold back and let her take the lead, but he prayed he could hold on. Just kissing her was about to drive him wild with need.

He did not have to wait long. Muren tugged at his tunic, and at the moment their kiss broke, he gazed down into her eyes. She was the most incredible creature he'd ever beheld in that moment. Lips swollen, eyes half closed, and hair tussled from their earlier passion, she was a perfect depiction of womanly passion, and he thanked Christ she was his.

Rorie tossed his tunic to one side and lifted her shift. Muren lifted her bottom so he could pull it upward and over her head. He traced his hand down across the side of her breast and farther down to grip her hip. She spread her legs in response and held on tight to his shoulders.

"I want you inside me, now," she whispered.

He'd never seen such conviction in her. Who was he to deny his lady? Rorie grinned and positioned himself so that he pressed against her, but would not enter her. Their earlier passion had been fervent, so he wanted to make sure he was gentle with her this time.

Muren shifted her hips, allowing just the tip of him to slide inside. Her body squeezed around him, urging him forward. It was everything he could do to not pound into her as his body so desperately wanted.

"Rorie, please," she whispered.

He slowly pushed into her, revelling in her tight, hot sheath. His blood pounded in his veins as his excitement built, but he would not quicken his pace. Muren's hips moved upward to accept all of him and, once fully joined, her head fell back in a gasp. The sight of her beneath him, heavy breasts heaving upward, head back with her flaming red hair splayed out around her, with her eyes closed and her mouth open, was his undoing.

Rorie pulled back and then slammed into her. She groaned and gasped. "Yes, Rorie, harder."

God, this woman was his perfect match in every way. Her legs wrapped around his waist as he thrust into her again and again until he felt her body pulse tight around him. He could hold on no longer as his climax washed over him and his erection thickened and his seed spilled into her. Rorie's body shook above her as the waves of his passion lapped through him.

When he was fully sated, he slipped out of her and lay back on the grass, staring up at the sky. He could not help but smile. He'd wanted her from the first day they met, but nothing could have prepared him for this. His mind buzzed with all the ways he wanted to have her, all the places, too. Something told him she would be willing to try just about anything.

Her warm body curled up beside his. She slid her arm and leg over him and placed her head on his shoulder. Rorie stroked her arm and side, and let his eyes close. This very moment was the most relaxed he'd ever been in his life, and he was certain he could stay like this forever.

A cool breeze made him open his eyes. When he looked up, dark clouds now covered the sky. Muren breathed deeply beside him and, though he hated to wake her, he did not want them to get caught in the rain.

Sitting up, he kissed her cheek and said, "Muren, you must wake. It's going to rain. Come on, love, wake up."

She blinked her eyes open a little then looked up. Upon seeing the same dark sky, she turned to him with a worried look. "We must return straight away."

"Aye, love. Are you well?"

She paused for a moment and then smiled at him. "This is the happiest I've ever been in my life."

"Then why do you look so sad?"

"I am not sad," she said.

"You're still thinking about what Ada said, aren't you?"

"I cannot help it. But I will try, Rorie. For you."

He stood and helped her up. Donning his tunic quickly,

he then set about to aide her. He was not the most adept at women's clothing, but he fared well enough so that she was dressed and they were moving toward the path as the first drop of rain fell.

By the time they reached the lodge, the skies had opened, and they were satched to the bone.

"Where have you been?" Morag asked as they entered the lodge. "I've been worried sick."

"We were walking and exploring the area around the pool and the watch tower," Rorie said.

"Well, you're both soaked, so come, Muren. You need to get out of those wet clothes."

As Muren and Morag retreated to the back chamber, Rorie stood by the fire to dry himself. He stared into the flames and thought about what he and Muren had shared. She was his wife now by natural law and would be by God's law in the coming days. He intended to ensure she was not bothered by anyone again. He was not sure how he would manage it, but he was also determined that these dreams of hers would cease to steal her peace. Surely Ada could do something for her. And speaking of which, he intended to find out exactly what the old woman had said to her.

Rorie looked around the lodge and found Ada sitting alone by a smaller hearth in the cooking area, working on a cloth with a needle and thread.

"How do you fare, Ada?"

She looked up at him and smiled. "I am well, my lord. How is your lady? You were caught in a downpour."

Sensing a double meaning, he asked, "Exactly what do you know, Ada? What did you tell Muren?"

The wrinkles around her eyes softened as she took on a saddened expression. "I do not believe I should be the one to tell you that. 'Tis her dream, and she is the one who knows what to do about it."

"But you know what it is."

"Aye, that I do, but 'tis not my place to tell something of that sort. You asked me here to do what I can to help her. I can only do so much. She needs a seer more than a healer. Sure, I can concoct a tincture for her at any time her pain comes on, but what's happening to her is much more than a headache. Surely you know that."

"I don't know anything, Ada. That's why I'm asking you. I do not pretend to ken how your healing remedies work any more than I understand how a dream can affect a person so."

"You still believe they're dreams?" she asked with that scolding tone which brought back many memories of when he'd heard it from his own mother.

"What else could they be?"

"Sit with me a while, Rorie." She placed her stitching aside and folded her hands in her lap. When he pulled a chair over, she smiled and said, "There are things in this world we do not understand. For you, seeking out the counsel of a priest or an elder is the usual way to go. For me, I seek answers in all the living things around me. If there is sickness, 'tis sure it came from this land, and the remedy can be found there, too. Sometimes it's a little harder to find, but the land provides everything in balance."

"You are pagan," he said. Though he'd suspected it—most healers were—he'd never actually had a conversation with one before. For sure, Father Iain would bless Muren when he came and offer communion, but his form of healing for her would come in the form of prayer. There was an interesting contrast between the two. One was in the spiritual form in heaven; the other in the spiritual form beneath their feet.

"Aye, does that bother you?"

"No, not as long as you understand that Father Iain will be here in a few days and he will likely engage Muren in a series of prayers, as well as your healing remedies."

"No, lad, I do not mind that at all. I believe there is a place for both of us in her healing."

"And you will not tell me about her dreams?"

She smiled again. "No, lad. I will not. 'Tis not my place."

"I respect that. Is there anything you need? For yourself, or to help Muren? I can have the lads scour the island for anything that grows here."

"Thank you, they have already offered and have been searching for wild yarrow for me."

Rorie stood at the sound of voices in the main hall. "If you need anything at all, you let me know or you let Morag know."

"Aye, lad. Morag is a pure soul like her daughter. She has already offered to help."

Rorie nodded and left Ada to her stitching. At the threshold of the kitchen, he turned. "What are you making by the way?"

"Panels for a bairn's quilt."

Rorie stared hard at her for a moment. Whose bairn, he dare not ask.

CHAPTER TWELVE

*M*uren wished she had a mirror nearby, like the one Freya kept in her bed chamber at Dunrobin, but there would be no sensible way to transport something that large here by ship. As it was, that morning a ship arrived with Father Iain from Eilean Donan, along with Rorie's brother, Ewen, and two of their sisters, both of whom had presented her with beautiful gowns from which to choose.

Placing a wreath of hawthorne on her head, her mother smoothed Muren's hair around her shoulders. She picked at the ties on the arms and at the back of the crimson velvet gown that fit her frame like a glove. Never had a gown quite accentuated her breasts in this way; it actually lifted them slightly. The gold stitching on the square neckline and long dropped sleeves matched that of the gold girdle now fastened low on her hips. It was quite pretty and far better to get married in than the woollen gowns she'd been wearing since arriving on this island.

"There, you are perfect, my precious lass."

Muren looked at her mother and smiled. She had no

doubts left about marrying Rorie. Well, none that she would voice or give credence to. She had not had any hint of a headache or a dream in the two days since she and Rorie had given themselves to each other near the pool. And though she would have loved to take him to bed and stay there until the time had come for them to be wed, they had decided to hold off until tonight.

It was near torture being near him without touching or tasting him. Muren's body trembled and tingled when he was near, as though he was the only medicine she needed.

The door burst open, and Rorie's two sisters entered the chamber and closed the door behind them. They stopped just inside and stared at Muren.

"You are stunning!" Agatha said. Then, nudging Lena, she said, "I told you the crimson would suit her better."

"I am sure you'd say that even if it looked like a sack on her," Lena said. Then, turning to Muren with her hands held out, she said, "Not that it looks like a sack on you."

Muren liked Rorie's sisters. She'd taken to Lena especially right away. Being close to the same age and of similar temperament, they hit it off immediately. At least, that had been the case two years ago. Now Muren regarded the woman in a different light. And, in fact, it was Agatha's bold nature Muren found herself relating to more than Lena's reserved manner. Still, she regarded both with respect and gratitude for their kinship.

"'Tis beautiful. Truly, I have never seen such a gown."

"It was our mother's. Agatha had it freshened up when you returned with Rorie a fortnight ago," Lena said.

"We were certain at the time that a wedding was impending, so we wanted to be prepared," Agatha said.

"We would never have imagined the complications that would keep you from making this day happen, but we are so glad it's finally here."

Muren was, too. She prayed that once Ronan learned of her marriage to Rorie, the whole business would be dropped and they could begin their lives together.

A knock sounded at the door, and her mother went to answer it. She nodded and closed the door again.

"Who was it?" Muren asked.

"It was Ewen. He said Father Iain is ready and awaiting us at the chapel."

Muren drew a deep breath and let it out slowly. This was the moment she had longed for, and now that it was here she was filled with trepidation. Not because of how she felt about Rorie, but of all the other things that would be affected if she went through with it. Was her marriage to him somehow connected to the wound he would receive? If, in fact, there was any possible truth to the dream she had, as Ada suggested.

Her mother pulled her into an embrace. "You carry the weight of a castle on your shoulders, love. You always have. Today you join with an honourable man who will share that burden with you."

Muren had not thought about it that way. Mayhap marrying Rorie would prevent his injury. Mulling over the future was starting to bring on an ache in the back of her neck that she dreaded. God, please not now. Muren drew another deep breath and let it out slowly. Her mother passed her a small pouch.

"This is from Ada. She said to smell it at the beginning of a head ache, and it will help keep it at bay."

Muren took the pouch. Though she had a nagging feeling the woman did not know lungwort from hogwort, she did trust that her intentions were pure and that she would not intentionally harm her.

As she inhaled, she tried to determine what the pouch contained. Aside from pepper and valeria, the primary scent

Muren could detect was rosemary. As soon as she inhaled, her whole body relaxed. Muren looked at the contents closer and, sure enough, there was crushed rosemary inside. She inhaled again, and the ache in the back of her head subsided completely. Tucking it into her sleeve, she smiled at her mother.

"The woman might be good for something, after all."

"Muren!"

The comment was too harsh by far, and in truth, Muren was not quite sure where it came from. "I am sorry."

"You have been under much pressure, love. But, despite these things, never forget who you are. And highlighting someone else's faults only highlights your own."

Her words resonated with Muren. And there was no doubt that the effects of the last fortnight had taken a toll on her and her usual ability to see more than one side to a situation.

"Thank you, Mama," she said. "I am very fortunate to have you to guide me."

A knock sounded at the door again. This time, it opened, and Ewen stepped inside. "Are you ready, or do you need another hour?"

Muren smiled. He was so much more carefree than Rorie, which made sense considering he did not carry the weight of clan responsibility. Muren liked him, despite his reputation with the ladies.

"Aye, Ewen. I am ready."

Ewen offered his arm and proceeded toward the entrance of the chapel. Muren squared her shoulders and held tight onto Ewen's arm as they proceeded up the aisle and toward Rorie. Her breath caught. He was dressed in a deerskin tunic with gold belt, and his plaid over his shoulder with his brooch pin holding it in place. The clan's motto was *I Shine Not Burn*. This would soon be her motto, too.

As she neared him, Rorie smiled at her. All the trepidation and worry fell away as she beheld the promise in his eyes. When they were together, she feared little.

When they were apart, she feared almost everything. And she despised fear. She prayed that this union would do just as her mother had predicted; help shoulder the burden she had carried alone for so long.

Rorie had witnessed many of her headaches now, and even when it was really bad, he had not abandoned her. Rather, he had stayed by her side and protected her when she was at her most vulnerable.

He was her lifeline. Now she would be his, too. He deserved more from her than she had given of late. Regarding him now, she made a silent promise to love and cherish him forever. When she smiled back at him, she heard the air hiss through his teeth as though he'd been holding his breath. His dimples deepened and his eyes crinkled. Muren's heart soared as he took her hand and squeezed.

I love you, she mouthed.

~

*R*orie's heart was near bursting when he realized what she had just said to him. This woman was more important to him than his own life, and she was about to be his now and forever. The exchanging of vows was like a blur to him. After what felt like seconds, the priest told him he could kiss her and she would be his.

Rorie cupped her face with his hands. He bent low and brushed his lips across hers. The scent of the flowers in her hair and the softness of her made him want her like he'd never wanted anything more in his entire life.

"You are finally mine," he said as they sat together at the table, while a feast was laid out before them.

"I have always been yours," she said.

"Not always," he said. "There was a time recently I was not so sure."

"I think even then, in my hour of doubt, I knew deep down I was yours, and you were mine."

He leaned close to her and kissed the delicate skin beneath her ear. "I cannot wait to show you just how much you mean to me. Do you think anyone would mind if we retired early?"

He loved the sound of her laughter that followed his scandalous suggestion. Of course, they were expected to remain, and feast, and celebrate with his family. But secretly, he wished they would all get up and leave.

After hours of eating and storytelling and well wishing, the time finally came for them to retire. One by one, the servants cleared the table and his family, clansmen, and Morag, left the lodge to retire to the other further dwelling. They would walk there together, with lanterns so as to find their way in the dark. Before long it was just Rorie and Muren seated at the table, with the fire slowly transforming into a red glow.

"Will you join me in our bedchamber, my lady?"

She took his hand and squeezed. "Aye, my lord. Nothing would give me greater pleasure."

"And great pleasure you will receive, my lady."

Inside the chamber, Rorie slid his hands around Muren's waist and pulled her against his chest, pressing his pelvis into her behind. When she wiggled her hips, she stoked his manhood, bringing him to erection quickly. He pulled her hair to one side and grazed his teeth across her neck, making her gasp.

Two could play at that game. Rorie unfastened her girdle and let it slip to the floor. He then gripped her skirt and tugged up until his hand caressed her inner thigh. Muren laid her head back against his shoulder as he stoked the delicate flesh between her legs. With his other hand, he reached up to cup her breast and squeezed hard. She gasped again and broke free from his grasp.

Turning toward him, she slipped one shoulder free from her gown and started to untie the sides so that the gown was let loose. Rorie reached for her, but she stepped back from his hand. Giggling, she slipped the gown over her head and tossed it at him. He quickly tossed it over his head and undid his belt, letting it drop to the floor with a loud thunk. He let his plaid fall to the floor then and removed his tunic so that he stood before her wearing only his boots. Slipping them off, he took a step toward her but again she stepped back.

"Do you mean to tease me all night, wife?" he asked in a hoarse voice. Her nipples were hardened and poking through her thin shift. She removed her wreath of flowers and also tossed that at him.

"I want to enjoy our time together tonight, not have it over with too quickly," she said in a teasing manner.

"Oh, you will be pleasured, my lady. That I assure you," he said and stomped toward her. This time he caught her around the waist. In one swift move, he removed her shift and tossed it aside. Now that she was completely naked before him, he held her by the shoulders and gently pushed her back onto the bed so he could admire her form.

Her firm breasts begged for his touch, but he took his time and let his gaze drift downward across her flat belly, and further to the apex of her thighs where they would soon join.

"Please touch me," she said.

Rorie needed no further encouragement and joined her on the bed, lying partly on top of her. He stroked the outside of her thighs, slowly working his way inward as he reached down and pulled on one firm nipple with his teeth. He let go and then sucked hard. Muren's hips raised in response, allowing him to slip his hand in between her thighs and discover the wetness awaiting him. She was ready, but he wanted her to be pleasured many times this night. He would hold onto his own climax for as long as he could.

Rorie spread her thighs and slipped two fingers inside her as he sucked hard on one nipple then another. When her hand enclosed around his erection, he was sure he would lose his seed, but instead, he pulled back and repositioned himself so that he could taste her sweetness.

Slipping one, two, then three fingers inside of her and stroking deep, he located her hardened bud and sucked hard. He increased the rhythm of his fingers in time with this sucking motion, marvelling in the way her body arched higher and higher off the bed. He looked up to see her gripping the bedclothes, with her head back and her breasts thrust upright. Christ, he needed her now.

In a swift move, he thrust hard and deep within her and then hesitated as he realized that this was only her third time and her body may not be prepared for the force of his passion.

"Oh God, Rorie, don't stop. Please don't stop."

Rorie slid his hands underneath her shoulders and thrust deep within her again and again, pounding hard into her as he chased his own orgasm. Her body squeezed around his erection, and her legs tightened around his waist as he felt her whole body tighten around his. He was close, but he could still hang on just a little longer. With each wave of her climax, she shuddered a little more until he felt her relax. Rorie slowed his pace until just the tip of him entered her over and over. Her body squeezed around him as her passion built again.

Rorie leaned down and captured her lips with his as he thrust harder and faster than he ever had in his life. She tugged on his shoulders and ground her hips into his until he could barely move within her. A tingling began in his lower spine and spread through his pelvis. At the moment when her body pulsed around his for the second time, his orgasm washed over him. He thrust forward hard, holding there for a second before he shuddered and thrust forward again. Each time he stopped, buried deep within her, he could feel her body squeeze around him then release. Her climax never seemed to end, only prolonging his.

Rorie opened his eyes to watch her tightly-shut eyes and furrowed brow. He slowed his pace and stroked while watching and feeling her body twitch in response to his. When she let her arms and legs drop, he slipped out of her and lay by her side. His heart raced, and his body was covered in a sheen of sweat from their passion. Rorie lay flat on his back staring up at the canopy made from various coloured plaids. He wondered if there was a way for them to simply stay there forever, buried in each other's arms, and loving each other until they were totally depleted. What a dream that would be. But it was just a dream. They needed to face reality soon enough and return to answer for the decision they had made this day.

Rorie hoped that in the days and weeks to come no harm would come to her or to his family. The king was stubborn—nothing was certain at this point.

CHAPTER THIRTEEN

*M*uren had the most wonderful dream. In it, she and Rorie rode through the countryside on horseback, his strong arms wrapped around her, holding her tight, while his heart pounded in time with the horse's hooves and his thick erection pressed against her backside.

She pressed back against him and let her head fall back on his shoulder.

Slowing the horse to a trot, he held onto the reins with one hand and used the other to cup her breast. She loved the feeling it drew from her body, loved the way he touched and caressed every inch of her in his adoration, and the pleasure he gave her so freely.

A huge clap of thunder drew their attention to the south close to the castle, and so they turned the horse in that direction and galloped toward it. Another large clap, followed by another and another, made Muren cower from the coming storm. Rorie placed his plaid around them both and rode harder as the rains pelted down onto them and lightning flashed in the sky.

A deafening boom, boom, boom, made her sit up in bed

with a jerk. Rorie was snoring beside her, and a thick quilt had been tossed off them both.

Boom, boom, boom.

Muren shook Rorie's shoulder. "Do you hear that?"

"What?"

Boom. Boom.

Rorie then sat upright.

"Someone is pounding on the door."

"Aye," she said, wanting to hide under the bed. "What should we do?"

Rorie slipped out of bed and threw his tunic over his head. He looked back at her from the doorway with a grin. "We answer it."

When he closed the door. Muren grabbed her shift and woollen gown and quickly put it on. If her brother had finally caught up with them, she would at least go dignified. Looking around the chamber, she spied an axe and two long swords mounted on the wall. Climbing up onto a trunk, she pulled the axe from the wall and approached the door, pressed her ear to it, and listened. The only sound she could discern was muffled voices.

She lifted the latch and pulled open the door. Creeping out into the hall, she was careful not to make any noise that would give away her presence.

"You have no right!" Rorie said.

"Aye, that we do and you know it," a second gruff voice said.

"Tell me why you come yourself, instead of sending your war chief."

"You know why."

"Nay, I do not. 'Tis my wedding night you have interrupted for this nonsense, and I will have a reason for it and not some foolishness about who owns this island."

Muren crept farther toward the outer hall. Peeking

around the corner, she could see Rorie's back, and it looked like his arms were folded across his chest. His legs were spread apart, and overall, he looked like he was not threatened by the other man.

He was as tall as Rorie but broader if that was possible. With long, light brown hair and a well-kept beard, the man wore a formidable expression, with a stare that she was sure could turn a man to stone.

"Your wedding night?"

"Aye."

"Christ's teeth, man, I didn't know that. I didn't mean to interrupt."

Rorie shook his head. "Well, now that you are here, you might as well sit and tell me what has made you cross to Rona at this early hour."

It was then Muren noticed the soft grey underneath the door. All the window shutters had been closed so she could not tell until then what time of day it was.

The two men sat, and Rorie reached for a trencher and two goblets that had been left out for them. She leaned closer to hear better when the floorboard creaked beneath her feet. Rorie turned around and locked gaze with her then grinned.

He flicked his head in her direction as he turned back to the man. "I have all the protection I need, William."

The man named William looked at her and smiled. "You've no need to be afraid, lass," he said. "I am William MacLeod. I come with news for the MacKenzie, and I suspect you are the Muren I've been hearing so much about."

Muren moved closer and took a seat across from both men. Rorie passed her a goblet of ale and poured himself another. Did he think she needed alcohol in order to receive the news MacLeod would share?

"You cannot stay here."

"I can stay here," Rorie replied. "I told you our grandfathers had an agreement."

"That's not what I mean, and you know it. If it were up to me, I would say stay here as long as you want. But the reality is, if I could find out you're here so easily, I'm sure the king's scouts could as well."

"There was someone here a sennight ago," Muren said.

"Aye, those two were my men. My scouts saw the ship heading to Rona, and we had to be sure who it was. But since then, I've had a pigeon from Ross saying there are rumblings of the king heading north with an army."

"Christ's teeth, how did he manage that so soon?"

"I do not know, but I am certain the Douglas has something to do with it. MacKenzie, you know we'll stand with you, but I have to know something."

"Anything."

"Did you accept MacDonald lands from the king, in exchange for your broken betrothal?"

"No. He did offer that, but I refused."

"That's what I figured. The king must have had someone spread a rumour in order to pit you against the MacDonalds, so now they are saying they will not support you if you raise arms against the Stewart."

"But is it not just a simple matter of contacting the MacDonald and clarifying the truth?" Muren asked.

"Have you met him?"

"No, I have not," Muren said.

"He's as stubborn and pig-headed as his father was," MacLeod said.

"Aye, that he is, but he assured me of his allegiance when I told him I would not accept the king's offer. He assured me he would aide my cause."

"Something has to be done about the Stewart."

"Those are treasonous words, and I will not be a part of

any plot," Rorie said. "I have too much at stake and have offended him quite enough."

"They are just words," MacLeod said. "And I am not the first one to voice them. He has done much damage since his return, and if we want to preserve our way of life, we need to do something about him."

"Who has spoken such words?"

"Albany."

"Albany is just as power hungry as the Stewart. Believe me when I say we are all better off staying out of any conflict between those two. I suspect they will destroy one another before this is all over," Rorie said.

"Suit yourself. But you do understand that you are not safe here." "Then I am not safe anywhere."

Muren tried to make sense of their conversation. Was she really at the root cause of all of this conflict? Just because she had chosen love over an arranged marriage of the king's choosing? If it were even half true, she could not bear it.

"There is one way we can be safe," she said.

Rorie shook his head. "No. You are not going back there. We are married now, and I forbid it."

Muren couldn't believe her ears. Was this how he was going to be? "You cannot forbid me to see my own family."

"Aye, I can and I will if it means you are in danger. What do you think Sutherland will do if he gets his hands on you?"

"He will let me explain, and then he will let me return to you."

"No, he will put you before the bishop, and he will have our marriage annulled and you married to the Douglas within a sennight. You cannot go home."

Muren's body shook with anger. How dare he dictate to her that she could no longer see her family. "You spoke nothing of banning me from my family before we wed. And now that the deed is done, you will treat me as all the others have treated me, like a possession? I will not have it."

Rorie stood. "MacLeod, if there is nothing else, I must speak with my wife alone."

"There is one more thing, MacKenzie. You have not yet given me your blessing to court Mairi."

"And nor will I give it until I am certain all of this business has settled down. We are all in danger now, and I intend to keep my family very close to me."

"You cannot do that if you are dead," MacLeod said. "Is that a threat?"

"Don't be daft, man. You know it's not a threat from me. But it very much is from the king, her brother, and the Black Douglas."

With that, MacLeod went to the door and opened it. "I hope you reconsider about Mairi. I wish to link our clans, and she is my choice."

When the door closed, Rorie turned to Muren. For a few moments, he said nothing but just stared at her. He opened his mouth once and then shook his head and walked to the bedchamber.

Muren waited as she heard the clanging of his sword, and when he returned he placed his weapon, belt, and plaid on the table. As he dressed, he said nothing. The silence stretched between them, and Muren's heart beat hard with every agonizing second that passed.

After what seemed like an age, he said, "Do you really want to leave me to return to your brother?"

She did not. But he had to admit it would resolve much. "I do not see a better solution."

*R*orie could not believe his ears. After what they had shared and what they had confessed to one another, she did not trust that he would protect her? Well, by God, she was not leaving him again. He'd do whatever it took to keep her with him, even if it meant she never spoke to him again.

Rorie finished dressing and left the lodge. He walked up the path toward the watch tower and further beyond to the other dwelling. Halfway there, he realized he'd been so caught up in his anger that he'd left her alone with no protection. He turned back to collect her, and it was only then he discovered that she had followed him.

"I was about to return to you."

"I know," she said in a small voice.

His heart squeezed. "Muren, I do not want to lose you," he said.

"I don't want that either, but you have to admit, this would all be easier if I just did what they wanted."

"No, it would not. The king would find another reason to strip us of our rights, and besides," he said, and pulled her into an embrace, "you are mine now in the eyes of God and the eyes of man. I do not care what this king says. You are my wife and may even be carrying my child. I will not let anyone come between us."

Even as he said the words, doubt entered his heart. Something still was not right about the situation. As soon as he had mentioned a child, Muren had stiffened. He thought he understood why. While they could go into hiding for a time, it would be much more challenging with a small child or children in tow, and it was a rough way to raise a family. And then there was the matter of his family and his clan. He was responsible for far more people than she allowed for. There was no way he could hide any longer. It was time to put an end to this business one way or another.

Holding her hand, they walked together to the other dwelling. Once there, they found Morag up, with the fire stoked and something cooking in the pot.

Her brows were raised as she turned toward them at the door. "I do not think there has ever been a newly-wedded couple who's left the marriage bed so early. You either dislike one another completely, or something is amiss."

"You're very perceptive," Rorie said.

She sat at the table and folded her hands. "Then tell me. It's Ronan, isn't it? I curse the day his father took him from me."

"'Tis the king. He's amassed an army and is heading north. We must return to Eilean Donan and prepare for a siege."

"God's bones," Morag said. "We can be ready to leave within the hour."

"Good," Rorie said. "The sooner we are behind the stone walls of the castle the better."

Rorie left Muren to help her mother and his sisters pack. He rounded up all the men, who were tasked with gathering up their belongings. Within an hour, they were aboard two birlinns and heading east to Loch Duich. Rorie watched the scenery pass by and contemplated on how many disputes had occurred over land and property. In this case, Muren was that property, and much of what she said about being a part of decisions that affected her life made sense. Still, it did not change the fact that she was his wife and his to protect, like the many people who worked at Eilean Donan and those who lived in the nearby villages.

By the time they docked, Rorie was more than ready to dive into preparations for the upcoming confrontation with the king. If the estimations were correct, the army would be there within four days; much closer than he had originally thought.

He ordered Ewen to assemble his war council. They would need to reinforce a portion of the back courtyard and block off access to the bridge. The great thing about the bridge was that it would bottleneck an army and, in the meantime, their ships would be docked and waiting should the king use stronger force than the castle could withhold.

Once his council had convened, Rorie took stock of his assets.

"Our walls are thick enough to keep men out, but will not withstand cannon fire," he said to Ewen.

"Aye, we have stocked the larder and can remain here for months. Besides, our birlinns will provide escape should the siege last for longer than our stores."

"Have we heard from MacDonald?"

"Not yet."

"We need him onside. It is possible for us to be blocked in if MacDonald sails against us. We absolutely need him not to take up arms against us."

"And if he does?"

"Then we will have to sail to Skye and seek shelter with the MacLeods. I've already spoken to William, and he agrees that now is the time for the clans to band together. We cannot allow this king to pit us against the other. Sutherland's and MacDonald's crimes against this clan are great, and they should pay for them. But I will not start a war with either of them while this threat from the king exists."

The more Rorie thought about it, the angrier he became. His family had worked hard to build the clan and thrive, and the king should not have the right to pick and choose whose life he changed nor who he wished to reward. The whole thing was a gnarly mess. And none of it was Rorie's or the MacKenzies' doing.

"We must fight back instead of retreat," Rorie finally said.

Ewen's eyes grew wide. "I thought you wanted to avoid confrontation."

"I did. But enough is enough. The elder Sutherland and MacDonald destroyed an entire village in order to blame MacKay so that Sutherland could gain control over his lands. I see the king as no better in what he is doing here. He offered me MacDonald lands as compensation for Muren. Lands he does not own. He cannot be allowed to continue on this path."

"We're prepared for a siege, Rorie, but not for war," Ewen said.

"Then get every able-bodied man to come here and fight. If we don't have the numbers, we'll make the numbers. Send a missive to MacLeod. Tell him to block the seaways. I have a bad feeling about MacDonald. His wife is the queen's cousin. It was always a stretch that they would help us."

Ewen grinned. "Aye, Rorie. I will do all of that. What about Fergus?" "Send a missive to him, too. Tell him we need his army to march south."

Rorie looked at the map laid out before them. He would have reinforcements by sea and from the north. If only he could secure MacDonald's from the south, but he was sure that would not happen. And then he looked farther east.

He looked up at the oldest man in the hall. Hugh Ross. "Hugh. What about your kin?"

The man was as strong as an ox in his day, and could still wield an axe when needed. He'd been indebted to Rorie's father, and so ended up in service to him. He was a great asset to Rorie's council, but Rorie would award the man anything he wanted if he could secure the chieftain's aid. In essence, they could cut off Sutherland's access and lessen the king's presence. Rorie was certain that's what the king intended.

Hugh smiled. "I believe, in this case, they will gladly come to your aid."

"I don't need them to go anywhere. I just need them to keep Sutherland's army separate from the king's."

Ewen came closer as Rorie's finger positioned the Ross army. "If only we had another ally to the south who could keep the king from crossing Loch Ness."

"That would take Grant and Cameron, and we both know that's not going to happen. Nor can we count on MacIntosh. He was convinced once to stand in unison, to make a point against the king, but we can ask no more of James MacIntosh. He's too loyal. What about Fraser?"

Rorie looked at the map again and shook his head. "We have the vantage point in terms of a siege. But we do not as far as a battle. We cannot let him come to us. We must go to him."

"Where?" Ewen asked.

"On the southern edge of Loch Ness."

Rorie instructed Ewen to send missives to MacLeod, MacKay, Ross, Fraser, and Grant. They had little time, but just enough if they left on the morrow. In that case, he had a lot of work to do.

CHAPTER FOURTEEN

uren stood at the top of the tower and looked at the way three lochs met pretty much right where the castle was situated. She was eager to learn of the results of the war council. She did not know much about the ways of war but, looking around, she did not think that it made much sense sitting here and waiting for the king and her brother to show up with their armies. While the larder was well stocked and they could stay here comfortably for quite some time, what if the king brought cannons? What if sailing vessels came in from the sea, belonging to someone with whom they were not allied?

The more she thought about it, the more staying here made little sense. She must find Rorie and talk to him about it.

As she turned to retreat down the stairs, she saw him coming up. "I thought I'd find you here," he said.

"Aye, I was just looking around at the location of the castle."

Rorie's brows raised. "And what did you conclude in your examination?"

"That staying here does not make sense if the king truly is bringing his army to attack us."

He smiled, and her heart fluttered a little. "You have a keen mind for strategy. How did I miss that before?"

While she was pleased that he admired her, she was even more pleased that she did not need his admiration. The old Muren would have longed for his approval, but the new one was more concerned with pleasing herself. She liked this.

"Mayhap you were not paying close enough attention," she said with a grin.

Rorie slipped his arms around her waist and drew her closer. She slid her hands up and behind his neck, drawing him down for a kiss.

Just as his lips were about to touch hers, he said, "I promise to pay much closer attention from now on." He brushed his lips across hers. "I want to spend the rest of the day watching your face as you reach your pleasure."

Muren's body pulsed at his words. He could bring her excitement to the surface in seconds and, if he wanted to, he could have her right then and there. She was ready.

He deepened his kiss and Muren slid her hands into his hair, pulling him closer. After a moment or two, he said, "I have much to tell you, and we have little time."

She smiled and took his hand, leading him downstairs to their chamber. "Do you have at least a little time?"

"Aye, lass. I will make time." At the bottom of the stairs, he drew her toward the bed and lifted her skirt. "Bend over," he said.

Muren hesitated. What did he mean to do?

Rorie cupped her face with his hands and kissed her sweetly. "Trust me, love. You will enjoy this, I promise."

She let him bend her over the large bed, and waited as he lifted her skirts. Muren's heart pounded as he exposed her bottom and gently spread her legs.

"Rorie," she whispered, as he stroked the back of her thighs and brushed his hand across her now quivering flesh.

"I am here, love," he said, as he slipped the tip of his hard erection into her.

Muren gasped at the sensation and the wicked, wanton feeling of making love with their clothes on in the middle of the day.

"Are you ready for me?" he asked.

She was always ready for him. Biting down on her finger, she pushed her hips back, taking more of him inside of her in response.

Rorie grabbed hold of her hips to slow her movement. He thrust hard and deep, and her body shook as desire flooded her veins. He pulled out agonizingly slowly and thrust hard and deep within her again.

"Oh God, you feel so good," he whispered. "Muren, you feel so good."

On the third thrust, Muren could not take the slow pace any longer and pushed back against him. "Faster, Rorie, please."

He obeyed and increased the pace of his thrusts. Two, three more, and Muren's orgasm overtook her. Her body shook as he pounded into her deeper than she ever thought possible, stroking her to her very core.

One final thrust and Rorie stiffened behind her. His body trembled and quaked as their climaxes took hold. He did not remove himself from her until the last wave of her pleasure had passed, then he gently lowered her skirts and lifted her from the bed.

Embracing her and burying his face in her hair, he asked, "Did you like it that way?"

She wrapped her arms around him and held on tight. "Aye, very much. Can we do that again?" And she really did mean now. "And can we do that in other places besides our chamber?"

Rorie leaned back and gazed into her eyes with a grin. "We can do that anywhere you like any time. Mayhap even in the guards' room above the great hall, when people are there but do not know we are."

Muren loved the delicious feeling the image of that gave her. Desire washed over her again. God, how much she loved him. But reality dawned on her when he frowned.

"What is it?"

"Your calculation of our location was correct. We cannot stay here and wait for the king to bring his army to us."

"What does that mean? Where will we go?"

Rorie shook his head. "You will stay here, and I will take our army east to meet the king somewhere that will give us an advantage in the fight."

"I do not want you to go," she said and squeezed his arms. "Rorie, what if something happens to you?"

"Nothing will happen to me, Muren. We are calling on the clans to come to our aid. If they all reply in favour, we will have the numbers to meet the king."

"But can they assemble in time?"

"Aye, but just barely."

"I do not understand how," she said.

"Come, and I will show you," he said and took her hand.

He led her to the great hall where a large map was laid out. Wooden carvings lay on it with inscriptions she did not recognize, but the symbols she did. Her own Sutherland clan crest lay near the water on the east coast. Underneath it was a drawing of a castle. Dunrobin.

"Tell me what you see," Rorie said.

She pointed. "That's Dunrobin, and the clan crest on that piece is Sutherland's."

"Aye, what else?"

She scanned the map.

"I see a lion on that piece and a unicorn. That represents the king, and you have him on one side of a long loch."

"Loch Ness, aye. And what else?"

She peered closer at all the pieces together and saw a crest with a fire on a hill, another with a hand holding a knife, one with a stag's head, and one with rocks and a flame. "Which one is you?"

"Our crest is the fire on the hill. Our motto is *I Shine Not Burn*. Do you understand what that means?"

"Aye, it means you're not a hothead like my brother."

Rorie smiled. "The other pieces represent MacKay, Fraser, and Grant." As he said each name, he held up the piece.

There was one piece he had not yet mentioned. The one just beneath Sutherland.

She pointed to it. "And what is this one?"

"That's Ross."

"Why do they not join you in the battle?"

"Muren," he said in a low voice, "they are tasked with preventing your brother from joining his army with the king's, against us."

"Do you really think he would fight you?"

"I cannot risk thinking anything else."

Muren noticed the quiet tone his voice had taken. "There's something else, isn't there?"

"I do not wish to upset you. He is your brother."

"Aye, that he is. And even though he made a bad decision regarding my betrothal to you, he is still my family, and I would not see him harmed."

"I understand that, Muren. Believe me, I do. But if we do not act, I cannot guarantee that you will still end up in the clutches of the king. Even though we are married and that marriage properly consummated. I do not trust the man, and I have to do everything to protect those for whom I am responsible."

"What are you saying, Rorie?"

"I intend to retaliate against your brother for the broken betrothal."

"No!"

"It must be done, Muren, or else this will never end. I know this is not what you wanted to hear, but there is no other way. We cannot wait for them to remove any opportunity from us regarding resolving this mess. And a huge mess it is. Several chiefs have already received decrees from the king, just northwest of Stirling, stating that their properties and tenants now fall under his jurisdiction."

"How can he do that?"

"He is king, and figures he can do whatever he wants. You of all people should know that. He will use anyone and anything to advance his own purpose, and the time has come to put an end to it. We must fight back."

Muren's head hurt trying to keep it all straight. She was angry with Ronan for involving her in such a scheme, and she was angry at the king for his arrogance and tyranny. But she could not regret the opportunity the circumstances had afforded her. Without these events, she would have never gotten to know herself. And for that one thing, she had to be grateful.

∾

*R*orie watched the expressions on Muren's face change from anger to acceptance. She drew a deep breath and placed her hands on her hips.

"And exactly what am I supposed to do whilst you are off warring with half of Scotland?"

"You will remain here with your mother, under guard.

The MacLeods will protect the sea to the west in the event MacDonald decides to side with the king." Rorie pointed to the place on the map where the sea narrowed between the mainland and Skye. "MacLeod will lay in wait just here, and if MacDonald tries to sail through the narrows, he will be stopped."

"But I thought MacDonald was sympathetic to the Highlanders' plight against the king. Did not his father endure imprisonment for his plots to overthrow the king?"

"Aye, that was the father. The son wants peace and assumes that taking a wife who is a relative of the queen is one way to do that. The other way is to stay away from clan battles, and especially those with the king."

Rorie was impressed that Muren understood the complexities of the situation. He wished there was something he could offer by way of assurance for her brother's safety, but the base of the matter was that anyone who would threaten them must be stopped. There truly was no other way.

"Do you have any questions?"

"When do you leave?"

"On the morrow."

She had one night to have him to herself, and then heaven only knew when she would see him again. Muren lowered her head. "Will we ever find peace?"

Rorie walked toward her and gently lifted her chin with his finger. "Muren, I will make this right. You will have nothing to fear once this deed is done."

"Will you try to protect my brother from coming to harm?"

He dropped his hand and took a deep breath. "I cannot promise that, but I will say that I do not intend to bring harm to him, rather stop him from coming after you."

Muren could accept that, but she was also aware that a

battle would have to occur in order to stop Ronan. Wasn't that the way of men? Rather than talk it out, they drew their swords. And while Rorie had tried other measures first—and she was grateful for that—in the end, in his view, violence was the only way. But there must be another solution.

She looked at the map again. Even in the best-case scenario, men would lose their lives in this mess. Husbands, fathers, brothers, would be ripped from their families for someone else's cause. The whole lot of it made no logical sense to her. Why did some men covet that which was not theirs? She had no answer for it. But she would not accept Rorie's plan as the only solution either. She would find a way to get through to her brother and make him stand down. At this point, he did not even know they were married. Mayhap, if she could communicate with him, he would not seek retaliation.

Muren returned to her chamber while Rorie went to make preparations to leave. Her mother knocked on the door a time later and came to sit with her by the hearth.

"Do you know what passes?"

"Aye. Rorie told me that they are amassing the army and plan to intercept the king near Loch Ness to increase their chances."

"Why do they not just wait it out here?"

"Because, while this is a great place for a siege, it is not tactically advantageous to withstand a battle. Rorie does not have a clear sense of numbers, nor what weapons the king plans to bring with him."

"And yet he rides into battle alone?"

"No, he has called on other clans to aid."

"And what about Ronan?"

"Rorie plans to use Ross's men to keep Ronan from joining forces with the king."

Her mother shook her head. "Will he battle Ronan?"

"I do not know. I have asked him not to allow Ronan to come to harm, but he said he could not guarantee."

"Then we must warn Ronan."

"I cannot do that, Mother. I cannot undermine my husband when I know what he is saying is true. But I cannot sit here and do nothing either."

"What do you mean?"

"I need to speak with Ronan. I need to tell him Rorie and I are now married, and he needs to make peace with that."

"Muren, you know your brother. You know he will not go back on his word so easily. He's made an agreement with the king. He would not put his clansmen in danger any more than Rorie would his."

Her mother's words resonated with her, but Muren was convinced she could get through to Ronan if she could only speak with him alone. But that would involve travelling to Dunrobin, and Rorie would never allow it.

Yet Rorie would be gone on the morrow, and if she left the day after that, she could make it to Dunrobin long before Rorie and his men were finished with the king. She swallowed a large knot in her throat. *If* he won.

"What are you planning to do?" her mother asked.

"I will go see Ronan. 'Tis the only way, but you must say nothing to Rorie. He will not support it, but he will be gone tomorrow, and I will leave the day after that."

"You will not go alone."

"Aye, it will be easier for me to be undetected if I ride alone."

"No. I will go with you."

"Mother, you are safer here."

"I do not care. I will not see either of my children harmed. I am coming with you, and there's nothing you can say to stop me."

Muren had to admit she did feel safer knowing her mother would accompany her.

A slow, dull ache began at the back of her neck. Not now, please not now.

Muren stood, and as soon as she did, pain shot to her head and intensified with each passing second. She doubled over and vomited on the floor.

Her mother rushed to her and guided her to the bed. "Sit on the bed, Muren. I will get cool cloths and draw the curtains."

Muren could barely make out what her mother said. The room spun, and her guts heaved again. Her stomach contents landed on the floor beside the bed, and darkness reached out to her. Muren fought to remain conscious, but the blackness rushed at her too fast this time. Once more, her stomach heaved and vomit spewed from her lips onto the edge of her gown and the floor.

Please, please no. This was the most intense she had ever experienced the headache in her life. She feared she could not hold on much longer while waiting for her mother to return. She peeked through her shut eyes, but the light from the window made her head hurt all the more. Muren gasped as the pain made her skull feel like it had split in two. She had no choice but to lay back on the bed while the room spun around her and her stomach threatened to heave again. The door opened with a crack, and her mother's footfalls sounded like loud claps of thunder.

"I'm here, love," her mother said.

Muren shook her head to tell her not to speak. The claws of the black edged closer to her. She sobbed, and the last thought she had before she was enveloped entirely was of an unborn child growing in her womb.

Muren opened her eyes to see a familiar cave, with the old woman beckoning her forward.

"Come and see," the crone said. "I do not wish to see," Muren said.

"But you must. Time is running out. You must come with me."

Muren followed the crone to the pool. How many times had she had this dream? She didn't know. But for some reason, she was not as scared as she had been in the past. Something drove her in a different way this time.

Once they reached the pool, Muren knelt to the side and peered in. The crone stood to the side and touched the water with her walking stick so that a ripple crossed the flat surface. Muren waited. She'd done this before but had been frightened when the images came.

A smoky hue filled the pool. Before long, images flashed one by one, and she tried to process their meaning. Once again, she saw Rorie being pierced with a sword and falling to his knees. She kept watching, hoping he would get up, but instead he fell over. She then saw a man wearing a lion and unicorn on the crest of his breastplate. He was atop his horse and in a great battle. In the next image, he was lying in his bed as men broke into his chamber and stabbed him where he slept.

The next image was that of herself. Muren closed her eyes. She didn't want to see her own demise. It was too much.

"Open your eyes, child," the crone said. "You must bear witness."

Muren opened her eyes and the cloudy image cleared. She saw herself holding a small bairn swaddled in a warm blanket. Tears streamed down her face in the image. Muren could not tell if the tears were from joy or sorrow, but the sight made her tremble. Was the bairn hers or someone else's? Did it live or was it stillborn? It was all too much.

Muren tried to turn away, but the crone turned her head back again.

"You must bear witness. There is no time left."

One more image emerged. In it, Muren saw her brother. He was lying on a pallet, unmoving, with his wife, Freya, holding his hand and weeping. No! She could not allow this to happen. Her resolve increased tenfold to get to her brother and make peace with him.

She simply must be able to affect change.

"I can change these events," she said to the crone. When she looked up, the crone was nowhere to be found.

Muren looked back to the pool, but it had returned to a flat surface with no further images for her to see. She got to her feet and returned to the standing stone. As soon as she touched the stone, warmth spread through her, completely surrounding her and washing all the darkness away. Muren opened her eyes to find herself in her bedchamber. Her mother was at her side, and Rorie stood at the edge of the bed, wearing a terrified expression.

CHAPTER FIFTEEN

*R*orie watched her eyes flutter and open. He drew in a deep breath and let it out slowly. He couldn't even speak as their gazes locked. The stench of vomit still hung in the air, and her face was deathly pale. He was certain he'd lost her this time. Her mother had called for him with such a panic that he'd left the armoury and run all the way to their chamber. When he got there, she was unconscious and her breathing so shallow there were moments he was not convinced she still lived.

"Muren love, how do you feel?" her mother asked.

Muren sat up and looked around her as if she couldn't figure out where she was.

When she made to get up, Rorie came around the side of the bed and held her hands. "Why don't you rest, Muren? You've been very ill."

She looked past him to the window and her brows knit. "How long have I been out?"

"Two days," her mother said.

"What?" She then turned to Rorie. "But you were

supposed to leave yesterday. Rorie, you wanted to intercept the king. Why did you not go?"

Rorie could hardly speak. They had even had the priest come and sit with her for a while. Now she sat up in bed as though nothing had happened.

"Muren," her mother said. "You've been so sick this time." Her voice cracked on the last word. "Is the pain gone in your head?"

She stood up and only stumbled a little, and then leaned on Rorie. "Aye, I feel perfectly fine. How could I have been asleep for two days?"

"I had Ada come see you, too, and she was convinced you would wake. We took turns waving the rosemary she left under your nose. She also waved burnt sage in the corners."

"For evil spirits? Surely she did not suspect dark magic to be a cause."

"No, but we were so fearful about what was going on with you that we tried everything."

Muren turned to him and smiled. "Rorie, I am truly better. I feel better than I have in a very long time."

"What do you mean?" her mother asked.

"My headaches never ever went away completely. There was always a hint of it, but now I don't feel it at all. I almost feel like I'm floating," she said and laughed.

Rorie lifted her over to a chair by the fire and helped her sit.

"Stay here with her," her mother said, as she went to the door. "I'll get the cook to bring some broth, and I'll send the maids to change the bedding and clean the floors."

Rorie sat across from Muren and held her hands. He studied the lines of her face, and his heart soared when she smiled at him. "I love you so much, Muren. I really thought I had lost you."

"I love you, too, Rorie."

"I don't want to go now."

"I cannot tell you what's right, Rorie. But I can say that I do not think challenging the king in battle is the answer."

"No, but battle will be on our doorstep if I do not."

"I know you think that. But maybe there's another way."

"There is not, I assure you. I have thought this through at every angle, and we are sitting ducks here. We must ride out to head him off. The more ground he covers, the less likely we will be able to have a tactical advantage, and we must have that."

"Have you heard back from the other clans?"

"Aye, all are on side."

"And Ross? Will they battle my brother to keep him in Sutherland?"

"Aye."

He hated the look of sadness that crossed her face. It was not an ideal situation by any stretch. While he'd sat with her over the last two days, he'd spent much time contemplating his options. He truly did not have another choice. Now that she was well, he would continue his plans to leave at daybreak. Tonight, he would hold her close.

❧

*M*uren's mother returned with a bowl of broth and crusty bread. As soon as the scent hit her nose, her belly rumbled. She pretty much inhaled the soup and bread and then reached for the pitcher of ale. It was not normally a drink she preferred, but for some reason, she was thirsty for the barley-flavour.

Looking down into the goblet, she saw her reflection and paused midway to drinking. The flash of her dream returned to her, making the goblet fall from her hand and clatter to the stone floor. The cold fluid soaked her night shift as her mother and Rorie fussed over her while the full impact of what she'd seen washed over her.

"Rorie, you cannot go."

He stood and looked at her with a shocked expression. Her mother stood, too. "Muren, what is it?"

"I dreamed. Full dreams this time, and I think it was images of what is to come."

Rorie shook his head and put a finger to his mouth. "Muren, you cannot be overheard saying such things."

"I do not care who hears me. I saw you getting hurt, and I cannot let you go."

Her mother drew her into the side chamber and lifted her wet shift off her, then helped her into another. They returned to the chair, and Morag placed a blanket over her legs and another around her shoulders.

"Muren," she said. "Rorie is right. Do you not remember what I told you about your grandmother?"

"Aye, I do. But if it is true, then what I saw in my dream will come to pass, and I cannot let the man I love go to his death when I can prevent it."

"Tell me what you saw," her mother said.

"I do not want to hear this," Rorie said. "You were ill, and you had a dream. Considering everything that has gone on in the last month, it is only logical that you have troubled dreams brought on by stress, which is also why your headache was so severe this time. I will call for Ada to bring more rosemary, and you will speak of your dreams to no one."

Muren did not like his tone, and she did not like him dictating to her what she could and could not do. He knelt before her and took her hand.

"Don't you see, love. I only want to protect you. People will not understand if you tell them you're a seer."

"Do you not believe me?"

"It does not matter if I believe you or not. You place yourself in more danger if you reveal what was in your dreams."

"I know now that they are not dreams," she said. "Muren, you must promise me to speak of it to no one."

"I cannot do that."

Rorie stood and raked his hands through his hair. "I cannot protect you if you do not let me."

"Don't you see?" she asked. "'Tis that I want to protect you."

"I cannot risk the lives of everyone here and allow the king to attack us here because you had a dream."

His words cut through her. Never in her life had she been so thoroughly dismissed. And coming from him, it was even more painful. "Then go," she said and turned her head toward the fire.

Rorie leaned his face down to her and kissed her cheek. She pulled away. "You can dislike my decision, Muren, but it stands. You are staying here, and I am leaving on the morrow."

With that, he left her chamber and slammed the door. Turning to her mother, she asked, "Do you believe me?"

"Aye, and that's why I agree with Rorie. You cannot tell anyone outside this room what you saw. Do you understand how important that is?"

"And what if what I know may save lives?" Her mother sat in the chair across from her. "Tell me."

Muren drew in a deep breath. "The first vision I had was of Rorie being run through. He dropped to his knees and then fell over."

Her mother placed her hands over her mouth. "Oh, Muren. Are you certain?"

"Aye, it was as clear as if I was watching it happen right in front of me."

"I understand why you would be upset. Rorie hardly left your side while you were out."

"I cannot let him go and be killed. I now have no choice but to leave as soon as Rorie does."

"Aye, we will make preparations to go as soon as he has left. Did you have any other visions?"

"Aye, I saw the king in battle, but later saw him being slaughtered in his own bed."

Her mother leaned forward. "That you must never repeat. Promise me, Muren. It is one thing for people to think you a witch, but those words are full-on treason."

"I know, and I promise to never utter the words again." Muren put her head down and wrung her hands.

"Was there another vision?"

"Aye," she said in a soft voice. She was not quite sure how to describe it. "Tell me, love, then put them all out of your head."

Muren looked deep into her mother's eyes. She barely had the heart to voice the words, but she did not possess the strength to hold onto such an image and bear the burden of it alone.

"The last image was that of me carrying a newborn bairn. The babe was swaddled, and I held her so tight."

"Did you know 'twas a wee lassie?" Her mother smiled. Clearly, she thought it was a happy vision.

"In the vision, I was weeping."

Her mother's expression turned to concern. "Maybe they were tears of joy?"

"Perhaps. I could not tell if I was happy or sad. Just that I looked upon the bairn with love and I was weeping." Muren had not the heart to voice the vision about Ronan.

Her mother came over to her chair and wrapped her arms

around her. "Oh love, you've been through so much. Why don't you let me put you back in bed so you can rest? Tomorrow will be a long day."

All of a sudden, weariness settled over her. She let her mother help her to the bed and cover her with the thick quilts. Morag tended to the fire, then blew out the candles and left the chamber.

Heavy slumber settled over Muren, and just as she was drifting, the door opened and closed again. The sound of a belt and other clothes being removed was followed by the quilts lifting and Rorie slipping in beside her. He must have assumed she was asleep because he rolled her onto her side and then contoured his body behind hers with one arm draped over her.

"I am awake," she whispered.

"I know," he said and kissed the back of her head.

"I do not want you to leave while you're angry with me."

"I am not angry with you, Muren. I only want to keep you safe, and the words you spoke earlier scared me. I can fight an army, but I cannot fight an angry mob wanting to burn you for a witch."

"I know. I told my mother about the visions, and I will never repeat them again."

"I am glad to hear it," he said, and cupped her breast and squeezed a little. "How do you feel now?"

Muren wanted the physical comfort he offered. More than anything. They didn't have to always agree on everything, but they had a wonderful way of comforting one another in a way that transcended common language.

She turned toward him and slid her leg over his hip, then pulled him on top of her. "I would feel much better if my husband would drive me mad with desire."

Rorie leaned down and kissed her so passionately she thought her heart would burst. She kissed him back with absolute abandon as if she would never get another chance. She spoke with her body, telling him that he had imprinted on her very soul. Their lovemaking was not hurried as the other times; this was slow and sensual and filled with such emotion that when her orgasm overtook her, tears of sadness and joy slipped down her face.

CHAPTER SIXTEEN

$\mathcal{R}$orie looked over his shoulder to check on the progress of his men. Two days into riding and he was nearing the closest he would come to a decent vantage point. The sun was still pretty high in the sky, and they had plenty of time to set up camp, but preparations for battle took much longer.

Ewen rode up beside him. "Here?"

"Aye. Here is about as good as we'll get. Did we get a pigeon back from our scout yet?"

"Aye. The king's army is about a day's ride away. No doubt they have scouts riding north as well, and he will be well aware of our position long before he gets here."

"Any word from the clans?"

"Nothing yet. It will take Fergus a few more days to get here, but I expect Fraser and Grant sometime today, considering the distance they had to travel compared to us."

"Get the men set up and let's take stock of what we have to our advantage."

"Aye. Rorie, I heard about Muren's visions."

Rorie's guts lurched. "How?"

"One of the maids was about to enter the chamber the other night to bring fresh linens when she heard your raised voice. She said she dared not enter because it sounded like you were vexed. As she was walking away, she heard you mention visions and keeping it a secret."

"God's teeth. Who is she? What do we have to do to keep her quiet?" "Nothing. She's auld Allain's daughter."

"The ferrier?"

"Aye, and just as quiet as he. She came to me this morning before we left, and told me."

"And you are certain you can trust her?"

"I am as certain as anyone can be with such information. Does Muren really believe she's had visions of future events? And what did she see?"

"She does. She says she saw me being run through, and that's when I cut her off. I do not want my head filled with such images when I need to focus on this conflict with the king. I cannot afford to have my head clouded. And we cannot afford for anyone else to think so. I expect this topic to never rise again."

"You have my word."

Rorie watched Ewen ride off to oversee camp being set up. The business with Muren was delicate and dangerous. Between him and her mother, and now Ewen and the maid, the list of people who knew was growing like a cancer. He thought back to the morning he'd left her, her soft body lying next to his. He had watched her sleep for a while before waking her to love her before leaving. She was so passionate. He was a very lucky man to have such a woman who was so free with her desires.

Rorie squirmed in his seat. He needed to put thoughts of her out of his head and focus.

From where they were situated at the head of the glen, they had a perfect view of the only road leading northwest.

Here they would pitch, and here they would wait. By all estimations, he would see the king's banners on the morrow.

Rorie rode around the encampment and watched the men erect tents, dig trenches, and sharpen posts. They had a lot of work to do in a short time, and he hoped he'd see his allies riding in before much longer.

Dismounting, he grabbed an axe and joined the men who were shaping the logs they had felled to make spears for the king's horses. If they rode hard against them, Rorie's men would have to stop or at least slow them, or risk being trampled.

An hour later, Ewen tapped Rorie on the shoulder. "Grant is here and said Fraser is not far behind."

"Excellent."

He followed Ewen to where Iain Grant was just dismounting. Rorie had met him before but a long time ago, and only briefly. The man was much larger than Rorie remembered, with flaming hair that hung to his shoulders and a thick beard, but the most memorable feature that captured Rorie's attention was his icy blue eyes. He looked almost wild, and Rorie was glad he did not have to face this man in battle.

"Grant.

"MacKenzie. You're bigger than I remember."

Rorie smiled. "Aye, and you. Thank you for joining our cause."

"Someone has to do something. This business has gone on long enough, and what you're dealing with could be any one of us."

"How many men have you brought?"

"Five hundred and change."

"Excellent. Well, we can put them to work right away, finishing the trenches and poles."

Grant nodded and signalled to his men to go with Ewen and do as they were bid.

A short time later, Fraser rode up. Rorie had never met the man before but knew of him by legend. With hair as black as night and eyes to match, he had the nickname of Raven. As the man dismounted and walked toward them, Rorie could see why he was so aptly named. Head to toe in black, the man carried an intensity about him that would be formidable for anyone who met him on the battlefield.

The Wildman and the Raven. An interesting pair, Rorie noted, as the two men clasped arms in greeting. Being such close neighbours, it would be near impossible to thrive if they feuded. And though they had squabbled in the past, they were close allies for the most part.

"Welcome, friend," Rorie said to Fraser.

"'Tis I should be thanking you for bringing us together in this cause."

"That's what I said," Grant said.

"Well, I'm saying it again," Fraser said. "But I said it first," Grant said.

"And I'm saying it now," Fraser said.

Listening to the two of them made Rorie's head hurt. "Enough, you two. Come, we have much work to do. Fraser, how many men did you bring?"

"Eight hundred."

"Excellent, let's put them to work. We only have an hour or so of daylight left and a lot of work to do."

"Aye."

Fraser went off to instruct his men, then returned to the tent where Rorie had set up his council. He'd laid out the map and positioned markers showing where everyone was located at the moment.

"Do you think Ross can keep Sutherland at bay?"

"If it was the elder Sutherland, I would say no, but Ronan is not his father. He will be stopped."

"I hope you're right. What about MacKay, and how many men can he amass on short notice?"

"He can pull together four thousand with a couple months' notice, but with mere days, he should be coming with a thousand."

"We will need to stay in contact with him to monitor his progress," Fraser said. "Aye," Grant said. "If Ross runs into trouble, MacKay may need to send some of his forces to their aid."

"What about Sinclair?" Fraser asked. "Will they join Sutherland or stay out of it?"

"They've answered the call before, but who is to say where their loyalties lie now. Being so close to Sutherland, they've never been reliable," Grant said.

"Understandable, since John Sinclair has been sickly. He's only been interested in keeping the peace. What do we know of the king's progress?" Fraser asked.

"He will be here on the morrow, and we will be ready for him."

"So, now can you tell us what this is all about? Why do you battle both the king and Sutherland when you are to marry Sutherland's sister?"

Rorie recounted the events leading up to that moment, including the fact that he was now married to Sutherland's sister.

"God's teeth, man, you must have balls of solid rock," Fraser laughed.

"It was the only way to protect her from the Douglas."

"Aye, I see that, but you've not only disturbed the hornet's nest but you've also beaten it down from the tree and danced on it."

It was an interesting analogy. Rorie scanned the map again and everyone's positions. Still no word from MacDonald, so he had no idea what to expect there. But MacLeod would block him if he meant to sail north and block his retreat.

Rorie bid his allies good night and lay on the straw pallet after dousing the candles. He covered himself with a fur and listened to the sounds of the night. He'd been in battle before and always found sleep hard to come by in anticipation of the dawn. One way or another, tomorrow would bring change to the situation.

~

*M*uren maneuvered her horse off the road, urging her mother with her when she heard pounding hoofs approaching. They hid behind a tree and watched as several riders passed by. With no distinguishable markings on their tunics, Muren had no idea if they were friend or foe and so waited until they were well past before venturing out onto the road again.

Her grey mare was used to her and was, thankfully, not easily spooked, but it would soon be necessary to take an older Roman road to avoid detection. The decrepit condition of the path would slow their travels, but it was a much-needed trade-off in order to risk not being caught.

They took a turn and ventured onto the overgrown road. Not many used this one anymore since it worked its way through the mountains versus down through the glens. Mostly scouts seeking the goings-on of the Pictish tribes had used this road. The larger roads that were still used now were how the Romans moved their large armies.

As they climbed, the air cooled. Muren wrapped her cloak tighter around her and prayed the mists would remain at bay. After riding for several hours, they came to a small loch. She dismounted and led her mare to it. Her mother did the same. The sun was just dipping toward the horizon.

"We should make plans to camp here tonight. I think it's about as good as we can expect for comfort, and the horses can drink freely here."

Muren walked around the side of the loch and found a small clearing that was well protected by trees. It would allow them to avoid detection in the unlikely event that anyone happened by.

The two women made a fire and shared some bread and meat. Her mother warmed the honey mead she'd brought, and Muren sipped the sweet drink, enjoying the way it spread comforting heat through her body.

"What is your plan for when we get to Dunrobin?" Morag asked.

"I plan to walk into the castle and find my brother."

"Do you think he will be there, or do you think he will be trying to break through Ross's defences to get to Rorie?"

"I do not know. But we will go to Dunrobin first. If he is not there, I will find him and talk some sense into him."

"I know that, love. Have you thought any more on your visions?"

"I do not need to. They were crystal clear to me. I know they mean that if I do not intervene, I will lose my husband."

"But you never saw him laid out. You only saw the injury, not the result."

"I didn't need to see the result. Those were mortal wounds. I know it in my heart."

Her mother did not press the issue any further, and Muren was grateful for it. Her mind buzzed with the possibilities of what she suggested. All she could rely on now was what she had seen and how that made her feel. In her heart, she was certain Rorie and Ronan were in mortal danger.

The next morning, they broke camp and continued along

the old road just as the sun was coming up. At times, Muren was awarded a stunning view of the lands that flattened out to the east, shrouded in a layer of mist. She breathed in the clean air, willing it to cleanse her mind from her troubled thoughts.

If Ronan was still at Dunrobin, she was certain she could get through to him.

Nothing she and Freya had said to him had managed to sway him from allowing the betrothal with the Douglas to go ahead. But now that she was already married, surely he would see that peace could be had. The Douglas could be compensated another way. They had more money than they knew what to do with. Surely the man could be paid off and sent away.

As for the king, she prayed Rorie would utilize a diplomatic approach and do everything he could to avoid a bloody battle. Her stomach lurched as the image of him doubled over flashed across her mind.

She pushed the image aside and focused on the journey ahead. Grateful for her mother's company, she was equally thankful she did not find it necessary to chat while they rode. The silence allowed Muren to mull over just what she would say to Ronan.

As the sun fell toward the horizon, Muren and her mother rode up to the drawbridge of Dunrobin Castle. Old trepidation welled up and bubbled to the surface, but Muren worked hard to tramp it down so she could maintain her courage.

They only had to wait a moment or two until the drawbridge was lowered and they were permitted entry.

Freya rushed out to meet them. "By God, you're a sorry sight!"

Muren dismounted and allowed herself to be pulled into a hug by a very pregnant Freya.

"It is good to see you, sister. Where is my brother?"

"He is not here."

Muren's heart squeezed. She was too late. "Where is he, Freya?"

"Come inside and let me get you fed and rested. You look like death warmed over."

"We have little time. I must find Ronan."

"What has happened?"

"I will explain, but first you must tell me where he is."

Freya looked from Muren to her mother and back again. "He was bid to the king, to aide him in a campaign."

Muren's heart sank. "When?"

"A sennight ago."

Christ's teeth. Rorie was walking into a trap. Ross would not be able to stop Sutherland because the king's army had somehow skirted around them before Rorie had even asked them to block the route. Rorie was not just waiting for the king's army; he was awaiting the added thousands in Ronan's army, too. There was no way MacKenzie, Fraser, and Grant numbers could match what approached.

Muren turned to her mother. "We must leave again at once."

"Our horses need the rest, Muren. We will ride them to their death if we do not let them rest."

"You must tell me what is going on," Freya said while rubbing her belly.

"We will come inside, but we will have to borrow two fresh mares. I need to warn Rorie."

Muren and her mother followed Freya into the castle and to the great hall. Chairs were moved to the hearth, and the women were brought bowls of stew and pieces of crusty bread along with a tankard of ale and goblets.

Muren recounted everything she knew to Freya,

including her visions. At the first mention of a dream, she halted Muren and then sent the servants away.

"We must be careful of that kind of talk."

Freya had always possessed a keen mind. She and Muren shared a strong bond and, regarding her now, Muren realized just how much she had relied on Freya in the past for her common-sense approach and vast courage.

Muren told her then about the visions, all except the bairn. She was not sure how Freya would handle that information, so left it out.

"You think Rorie is walking into a trap?"

"Aye."

"And you think you can convince Ronan to stand down now that you are married to Rorie?"

"Aye."

"Muren, Ronan has been going crazy trying to find you. He was convinced you had come to harm, and that Rorie had lost his wits and was holding you somewhere against your will."

"That was not true. I went with Rorie willingly."

"But could you not have sent word somehow to ease our worry?"

She supposed she could have. But that would have run the risk of drawing the king to Eilean Donan, and that would have removed any chance they had of coming out of this without massive casualties on their side. No. Rorie's calculations had been sound. But he didn't know about Ronan. She needed to get that information to him immediately unless it was already too late.

CHAPTER SEVENTEEN

*R*orie stood beside Grant, Fraser, and his brother Ewen and watched as the king's army proceeded up through the glen. It was midday, and a heavy mist hung in the air. With no wind to blow them away, the midges were thick, and Rorie was sure there was a level of hell containing nothing more than those tiny bastards for torment.

A scout in the night had told them that Sutherland's army marched south. How the hell Ross had missed them, Rorie did not know, but he intended to find out...if he got out of this alive. The two armies combined yielded far higher numbers than he could comfortably defeat. And Fergus was still a day away. He would either have to negotiate terms, delay the battle somehow, or yield.

His men were battle-hungry, as was normal in the circumstances. They had all been affected in one way or another by this king since he'd taken back the crown ten years ago. The man was greedy, and he cared not for the manner in which his politics affected the common folk of this country.

It made Rorie's guts burn.

"What's your position, MacKenzie?" Grant asked.

"A good question. If we battle them today, we are outnumbered. Fergus's army will even the score, but he is a day away. Sutherland managed to skirt around Ross before we asked them for help, but why they did not notice or bother to share with us that his army had already marched past them, is beyond me."

"Ross cares only about Ross," Grant said.

"We've no time to banter on the motivations of anyone not here," Fraser said. "We need to make a plan. Now."

Rorie turned to the other men. "I will not hold it against you if you want to take your men and leave. This is my fight and my burden to bear."

"Are you daft, man?" Grant said. "We didn't come to stand up with you only to run when the numbers didn't sit in our favour. We came here to kill some Scots."

Rorie noted the wild look in his eye. His blood was up, as it was with many of the other men. They were ready for a fight.

"Some of us came to reclaim our right to govern over our own," Fraser said.

"Pretty words, from a pretty wee man," Grant said.

"You'll see how pretty I am with my blade in your gullet."

"You wouldn't get the chance," Grant said and moved closer to him.

Rorie stepped between them. "There are enough men needing your blade in their gullet crossing the glen. No need to kill each other just yet."

Grant tipped his head back and laughed. "So, battle it is then?"

"Aye," Rorie said. "It would appear so."

Fraser shook his head and looked up to the sky then kissed an amulet around his neck. "I'll see you soon, love."

The man's wife had died the previous year. After that,

he'd been given the nickname of Raven. His heart had turned black, people said of him. But Rorie knew better. Grief could cause a man to withdraw, but there was always a balance in life. He'd pined for Muren for months, and now she was his. For how long depended on the outcome of his discussion with the man crossing the glen.

When the king was close to the halfway mark, Rorie rode out to meet him, flanked by Grant and Fraser. For several heartbeats, they simply stared at one another. Ronan flanked the king's right side, and MacIntosh flanked his other. Rorie was surprised at how fat the king had grown since he'd last seen him. What had once been a lean and muscular man was now plump. Rorie pitied his horse.

"You've something of mine in your possession, MacKenzie," Ronan said.

"Something of yours? I do not see how that's possible. What I have is my own."

"That's not possible unless you've taken her against her will and forced her to marry you."

"I assure you there was no force involved. She was quite willing."

Ronan was off his horse in an instant and striding toward Rorie, who jumped down to meet him face-to-face. MacIntosh jumped in between them before they even had time to draw their swords.

"Well, this is an interesting development," the king said, from atop his charger.

"Muren was always mine," Rorie said. "Our marriage has been blessed and consummated, so there is nothing for you here."

"I will have retribution for the damage caused to me," Ronan said.

"Caused to you? You're the one who broke the betrothal

and gave her away to someone else as if she were cattle. If anyone should be furious, 'tis I."

"You forget whose company you keep," MacIntosh said. "Your king is the only one who decides in such matters, and his decision was to break the betrothal."

"You have both broken your oath to me. You agreed to serve me as needed, in exchange for your authority to remain intact. You've broken that vow and leave me with no choice."

Rorie had a sense of what was coming. This would end in bloodshed today; he was not willing to give up his right as chief of his clan, and he was certain Grant, Fraser, MacKay, and even Sutherland would stand up to this tyranny.

"And what is that choice?" Rorie asked.

"I hereby strip you of your titles and claim your lands as my own."

"You do not have the right," Rorie said. "I have Fraser, Grant, MacLeod, and MacKay behind me, and we will not stand for it." He looked at MacIntosh and Sutherland then. "And if you go along with this, there will be a bloody war that will mean losses for all of us."

"You have no choice. My word is law," said the king.

"You will have a mutiny on your hands if you force this," Rorie warned.

"Are you threatening your king?" MacIntosh asked.

"No. I am merely stating a fact. You tried this at Inverness, and look what happened. We bonded together. You cannot take us all on. You do not have the numbers." Rorie was fed up with the arrogance of the man, king or not. He had interfered in their lives for far too long because of his own greed and lack of understanding of their Highland ways. Well, by God, no more. "If 'tis a war you want, a war you'll get."

Rorie turned around and remounted his horse. Without another look back, he kicked the sides of his horse into a gallop. He did not have to look back to know that Fraser and Grant followed. He didn't know what would happen next, and in truth, he was prepared for the worst. There was no way to reason with the king, and if that meant he had to be driven back to Edinburgh then so be it.

"What now?" Grant asked. "You have now officially started a war that we must all fight."

"We were never going to avoid that fight," Rorie said. "The Stewart would never be satisfied until he stripped us of everything we had."

"What about Sutherland?"

Rorie turned around and watched as the king retreated leaving Ronan in the middle of the battlefield alone.

"Come on, man," Rorie said under his breath. "Do the right thing."

Rorie blinked and watched as Ronan turned his horse toward Rorie's side of the glen. A second later, the king turned around and rode hard toward him. Rorie took off toward them and prayed he could reach them in time. Guards of the king surrounded Ronan and the Stewart, but before Ronan had a chance to even draw his sword, the king ran him through.

Ronan fell to the ground. A thunder of hooves sounded behind Rorie as he tore off across the glen. By the time they got to Ronan, he was deathly pale and surrounded in a pool of blood, the king and his guards having retreated to the other side of the glen.

"Jesus, Ronan! No!" Rorie knelt at Ronan's side.

Ronan's lifeblood spilled forth from him in great spurts. Rorie pressed hard on the wound trying to slow the blood, but it would not be contained.

"Take care of my family, Rorie," Ronan whispered.

"You're not going to die. Do you hear me? You're going to live, and we're going to fight the Stewart together."

"I never should have listened to him. I should have never broken the betrothal. Find her and marry her."

"I already have Ronan. She is safe."

Ronan locked gazes with Rorie and smiled. A second later, his body relaxed, and his head fell to the side. Rage and despair flowed through Rorie's veins as he screamed at the sky. He would make the king pay for this atrocity one way or another.

~

*M*uren held Freya's hand as her sister-in-law bent forward and drew in deep breaths. The agonizing howl that escaped her lips mirrored the war raging inside Muren, torn between going to warn Ronan and Rorie or staying here where Freya needed her as she brought her new bairn into the world.

"Did you find the midwife?" Muren asked her mother when she entered Freya's chamber.

"Aye, she is on her way."

"Thank God. Freya's racked with pain."

"Pain is normal, Muren. 'Tis not easy bringing a bairn into the world."

"She was not like this last time. The wee laddie had already come almost before the midwife could catch him."

Muren's mother soaked a cloth in some cool water and brushed it across Freya's brow. "Hush now, love, we're here."

"I want Ronan," she said when the contraction passed.

"A rider has been sent to him to let him know the bairn comes early." "I need him here," Freya said.

Muren held her hand tighter. "He will be here soon," she said. It was not customary for a husband to be present at a child's birth, but in this case, she supposed she could imagine an exception. Ronan had witnessed their wee lassie's birth the year before.

Freya let out another howl just as the midwife entered the chamber.

"Ooooh now, it sounds like someone is anxious to meet their mama," the older woman said in a calm, quiet voice that Muren found to be quite soothing. "Let's get her into bed," she said to Muren and her mother.

Muren watched as the midwife checked Freya for her progress. Freya seemed like she was lost to the pain, and Muren knew exactly how that felt. In that moment, she had an inkling of what it might be like for Rorie to have to watch her suffer when her pain overtook her.

The midwife stepped back and stared at Freya. "What is it, Euphima?" Muren's mother asked.

Wiping her hands on a cloth, she said, "I fear she's in for a long night. The bairn comes, but has not turned."

Muren placed her hands on her own belly. There was so much that could go wrong during childbirth, it was a wonder any made it into the world. "What can we do to help?" she asked.

"Just be ready to hold her hand when I tell you."

Muren sat next to Freya on the bed and held her hand. Her mother passed her a cool cloth, and Muren wiped Freya's brow. "'Twill be well, Freya. Your wee bairn will be here before you know it."

"I want Ronan," she said again.

The fear in her words was palpable. Freya was the strongest woman Muren had ever known, save for her mother. Her obvious concern drew images into Muren's mind of the vision with the bairn. Would it—? No. She would not ask that question.

She needed to focus on the here and now and do everything possible to see to Freya's comfort, including finding a way for her sister-in-law to focus.

Euphima rolled up her sleeves and then nodded to Muren's mother.

"Here," Morag said while placing a wooden rod in front of Freya's mouth, "bite down on this, love. And take my hand."

Freya did as she was asked, while Euphima lifted the sheet and reached underneath. Whatever she was doing caused Freya's body to go rigid as a mighty scream erupted from her throat. Muren's heart pounded in her chest and sweat trickled from her own brow. She and her mother held onto Freya's hand and helped her lean forward when Euphima said, "Push!"

A few pushes later, a baby's cry rang out loud and clear. Muren was sure she'd never heard such a glorious sound in all her life. She gently stroked Freya's hair as Euphima and Muren's mother cleaned the bairn up and swaddled her.

"Here is your wee lassie," the midwife said, as she passed her to Freya.

Tears streamed down the exhausted woman's face. "Your papa will see you soon, love. Hush now."

"You did well, Freya," Muren said but got no response. It was like the woman didn't even register anyone else in the chamber, so intent was she on the bairn. Muren supposed she could understand that. She was about to get another cloth when a loud knock sounded at the door.

Lifting the latch, Muren stepped outside to see who would dare knock on the lady's door whilst she was in such a way.

"Father Sinclair? What brings you here? The wee lassie was just born, and she and her mother both fare well."

He shook his head. "I've terrible news, Muren. In truth, I do not know how to share it."

Muren placed her hands over her ears. She did not want to hear whatever it was.

But Father Sinclair was insistent. Taking her hands from her head and holding them tight, he asked, "Where is your mother?"

"Inside, seeing to Freya,"

"She will want to hear this, too."

With shaking fingers, Muren pushed the door open and beckoned her mother, hoping Freya would not notice her absence.

When her mother was outside, Father Sinclair said, "A terrible thing has happened."

"To whom?" her mother asked. "Ronan. Slain, at the hand of the king."

Muren could not bear it. She'd seen his death but could not get to him in time.

That meant the other visions were true as well.

Her mother's knees buckled, but the priest was quick to help steady her.

Muren's heart ached so badly she was sure she would not survive this. Tears streamed down her face as a sob escaped her lips. Her mother pulled her into a tight embrace and sobbed on her shoulder as Father Sinclair prayed quietly.

When he was finished praying for Ronan's soul and for healing strength to be bestowed upon Muren and her mother, he said, "He is being transported here now."

Muren pulled back from her mother's embrace. The woman looked years older than she had but days ago. How could she tell her she'd foreseen this? Muren was ashamed of holding the information back now. Mayhap it could have prepared her mother for the worst.

Rorie. Oh God, she needed to get to him now more than ever. But she could not leave her mother or the new bairn.

And what about Freya? How could they tell her such news when she was in such a delicate and vulnerable state?

"We must tell Freya," her mother said through sobs.

"I will help you with that," Father Sinclair said. "Muren, go inside and make sure she is able to receive me."

Muren entered the chamber but could not look at Freya. She tried to act normally, but her body would not quit trembling. She tugged on Euphima's sleeve and beckoned her towards the door. In a low voice, she said, "Father Sinclair is outside and wishes to speak with Freya."

Euphima looked back at the bed and then back to Muren. "Now?"

Muren made the mistake of glancing at Freya. She was staring hard at her and frowning. "What is it, Muren?"

"Father Sinclair wishes to see you. May I let him enter?"

"'Tis Ronan, isn't it?" Freya asked, and made to move out of the bed.

Euphima moved very quickly for a woman of her age and was by Freya's side pushing her back into the bed. "You must not get up yet, Freya."

"Where is Ronan? I want to see him now."

Muren opened the door as soon as Freya was covered again. Euphima placed the bairn in Muren's arms, and the moment she did Muren's tears would not be held back. She sobbed as the beautiful wee lass opened her eyes and blinked at her.

Muren barely registered the door opening and then Freya's wail as she was given the devastating news.

Flashes of the boy with whom she'd played as a child and the man with whom she'd quarrelled, all passed in front of her mind's eye. She would never get to tell him that she forgave him for his choices, and she would never forgive herself for not warning him in time.

CHAPTER EIGHTEEN

"Christ's teeth, this could turn into Inverness all over again," Fraser said.

"He'd never get away with it now," Grant said.

Rorie could not speak. In his mind's eye, he could only see Ronan being carried off the battlefield by his bannermen. The king had forced his army to stay put and was no doubt putting the fear of God into them should they rise against him.

Inverness indeed. Up to now, that had been the worst this king had dared. Peace talks, he'd called it. How could that term be used when a good number of the forty chiefs had ended up imprisoned and three dead?

All of that aside, Rorie's only real thought was of Muren. He had to get word to Eilean Donan and let her know what had happened. If the fates were kind, he would deliver the news himself and comfort her properly. But this battle had not even begun, and already he felt a massive loss even though Ronan had fully intended to fight against him.

"What now, MacKenzie?" Fraser asked.

Rorie swallowed hard. He did not want this. Any of it.

Surely there was a better way to resolve their differences than slaughtering one another. And what exactly did the king gain by killing Ronan? The man already had an heir, so someone else within the clan would step in until his young son, Artagan became of age. Unless the king planned to place someone of his own choosing in such an exalted position. If that's what he had in mind, then none of them were safe.

"We wait for the king's terms," Rorie said. "We are as ready as we can be, and the longer we wait, the more likely Fergus will be here with his added numbers before the first arrow is let loose."

His strategy was sound, but his whole body itched as though an army of biting, irritating midges had hunkered down for a feast on his flesh.

As it was, they did not have to wait long for some action. Just as riders took off from across the glen to where the king was stationed, Fergus rode up alongside Rorie.

"What do you think he wants?"

Rorie turned to Fergus. Clearly, no one had told him yet, which was no surprise considering the delicate history between them. Their fathers being sworn enemies, Fergus and Ronan's elder brother, Artagan, had met and befriended one another. That was until Ronan's father caught wind of the occurrence and put a stop to it. He beat young Artagan so bad that the lad died from infection a month later. It was quite incredible that Fergus and Ronan had managed to secure an alliance despite the clan history, and that Fergus's own sister was married to Ronan.

"Fergus—"

The man watched the king approach and then fixed his gaze on a spot between them and Rorie. "Has there been a battle already?"

"No, Fergus, but—"

Rorie didn't know how to force the words from his mouth. "Whose blood soaks the glen?"

"Fergus, I could not reach him in time."

"Whose blood?" Fergus's voice became quiet and low. Deadly. "Ronan's blood, Fergus."

With that, Fergus took off across the glen. Rorie followed but, despite being an accomplished rider, could not catch up.

The king and his men stopped not long after Fergus tore off. Rorie could hear a thunder of hooves, no doubt the MacKay men were following their laird to protect him. Rorie was tight at their heels.

Fergus encircled the king and the three other riders he'd taken with him.

MacIntosh was among them, and Rorie noted the brief nod of acknowledgement between the two men. Were it not for MacIntosh, Fergus would have surely perished five years ago when Ronan's father and the elder MacDonald had plotted to pin a heinous crime at his door.

"You killed my brother-in-law," Fergus said to the king.

"Fergus, it is a lot more complicated than that," MacIntosh said.

"No, it is not," Rorie said, catching up just in time to hear the remark.

"Ronan had made a choice to stand with us against a king who would barter his people to line his own pockets at any cost, only to be run through by the same man."

"Those are serious accusations, MacKenzie. I would choose your words wisely," MacIntosh said.

"You call yourself a Highlander," Rorie scoffed, "but you're more interested in the scraps from the king's table than banding with us to protect the Highland way and her people."

Fergus encircled the men one more time then stopped directly in front of the king, pulling back on his destrier's reins so the beast's head was kept up to face off the king's horse. It was an aggressive move. The king did not flinch. Nor did his horse.

"If you can put a leash on your boarhound here, I will offer you my terms," the king said.

"Why should we believe anything you say? Your words have always been washed away in bloodshed."

"Because if you do not accept my terms, there will be massive losses on both sides this day. With MacKay's men, our scores are nearly even. How long do you think your patchwork army can stand up against mine who've trained together for years?"

Though he was right, every single inch of Rorie did not want to engage in any kind of agreement with this man who displayed such a lack of honour it made Rorie's guts lurch.

"You should hear him out," MacIntosh said.

Rorie was damned near sick of him and his politics. He'd hear the king out just to get MacIntosh to shut his pretty mouth.

"Very well. Say your piece. But you have slaughtered one of ours. You will answer for that," Rorie said through gritted teeth.

The king raised his brows. "You can say that even though he had planned to face you on the battlefield?"

"Only because of the position you put him in. It's true I had a quarrel with his father, but the son was an honourable man. You will get no sympathy in the Highlands after such an act."

"I don't need your sympathy. Only your fealty. And if I do not get it willingly, I will take it."

"At what cost?" Rorie asked though the answer was obvious.

"At any cost. The survival of the Crown is paramount to

any individual need." The man was bold. But he would not take what he wanted without a fight.

"Very well. Speak your terms." Rorie noticed MacIntosh open his mouth and shut it again; no doubt he'd been about to chastise Rorie for not using a formal address with the king. Rorie did not care anymore. This king's greed knew no bounds, and with his dying breath, Rorie would not stand for it.

"For defying my order relating to the betrothal of Lady Muren to William Douglas, I hereby revoke the MacDonald lands I previously offered, and decree that one of my magistrates will be sent to govern your lands in my stead. An additional tax will be imposed upon you for each seafaring man. You will pay me for each time a MacKenzie boards one of your ships. You will do this or lose your ships. Fitting, I think since those same ships were used in your deception."

Rorie shook his head. "Do you make up taxes in your head beforehand, or do you think them up in the passing moment?"

"Careful, MacKenzie," MacIntosh warned.

"And that will be enough out of you," Rorie said to him.

The king smirked and turned his horse around. MacIntosh and the other guards followed.

"This has to end," Rorie said.

"Aye, but for now we must think of Freya and Muren. Has anyone sent news to Dunrobin?" Fergus replied.

"I have not, but I cannot speak for the actions of the Stewart. He may try to claim their lands as his own, knowing him."

"He cannot do that. Ronan has an heir and, though young, it is up to us now to ensure a proper steward is put in place until Artagan comes of age. If we make haste, we can be there on the morrow," Fergus said.

"I must return to Eilean Donan to Muren."

"Muren is not at Eilean Donan, Rorie. She is at Dunrobin. Freya sent word as soon as they arrived."

"What? Why would she do that?" Rorie asked. He couldn't believe she'd put herself at risk!

"I do not know. All she said was that Muren was with her. I suspect she knew that Muren travelled without your permission."

"It was more than that. I told her to stay where she was. That woman will turn me into an old man," Rorie said, as he raked his hands through his hair. He took one last look out across the glen at the spot where Ronan's lifeblood had spewed from his body. "Fergus, I tried to reach him."

Fergus looked at Ronan's chest and arms. "He died in your arms. At least he was not alone."

"Do you blame me?"

"No, Rorie, I blame the Stewart. 'Twas his sword that ran him through, but I cannot speak for what my sister will think. She has a quick temper, and Ronan possessed the other half of her soul."

They galloped back to the men and informed them of their decision to ride to Dunrobin. Rorie instructed Ewen to return with the men to Eilean Donan. He would ride hard to Muren and comfort her, aye. But she would answer for defying him.

∾

*M*uren stroked Freya's hair as she sobbed. A full night and day had passed since the devastating news had been presented to them. Ronan's body was being held in another chamber, and Bishop de Strathbrook himself had travelled from Dornoch to oversee preparations for the funeral. Freya was told she must wait for his body to be cleansed before she could see him. It was everything

Muren and her mother could do to hold her down when she insisted on seeing him immediately. In truth, it was only the weakness from childbirth that kept the woman abed. Other than that, she would have surely torn the house apart.

Freya was the strongest woman Muren had ever known, and there was no doubt she would get through this, but right now there was only anguish. More than anything, Muren wanted Rorie. She had no idea where he was or how to get in contact with him. Comforting Freya whilst trying to reconcile her own grief, was exhausting. She had only slept but moments since the news had come, and the only moments of peace she received were when she was able to hold the child. In those times, a wondrous calm settled over her, as though something was telling her all would be well. Still, she would feel much better to see Rorie alive and well and in one piece.

Freya had just settled into a deep sleep, and Muren's eyes drooped when a knock sounded at the door. Muren placed the bairn in her cradle and crossed the room as quietly as she could. She lifted the latch and opened the door a crack. Her heart caught in her throat when she spied both Rorie and Fergus on the other side.

Muren slipped out into the hallway and closed the door quietly. The look of anger on Rorie's face confused her. And then she remembered; she was not supposed to be here. Going against his wishes seemed rather minor now, considering all that had transpired, and it had in fact been good that she had been here for Freya when the news came. Despite those logical thoughts, Muren's belly coiled into a knot, and her hands trembled.

"How is my sister?" Fergus's voice was hard, and it was everything Muren could do not to cower from it.

Muren cleared her throat and squared her shoulders. "She is very weak from the bairn coming early, and I fear the news has taken a toll on her."

"Her bairn came early?" Fergus asked, his voice a little softer.

"Aye, the day before we got the news about R-Ronan." Muren stole a glance at Rorie whose lips were set in a hard line. She could not meet his eyes. And then she became angry with herself. She had gone against his wishes, true. But she was not his prisoner, and she would not have the kind of marriage where her husband dictated to her what she could and could not do. Muren lifted her chin a little and met Rorie's gaze.

"I wish to sit with my sister. I will leave you two alone," Fergus said.

When the door closed behind him, a lump formed in Muren's throat. The fact that Rorie did not speak right away told her that he was angry with her. In her grief-ridden state, she was not sure she could bear it.

"Rorie," she said in a breathless voice.

A flash of pain crossed his features, which tore at her heart. God, she wanted his arms around her. Why was he holding back?

"You left Eilean Donan."

"Aye, Rorie. I was so worried about you and Ronan, I could not sit by and just let it happen. I came here to find Ronan and talk him out of coming."

Rorie's brows shot up. "You dreamed about Ronan's death?"

"Aye." She had tried hard not to think about the image, but now it came back with a vengeance. "I saw the king run his sword through Ronan's heart. I saw his blood spill onto the green grass."

Rorie placed his hands on his head. "I cannot hear this. Someone told you." "No, Rorie. No one told me. I saw it in my visions."

Rorie took her by the arm, not too roughly, but forceful

enough to make her come with him. He opened a chamber door and looked inside. He then entered with her in tow and closed the door, releasing her at the same time.

"I have told you to keep quiet about those dreams."

"Visions, Rorie! They were visions, and now you know what I saw came true. I can see it in your eyes that you now believe me."

"No, I do not. You never told me about Ronan."

"I did not have the heart."

"I do not believe you."

Muren gasped as though someone had punched her in the gut. "Are you calling me a liar?"

"I am saying that you must give up this business about the visions, or you will be in much more trouble than you've ever known."

That last statement was so pig-headed of him. How dare he presume to rank the dangers in which she was placed because of the greed of men.

"I came here to warn my brother that he was in danger, and then I planned to come find you and tell you the same thing. The fact that I was right about Ronan, and now the child, proves that. You were in my visions, too, Rorie, and you must heed me."

"I will not listen to another word of this, Muren. You must stop this right now. I will not stand by whilst you invite more trouble to our doorstep."

Muren could not have been more shocked had he slapped her. "You think I do this to invite trouble? How can you possibly say such a thing, when all I want to do is tell the truth and maybe help someone?"

"No, Muren. You only bring danger to yourself by sharing these dreams or visions, or whatever you want to call them. Do not bring it up again. For your own safety and for those around you."

She couldn't believe her ears. While there was some sense to being cautious, she would not forget these visions had come to her. Now more than ever. He was in danger, and there was still the king's slaughter. Muren could not stay silent. She would not.

"And that's your final word then, is it?"

His expression took on a sadness as he shook his head. "Muren, please. I just want to go home and start our life together. I do not want to quarrel," he said and reached for her.

Muren stepped back. "Back to your home, where you will dictate to me where I may go and what I may say? I think not, Rorie."

"Muren, I love you. You know that. I only say these things to protect you."

"You do not ask what I think. You only bark orders, and I will not have it. As much as I love you, I told you before that I will not be bartered, bullied, or belittled ever again. If you cannot accept that then—"

"Then what? You will have our marriage annulled? You will stay here with Freya? Honestly, Muren, I have done everything you wanted. I gave you the space you wanted, even when it went against my better judgement. I protected you, hid you, and moved hundreds of men to create a diversion so I could save you. But I will not let you bring harm to my doorstep in the form of a witch-hunt. My clansmen and the people under my care deserve better than that, and so do you. I know you're caught up in these dreams, and I know that you've suffered. But your brother is on a slab because of this mess, and I am saying enough is enough. We have a temporary peace with the king, and I want to put this behind us."

"You think this is all my fault."

"I did not say that."

"Aye, this business—as you put it—has everything to do with me. You protected me, hid me, moved men for me, and my brother is lying on a slab. That all has to do with me, and you just want to go home. Well, why don't you just go home, Rorie? I cannot escape the magrymes, and I cannot escape the visions. If I could, believe me, I would have done so long ago. Go home to your clan and keep them safe. The world I live in is a lot more complicated, and I cannot give up quite so easily."

Rorie clenched his fists. His jaw was set, and his eyes bore into hers. "You seem to delight in twisting my words. You are my wife, and I will not leave here without you. So, like it or lump it, we leave here as soon as your brother is put to rest. You might as well get used to the idea of being married to me, Muren. 'Till death do us part."

With that, he left the chamber and slammed the door. 'Till death indeed. Two of her visions had come true despite her trying to intervene. By God, she was not about to give up trying to protect him.

CHAPTER NINETEEN

*R*orie found Fergus in the great hall. His hand rested at the top of the hearth as he stared into the flames.

"How is Freya?"

Fergus turned. The man looked like hell. He could put fear into the hearts of men on the battlefield, but this man definitely had a soft spot for his sister.

"Not well. She will return to Tongue with me until she is recovered. She wishes to return and help run the clan and oversee the stewardship until Artagan comes of age."

"She is a very strong woman, Fergus." "Aye, that she is. As is your Muren."

Rorie shook his head. "These dreams of hers, Fergus, they're going to drive me mad. She insists she foresaw Ronan's death," Rorie said in a whisper.

"Christ. Then she cannot tell anyone about them."

"That's what I told her, but she insists by sharing them she can prevent harm."

"Did you know about her dream involving Ronan?"

"No."

"So she thinks that by not warning him, she is responsible?"

"Aye, something like that."

"What did you say to her?"

"I told her to forget about them."

Fergus chuckled. "And how was that received?"

"Not well, I fear. I told her we shall return to MacKenzie lands as soon as her brother is put to rest."

"And she agreed?"

"No, not really."

"What were her other visions?"

"One was about a child. I suspect she is convinced it is Freya's wee lass. And the other has to do with the king."

"The king? How so?" Fergus turned to him fully now. "She said she saw him being slain in his bed."

"Christ's teeth, those are treasonous words to speak even by repeating them."

"Aye, you do not have to remind me. If she keeps this up, I will have the king and every witch-hunter in Scotland beating down my door."

Servants entered with food and ale, lining the table in anticipation of the crowds who would gather to pay homage to Ronan.

Rorie took a trencher and filled it with meat, cheese, and bread. He filled his goblet with ale and downed it, then filled it again. A chair scraped on the stone floor behind him. When he turned to see who it was, he caught sight of the tapestry flicking on the other side of the hall. No doubt someone had been spying on their conversation. Until a steward was set up, there would be much speculation, and he doubted any chamber in the castle was safe from prying eyes and ears.

"May I join you, Laird MacKenzie?" a male voice said from behind him.

Rorie turned. The bishop filled his trencher with food and had already taken a seat next to him. "Since you already have, I suppose the answer must be, aye, you may join me, Your Grace."

"Ahhh, you are a keen one, Rorie MacKenzie, chief who does not want to be chief."

Rorie sat and took another long draught of ale. When he swallowed the last drop, he filled his trencher again and wiped moisture from his lips.

"What makes you think I do not want to be chief?"

"'Tis whispered on the wind," the bishop said.

"Is it now? And what else does the wind say?"

"That your lovely wife has a gift."

Rorie stood and toppled his chair. "What would you know of it?"

"Oh, do sit down, MacKenzie. She is in no danger from me. If I wanted to harm the lass, I could have done so any time whilst she took sanctuary at the abbey."

It was true. Rorie supposed he had no choice but to listen to what the man had to say.

"Very well. Why do you seek me out?"

"And what makes you think I seek you out?"

Rorie looked around the hall. There were only four other chairs occupied, and they were all well away from them and not within earshot. "Maybe because this table is not for want of space."

The bishop smiled. "No, it is not, indeed." He plucked a piece of cheese from his trencher and popped it into his mouth. After chewing for what seemed like ages then swallowing, he said, "You must protect your wife."

"You do not need to tell me that."

"No, I suppose I do not, but she is currently unattended and roaming the grounds. 'Tis not only protection she requires whilst on the road home, my Lord MacKenzie. 'Tis here within the walls of this castle, too."

"What do you mean?"

The bishop leaned in closer. "There are those still loyal to the elder Sutherland. A cruel man, who would have had Freya and little Artagan run through the moment they learned Ronan was dead."

"Are you telling me there is someone else who would lay claim to the earl's title and chiefship?"

"A cousin, aye. And the fact that Artair Sutherland is Ronan's father and not Muren's will matter not. She is Ronan's sister and, as such, is at risk. She is not safe here, MacKenzie."

Christ's bones, would it never end? Just when he thought he had a handle on one threat, another emerged. He needed to find Muren and secure her in a chamber, supposing he guarded her himself. And he knew without a doubt that she would be none too pleased about it.

Rorie located her down by the falconry. She'd told him about one particular golden eaglet whose wing had broken, probably on its first time out of the nest, so he wondered if he'd find her there. She was crouching low and speaking softly to the creature

"Muren, you must come with me," he said.

Her head whipped around so fast she stumbled and landed on her behind. "Why?" she asked, as she jumped up and swiped the back of her skirt.

Aye, she was still annoyed with him, and he could live with that, but he could not live without her, so she could pout all she wanted, but she was coming with him.

"We must speak in private."

She put her hands on her hips and cocked her head to one side. "What about?"

Enough was enough. Rorie hoisted her over his shoulder

and held her legs with one arm. "We will discuss this in private."

"Put me down!" She pounded on his back, and he was surprised at the power behind her tiny hands.

"If I do, will you promise to come quietly and make no fuss? We have some things to discuss, you and I, and the sooner we come to some agreement, the easier this will be on all of us."

Rorie continued to walk, and after a few steps, the pounding ceased. "Very well, I will come quietly, and I will let you have your say."

"Good." Rorie planted her on her feet so fast she struggled to stand. Without saying another word, he walked on ahead and did not break his stride until he was at their chamber door. He opened it wide and stepped to the side for her to enter. It was only then he realized that his height afforded him a much longer stride than hers. She was just coming around the corner when he looked back.

"What is so urgent that you make me practically run to catch up to you?" she asked, a little out of breath.

Rorie closed the door behind her and pulled her into his arms. He needed to know one thing before he laid down the new set of restrictions on her. He bent his head toward hers, noting how wide her eyes became and how they lowered once he brushed his lips across hers.

"You told me long ago that you trusted me," he said and pressed light kisses along her jawline and down her neck.

"Aye, Rorie. I trust you," she said with conviction, all the while tugging at the back of his neck to draw him closer.

He grinned. They still had this passion between them. An ocean of differences they may share, but they still had this core need for one another. He prayed it would get them through the challenges they would face in the months and years to come.

⁓

*T*o say she was confused was quite the understatement. Rorie was determined to get her alone, but his demeanour was not of a flirtatious kind. He'd urged her into a secret hiding place on many occasions, but this was something different. The urgency in him was not of a passionate nature, though if he continued to kiss her neck like that—and based on the growing erection pressing against her—she suspected that might quickly change.

But no. His reason for bringing her here was not to make love to her. She tried to reason it out, but his kisses stirred her, as they always did. If she had any chance of finding out why there were here, she would need to break this now. And whatever it was, she did not want to hear it after they shared their passion. She wanted to know before.

Muren pulled back from him and held him at bay with one hand. Holding up one finger, she said, "You wanted me to come here with you to discuss something very important."

Rorie reached for her again, but she stepped back. "No, Rorie. I want to know why you would fling me over your shoulder like a sack of barley, for everyone to see."

Anguish crossed his features as though he fought some inner battle and was losing.

Dropping his arms to his sides, he said, "You are still in danger." Rorie walked past her toward the open window. A great view of the sea lay beyond. She had studied every inch of it in the years since she'd come to stay at Dunrobin.

"Aye, from witch-hunters. Rorie. I am not afraid of them." And nor was she.

Witch-hunters did not burn noblewomen.

"I am not talking about witch-hunters, Muren. This threat has to do with your family."

Muren moved to stand by him at the window. "Because Ronan is dead?"

"Aye, love."

Rorie turned toward her and gazed into her eyes. Just being near him made her braver. She was sure she could face anything with his love to support her. And mayhap that was the lesson she needed to learn. That while she could stand on her own two feet, this was the man she was meant to be with and who made her stronger. The realization hit her like a blow. She'd been wrong to push him away when all he had tried to do was protect her. She would not be bullied by him, but she would listen to him, and together they would find the best way forward.

"Tell me, Rorie."

"The bishop came to see me in the hall. He said you are in danger because there are still those within these walls who are loyal to the elder Sutherland."

"Artair? No, it cannot be. Ronan worked very hard to ensure the loyalty of each man who remained here. He was very thorough, Rorie. Why would the bishop say that?"

Muren swallowed the rest of her words. It would do no good to rally against Rorie about something the bishop said. "I am sorry. Please continue."

Rorie smiled at her and cocked his head. Thankfully, he didn't probe. "These Artair loyalists may be out for Freya's and her bairns' blood. He does not think they will stop at immediate family. And though Artair was not your father, you, too, are Ronan's blood. Apparently, there is a cousin who would attempt to claim the earldom and chiefship."

"That will never happen," she said and shook her head. Over her dead body would she allow anything to happen to Freya and the bairns.

"Freya has agreed to stay with Fergus until she is well,

and you must travel to Eilean Donan with me the moment your brother is in the ground."

Muren winced. His words were blunter than she had anticipated. Whether there was truth to the threat or not, protecting those deemed dear to Ronan–including herself now—was the only course of action that made sense.

"But what of the castle? The clan needs a steward."

"Aye, that it does. The bishop has offered to oversee negotiations, and Fergus has offered to choose the man in Freya's stead. 'Tis not likely much time will pass before the man is chosen. In light of recent events, it will not be easy for anyone to hold the position, but Fergus said he has some ideas of someone with enough mettle to take on the job."

"So, that's it then?"

"Not exactly."

Something told her she would not like the next part of this conversation.

"Very well. When we return to Eilean Donan, what? You plan to lock me in my chamber, only to visit me for pleasure? Mayhap I will be allowed out for mass?"

Lord, she hated how bitchy she sounded. Even more, she hated that she had to hide and cower because someone might pose a threat to her. Yet when she approached Rorie with a threat that would happen to him, he dismissed her. Slowly, her anger built. It was not right that she was to take every word he said at face value, while her words were refused.

"Muren, you must heed what I say. I do not wish to upset you, but I will not risk your safety."

Oh God, he was serious. "You really do mean to shut me in, don't you?" Muren brushed past him and placed her hands on her head. Turning back toward him, she said, "For how long do you plan to keep me locked up? What if there is always a threat? I might as well be back on Rona, for at least there I could leave the lodge."

Muren paced. Any allowance she'd given him that he would approach this topic in a logical manner fled.

"I do not plan to lock you up, Muren. But you will have to stay within the walls of the castle at all times unless accompanied by Ewen or me. On that note, I will not budge. You may rant and rave as long as you like, but I will not bend, Muren." Rorie stepped closer to her. "If you push me, I can restrict your freedom to your chamber, if you like. As your husband, it is my right."

"As my husband? The man to whom I gave my hand and my heart, who now intends to prevent me from walking about freely and speaking of things that are of importance to me. What's next, Rorie? Will you restrict with whom I speak?"

"I will not place any restrictions on you that are not necessary. Of that, you have my assurance." With that, he brushed past her and left the chamber, slamming the door behind him.

Muren took off her shoe and threw it at the door just as a low knock sounded.

Stomping across the floor, she pulled it open, a mouth full of oaths—something she reserved for severe occasions—at the ready.

They died in her throat when she realized it was Freya, and not Rorie, who stood on the other side. The woman was pale as a sheet. Muren ushered her inside and closed the door.

Once they were both seated near the fire, Muren asked, "Freya, what are you doing out of bed?"

A single tear slid down her cheek. Dark circles surrounded her eyes. Muren's heart ached for her.

"They will not let me see him," she whispered.

Though spoken in a soft voice, the words were powerful enough to make a lump form in Muren's throat.

"That is not right. He is—was—your husband, and you have a right to see him."

"They say I am too weak, and that I should wait until tomorrow when I am stronger."

"Freya, you are weak, but you are the strongest woman I have ever known. If you want to see him, then muster your courage, and I will take you to him."

For the first time in a long time, Freya smiled, though it did not reach her eyes.

Muren feared the haunted look would last for a long time to come. "I would like that, please, Muren."

Muren took a cloth from her own washbasin and dipped into some cool water. She pressed it against Freya's face and then unbraided, brushed, and then braided her hair. If Freya wanted to pay her last respects to her husband, it was not anyone's place to tell her no, even if they were trying to protect her. Delaying her grief was not a kindness, in Muren's view; it only prolonged the anguish. Mayhap the same was true for her and Rorie. Waiting for danger to come to them would resolve nothing.

They needed to face it head-on and eliminate it.

Muren linked arms with Freya and walked to the chamber in which her brother lay. She drew in a steadying breath and knocked on the door. A stern-looking, elderly woman answered it and, when she saw who was there, stepped aside and opened the door for them to pass through.

The first sight of him nearly did Muren in. Her strong, kind, wonderful brother, who she wanted to rant and rave at sometimes, lay unmoving on the bed. He was dressed in a black tunic with a bright green crest on the front. His arms were folded over his long sword, and his hair was combed down straight. He looked at peace.

Beside her, Freya's knees buckled. That was when Muren noticed Fergus. He dashed out from the other side of the bed and caught Freya, lifting her easily and bringing her to a chair to sit beside her beloved Ronan. Freya reached out and grasped one of Ronan's hands and sobbed as it lay lifeless in hers.

"Can you both please give me a few moments alone with my husband?" Freya asked in a quiet, shaking voice.

"Aye," Fergus said, and walked toward the door.

Muren followed but looked back before leaving the room. The sight that met her was one she'd seen before. Freya was sitting by the bed holding Ronan's hand and weeping.

CHAPTER TWENTY

*R*orie gritted his teeth as Sutherland clansmen walked with Ronan's body toward the chapel. Dense mist had begun at dawn and had not let up all day. His heart was filled with just as much bleakness. This should not be happening. Ronan should be celebrating the birth of his child, not about to be placed in a cold stone crypt for all eternity.

He covered the hand Muren had tucked into the crook of his arm with his own. Her body shook beside his, making him want to carry her in his arms, but she would not appreciate him picking her up again.

"I remember when we were children and Ronan would try to get me to guess which of three bags held a special coloured stone."

"Something tells me you always got it right," he said and looked down at her.

The corners of her mouth lifted a little. "Aye, even when he left the stone out of the bags entirely."

Rorie knew the game well. He'd tried it on his sisters, but they were far too clever to be tricked. He suspected, though, that Muren's victories were of a different nature than his sisters'.

"I miss him," she said, her words torn from her lips in anguish.

Rorie wrapped his arm around her and held her hand. "I know, love. He was taken too soon."

"I cannot imagine what will become of Freya and the bairns. Who will look after them until little Artagan comes of age?"

"We all will, Muren. Fergus will ensure a reliable steward is in residence and, between us all, we will be there to support her in any way she needs."

"I curse the king for his brutality."

"Be careful of your words, love. I know they come from your grief, but there are far too many ears here who would like to turn them against you."

"I know," she said in a quiet voice.

Could it be true? Could he have finally gotten through to her? God, he wished so. He did not want to face her vexation at every turn. It had been far too long since he held her in a quiet moment. They needed that. So much had happened over the past months that he was determined that when this was all over, he would hide away with her in their chamber for a fortnight at least. He could not help but let out a small happy groan at the thought. Muren squeezed his hand.

"What is it?"

"I am thinking of a happy time in the future when you and I can settle into our new life together, away from terrible games such as the ones we have witnessed of late."

"Aye, I wish for that, too. Will you promise me something, Rorie," she said.

He wanted to say he would promise her anything, but he would not if it meant she would be at risk.

"What, love?"

"Will you promise me that when the day comes that I think my vision of you may come true, you will trust me?"

Rorie stiffened. It was beyond hope that she had let that topic rest. He hardly wanted to know what she meant by trust her. What could she possibly do if it was predestined for him to be run through? And, dear Lord, when had he started giving credence to her visions? Nay, dreams. They were dreams and nothing more.

"We will talk about this later, love. Right now, let us focus on seeing your brother properly put to rest."

Muren did not reply, only removed her hand from his. But she did not attempt to remove his arm from her shoulder, and for that, he held on to some semblance of hope that she was not completely furious with him.

They entered the chapel and stood close to the front whilst the bishop conducted the service. His words barely registered with Rorie. How many lives had been lost and services such as these held since this king returned from England? So many that Rorie had lost count. The man was fat in form and fat in greed, and would not be satisfied until there was nothing left of the Highlands to claim. He would rape the land and starve its people, in order to pile more gold and garish decorations into his palace at Linlithgow.

Something had to be done about him. For Ronan's sake and for all others who had stood against him and lost. But to whom could Rorie turn? Albany was no better than the king, for he'd displayed a greed that benefited no one but himself. If the clans rose up against the king, then what? They might band together to fight off a common enemy, but they would never agree to form a sovereignty. They could hardly keep from slashing one another's throats as it was.

No. There must be another solution that would satisfy the needs of the greater good, but still afford each clan their own right to govern. But greed was a quiet menace slipping into the hearts of even the most righteous of men. For some, there was never enough land, never enough gold, and never enough power.

Rorie wished he could live a life where none of it mattered. A small cottage on Rona, with Muren and a couple of paid men to help out, would make him happy for the rest of his days. These games played by the king and his nobles made his guts burn and left a foul taste in his mouth. By God, he would find a way to ensure peace for himself and his family. He would do it, or die trying.

The bishop offered a final benediction, and Ronan was moved down into the crypt. Muren, Freya, and Fergus were the only ones permitted to enter. A stone slab had already been carved out for Ronan. It had been commissioned the same day he'd taken on the earldom and chief of the clan. Rorie's clan had no such display. A simple burial and some reverent tunes were their custom.

Upon leaving the crypt, Freya said, "Fergus, can we leave here today?"

"Aye, love. We can travel on ahead and have your and the bairns' things sent after."

"Good," she said. "I need to be somewhere else for a while."

Rorie could not argue with her. She'd suffered the worst kind of loss, and sometimes stepping away from the place holding the most memories helped in the healing process. Muren squeezed his hand. He looked down at her lovely face. He disliked quarrelling with her so. 'Twas loving her and cherishing her he wanted, not bickering. They'd both become caught up in the circumstances around them, and he was determined that as soon as they returned to Eilean Donan, nothing would be more important than settling into their new life—a quiet family life. Well, as much as he could afford, in any case.

~

*M*uren trotted along beside Rorie on the road leading home. Her mother would not journey with them; she intended to help with the bairns until Freya was in better condition. When Fergus had tried to tell her that there were plenty of servants to help at MacKay House as well, Morag scoffed at him. Muren could not help but smile now. That dynamic would surely help bring Freya's spirits back up.

"What I do not understand is how you and your mother were not seen on the road travelling to Golspie," Rorie said.

"We took the old Roman roads." "And they were passable?"

"Aye."

"Well, that explains—"

Rorie's words were cut off by an arrow which pierced his shoulder. His horse reared and threw him to the ground

Highwaymen! Would their misfortunes never end? Muren dismounted and ran to Rorie's side. She rolled him to his back and inspected the arrow. He groaned when she pulled him to rest on his good side.

Both horses were distressed, so she put her hands up before her and shushed them to calm. She then tied them each to a tree and scanned the area. Rorie was still on the ground and groggy from the fall. When Muren was sure she could not see anyone nearby, she went to inspect him closer.

"Are you hurt anywhere besides your shoulder?" she asked in a whisper.

Rorie shook his head and looked past her with a frown. Something cold touched her neck.

"You will both live if you empty your purse, my lady."

Muren looked at Rorie lying on the ground. Mayhap this was the encounter that left him with a blade in his gut? No, by God, not if she could help it. She covered his brooch pin so that the highwayman would not be drawn to it, for it would surely give away Rorie's status as a nobleman.

"Stay down," she whispered and looked away as his eyes flashed in anger. "You may have our purse and ten times that if you let us go."

"Ten times that, you say? Well then, get up, my lady, and let us make acquaintance. For if you can offer me that much coin, then you must be someone of more import than I first gave either of you credit."

Muren stood and turned to face the lout. She had no intention of paying him anything in addition, but to find an excuse to lure him to where help could be found. They were not far from MacKenzie lands, by her estimation. Surely she could entice them into a trap by the promise of coin. Surely greed was an easy weapon to wield.

"I am Morag Grey of Strathnaver, and you have injured the man who promised to keep me safe."

"Aye, and a fine job he did of that, too, my lady. Now to the business of your purse," he said and reached out his hand.

Muren untied her small leather purse from underneath her cloak and tossed it to him. While his eyes were transfixed on her, she scanned the area behind him. There was no sign of movement in the bushes other than at one point. Squinting her eyes, she could just make out a figure peering out from behind a large oak. So, there were at least two of them.

"Now his purse, my lady," the highwayman said.

She took stock of his features to be sure that she could give a good description of the man, to allow Rorie's men to chase him down and bring him to justice. Tall and lean, the man's black hair was pulled back and fastened behind his neck, accenting his angular features. His brow was thick and dark, and his skin looked tanned; his eyes were as black as night. She'd noticed his accent when he first spoke. However, she did not know enough of the world to discern from whence he came. But she was certain he was not from Scotland, nor England, nor Wales. He was a foreigner, and she would not ever forget his face.

Muren crouched over Rorie and unfastened the leather pouch tied to his belt. In it was surely several pieces of silver coin; enough to keep the man in women and drink for a long time. For surely that was all a man of his ilk stole from others to procure for himself.

Whilst crouching over Rorie, she pulled a dagger from its sheath on his belt and slipped it up her sleeve. When she stood and turned, the highwayman had his arms folded and was grinning at her.

"My lady, if I had more time, I would show you how to effectively hide a dagger in your sleeve." He then grabbed her wrist and pinched until she was forced to drop the dagger. He picked it up and inspected it. "This is quite lovely. I will take this, too," he said and turned toward Rorie's horse, then mounted it in the smoothest movement Muren had ever seen. He was almost graceful if that was possible for such a brute.

A crack behind her, and then the unmistakable sound of a sword being unsheathed, made the hairs stand up on the back of her neck. Why could he not simply stay down? Turning around, she noticed that Rorie had broken off the arrow and was now standing with his sword arm outstretched, pointing at the highwayman.

"Really, Highlander? You think you can best me? For the sake of some coin and your horse, you should have stayed down."

The man jumped down and unsheathed his sword. It was not large and clunky like Rorie's broadsword, but thin and long. And according to the way the man flicked it about, the weapon was also much lighter.

"You will not take my horse," Rorie said.

"Will I not, Highlander?"

"Rorie, just let him go," Muren said. "We can make do on my horse."

"You call him by his given name? Not 'my lord' or by his surname? Curious. That can only mean one of two things. And since you look nothing alike, I would say you are not brother and sister."

The highwayman grabbed Muren and had his blade to her throat before she could react. The look of fury on Rorie's face sent chills into Muren's heart. He should have stayed down! Blood soaked the left side of Rorie's tunic, showing just how injured he really was. Despite this, he held his sword in his right hand and stared hard at her captor.

"Release her and I will let you live," Rorie said.

"I do not think so. In fact, I am starting to think you are more than just some common Highlander. That brooch pin on your shoulder. That signifies your importance in your clan. Unfortunately, I do not know all the clan mottos, and I dare not get too close to you, lest your blade find its way into my delicate skin."

"I am no one," Rorie said and stepped forward.

The highwayman threw Muren to the ground and lashed out at Rorie. Their swords met in a loud clang that rang in Muren's ears. Clashing metal and feet scuffing on the ground were the only sounds audible as she leapt to her feet.

"Stay back!" Rorie said to her.

"No, by all means, join us," the highwayman said. "I suspect you're more of a man than your husband."

Rorie should have known that the man was taunting him to lose his temper. The highwayman moved in close enough to kick Rorie's feet out from under him. He landed on the ground with a hard thud, his sword tossed from his hand in the fall.

The highwayman's face turned ugly as he raised his sword high. Muren jumped in front of Rorie to stop the man and tell him she would go with him, but he had already pushed forward in this thrust.

A stinging sensation caught her well below her heart. For a moment, she could only stare at the stranger. His eyes went wide and, for a brief moment, she thought she almost detected remorse.

Then he masked his features again. "You foolish wench," he said, as he pulled his sword from her body, resulting in a burning sensation forcing her to drop to her knees.

A loud swoosh sounded somewhere above her, then a black-haired head fell to the ground beside her with a thump.

Muren closed her eyes and vomited.

Rorie pulled her hair back from her face and held her as she retched. "Christ, Muren, why would you do that?"

"S-save you," she said through chattering teeth. The burning in her side was getting worse, but was manageable, and was nowhere near the pain she experienced from her magrymes.

"No, love. No, I never wanted you to do that."

"I s-saved you," she said. And she had. She had changed one of her dreams.

Despite the pain, her heart filled with joy. She had saved him.

Rorie turned her onto her back and inspected her wound. "Christ," he said. "Muren, I need you to stay still."

A ripping sound drew her attention to what he was doing, kneeling beside her. He pressed a part of her shift into the wound, sending sharp pain through her side. "It went clean through and should heal, but we need to get the bleeding to stop before I can move you."

Rorie held the cloth to her side for a long time. Muren drifted in and out of consciousness during that time. Flashes of the pool and crone came to her; the old woman did not look pleased.

Muren woke to the sensation of moving. She blinked her eyes open and spied the arches of the stone bridge leading to Eilean Donan Castle. She was cradled in Rorie's arms. She reached up to touch his handsome face and noted the moisture on his cheeks.

"Rorie," she whispered.

"Hush, love," he said, his voice cracking. "We're almost there, and then we will get you all fixed up."

Muren brushed a tear that had slipped down his cheek. "Why do you weep?"

Rorie cleared his throat. "I am not weeping."

"Aye, you are," she said and tried to smile as he brushed his hand down over his face to wipe it clean.

"You're badly wounded and delirious, love."

She loved the way his lips curled ever so slightly. "That may be, but I have never seen more clearly."

Rorie gazed down into her eyes. They were wet with tears still. "I thought I had lost you," he said in a hoarse whisper.

"Never. I broke the cycle. The visions were meant to be a warning. I know that now, and if I had acted sooner, I could have saved—"

"Do not think that, love. You must stop torturing yourself. Here, we are home now where we are safe and can start working on the dozen or so children we will have."

"S-so many?" she asked, though she would bear twenty if he wished it and the Lord blessed them.

Her body jolted as he dismounted with her in his arms, sending a fresh wave of pain into her side. She winced, and then blackness enveloped her.

CHAPTER TWENTY-ONE

*R*orie slammed his fist on the table, making the candlesticks and one goblet topple over. He'd been in a rage from the moment the Spaniard's blade pierced Muren's side. Never in his life had he wanted a man's head more than in that moment.

"He was not alone," Rorie said through gritted teeth. "You find his companion, Ewen. Find him and bring him to me."

"Aye, Rorie. We will find him."

Ewen left the hall with six other men. Rorie slumped into a chair just as Ada rushed to his side.

"You must let me tend to you now, lad."

In his haste to bring Muren to safety and send Ewen to find the highwayman's companion, Rorie had put his own injury aside. Now that attention was drawn back to it, a dull ache emerged all down his left side.

"How fares Muren?"

"She is resting. Her wound is clean and I believe will heal with no complications. She is much stronger than she appears, that one. If she stays abed as long as I tell her, and the dressings are replaced when I say, she should be up and about in a sennight."

"Thank you, Ada," he said. It was merely an oversight on his part that he had not made arrangements for Ada to be sent home after their return from Rona. He was now grateful for that since her healing skills were much needed at the moment.

Lifting his plaid and poking around the arrow entrance and exit, she said, "You did well to break off the arrow, but it needs to be removed, and the wound needs to be burned, else you will suffer greatly in the coming months."

Rorie did not look forward to the pain he would have to endure this night, but endure it he would. He'd seen plenty of men's wounds fester and cause a feverish sickness. Ada was right, his shoulder needed to be tended now.

"Let us not waste any time on comfort, then. Where should we do this?"

"We go to see the blacksmith," she said. "Only his fire will be hot enough to seal that wound once the arrow is pulled clear."

Rorie trusted her enough to follow her lead, but he'd never heard of a blacksmith being involved in healing before.

She sat him on a stool near the anvil in the blacksmith's cottage. "Come here," she said to the smith and his assistant. "What is your name?" she asked.

"I am called Bane," he said.

"And you?" she addressed his assistant. "What is your name?"

"Go on, boy," Bane said.

The boy winced and gave Rorie a wide-eyed look he did not understand. "I am John," he said, and again stared hard at Rorie and then at Bane.

Rorie looked at the smith a little closer. The man was quite tall and muscular, with whitish blond hair and icy blue eyes that looked familiar. Rorie estimated he was close in size to him, and then his thoughts cleared.

Their old smith had passed on but three months earlier, and Ewen had said they'd started a new smith who was of such slight frame that Ewen was in awe at the power the man wielded behind the hammer. The size of this man did not fit such a description.

The boy was trying to tell him something, and he had an inkling what it was.

"Been smithing long?" Rorie asked the other man.

"Aye, many years," he said with an accent Rorie could not quite place. It was harsh, almost like the Norsemen of Orkney, but even more so.

Rorie watched Bane stoke the fire. It did not flare in the way he'd seen when the old smith tended it. Rorie smiled as the bellows in behind lay flat, and the more Bane tended the fire, the smaller it became.

When the boy made to work the bellows, Bane swatted him out of the way and did it himself. Ada had set about cutting and peeling away the sticky, blood-soaked tunic and plaid on Rorie's shoulder.

Just what did this Bane intend? If he was the Spaniard's companion, why had he not come to the man's aid? And where was the real blacksmith? Did the man presume Ada would bring him here? Unless—

"There," Ada said, "he's all yours now, love." No!

Bane turned around with a sword instead of a hot piece of metal to cauterize his wound. Ada had, in fact, pulled Rorie's tunic down so that his arm was bound to his side, leaving him with only one arm to defend himself. He stood quickly, toppling the stool, and grabbed a hammer that was resting on the anvil.

Bane shoved the sword forward as they circled one another. "Why?" Rorie shouted at Ada.

"Because you all think you are so much better than the rest of us. My Bane is as good as any of you, and you never offered him a lofty place on your war council. No, you wanted him to remain a farmer forever. Well, my son is worth more than that."

Rorie stepped to the side out of the way and tripped over something. He looked down at the body on the floor, and his heart squeezed hard in his chest. Christ, Muren!

"What have you done to my wife?"

"I have not killed her if that's what you want to know. I have healed her properly. She will come in handy when the time comes for us to need more coin."

"Muren!" Rorie yelled her name as loud as he could. He would not let them take her. "Muren, wake up!"

He prayed the lad, John, was not a part of this treachery and could aid him in some way.

"Run away, boy. Run to my brother."

The lad skirted around Ada and tore off across the bailey. Rorie and Bane continued their deadly dance. Rorie, holding only a short-handled smith's hammer, could barely ward off the repeated blows coming from Bane. He really was a skilled swordsman, and Rorie wondered at what point they had spoken to his father and why they had not then approached him.

"You should have spoken to me, lad," Rorie said.

"We did," Ada said.

"No. I have no recollection of either of you coming to me since my father died."

"It was a long time ago, and you were on the road leading east. We waved you down, but you ignored our request, and your brother flicked us some coin. You who are too good to speak with an old woman and a cripple boy."

Rorie remembered now and stepped back. A few years back he'd been riding to see Sutherland with his father, and in truth, he'd been so caught up in clan business and the threat of the king riding north to claim all authority, he'd not paid any heed to those in need on the side of the road. Still, this was a pretty severe retaliation.

"You cannot imagine how pleased I was when you came seeking aid for your witch."

"'Twas you who spread the rumours." God's bones, he'd brought this madness into his home. She could have killed Muren at any time.

"The lass will be dealt with in her time. For now, I will not harm her whilst she carries a bairn."

Rorie stopped and looked at Ada and then back at Muren, who was now standing and looking at him with horror in her eyes. Was there something wrong with the bairn or—

"Rorie, look out!"

He turned around just as Bane stepped forward and thrust his blade into his belly. The ache in his shoulder was nothing compared to this pain. Rorie doubled over when Bane pulled the sword back out. Delicate hands held onto his shoulders as he fell to his knees and blackness drew near. The last thing he heard was dozens of feet running toward the blacksmith's hut.

～

*M*uren turned on her side so she could watch Rorie sleep. His wounds had been cleaned and treated by a woman in the village named Lyn. She'd scoffed at the prospect of burning the wound to seal it, and instead packed it tight with what Muren did not know, nor had she been in a fit state to ask.

When Lyn was finished with Rorie, she then saw to Muren's wound and flushed it with water before packing it tight with her own concoction.

"He should have come to me first," she said. "Even about your headaches, my lady. I could have cured those, too."

Muren smiled at her. She had a kind face even when she was chastising them. "I thank you, Lyn," she said. "You shall be paid with an amount of your choosing."

The woman flicked her hand. "I do not need payment," she said. "I only need the chief to protect us."

"You shall have that by any means necessary."

For the next two days, Muren drifted in and out of slumber. Lyn returned every few hours, and flushed and then packed their wounds again. Muren had to admit, her side hurt less and less. Rorie had not yet woken, though Lyn insisted he would live and heal fully.

On the third morning, Muren woke with an odd sensation in the pit of her belly. She just managed to climb out of bed and make it to a chamber bucket when her guts spewed forth. She waited for the pain to start in the back of her head, but none came.

Muren stood and wiped her mouth. Another wave of sickness doubled her over, and again she waited for the pain to begin.

The door to their chamber opened and closed again. "You are unwell, my lady?"

Muren turned around too quickly and had to hold on to her side when a needle of pain shot through her. "Just a little sick." Still nothing in her head. She did not understand. She'd vomited plenty of times but never without the pain following in her head.

She sat near the hearth as a couple of servants entered with some food and mead. As soon as they removed the bucket of sick, Muren's stomach rumbled. The thought of placing meat in her mouth brought on a new wave of upset in her belly, but it quickly settled when she took the cheese.

After two goblets of mead and several pieces of bread and

cheese, Muren's strength reared. She stood and walked over to the stairs to walk up to the tower.

"Now, just where do you think you're going, lass?" Lyn said.

"To stretch my legs. I fear I will go mad if I do not move about some."

"Very well, but take it slow. Your wound has not fully healed."

"Aye, I will take it easy, I promise," she said. She glanced at Rorie again before heading up to the tower overlooking the lochs.

The cool sea air kissed her very soul. She needed it. Her actions, resulting in her own injury, had not prevented her vision of Rorie's from coming true. That meant the king was in danger. But Rorie was right. She could not speak of it, lest she be burned at the stake or hung for treason. No. She would speak of these visions no more and prayed she never had another one.

Noise from below drew her attention to the stairs. She made her way slowly down and smiled as she drew nearer to the ruckus.

"I want her brought back down now!"

His familiar voice made her heart soar, even though he was barking orders again.

"Hush, Rorie. I'm here," she said, as she stepped back into the chamber.

The moment her eyes met his, she stopped. His were filled with worry and dread. Muren moved to the bed and took his hand.

"I am here, love. You need not worry any longer. I am well and healing, thanks to Lyn."

Rorie looked at the woman fussing about the chamber and then back to Muren. "I thought you were gone," he said in a hoarse whisper.

"I am here, and you are healing," she said and smiled at him. "What has happened to Bane and Ada?"

"I do not know. This is my first time out of bed myself in three days."

"Three days!" Rorie said and tried to sit up. He winced and clasped his gut, then lay back down.

"Now, stop that," Lyn said and came over to him. "If you do not stay put, you will be laid up for the winter, do you hear?"

Rorie smiled. Muren didn't think many had spoken thusly to him, besides her, in a very long time. She was pleased he did not challenge the woman.

"Thank you, Lyn," he said. "Would you send for my brother, please?" he asked her.

"Aye, but only a short visit."

She left then, and Rorie took Muren's hand. "Come back to bed," he said. She smiled and gently crawled over him until they were tucked back into bed together. Her side was forgotten for the moment.

"I knew you were not in bed with me," he said. His brows were drawn in tight, as though he was trying to figure something out.

"You must have woken to my retching."

"You were sick?" he said and leaned forward to kiss her forehead.

"How does your head feel now? I am sorry I was not able to help you."

Muren shook her head. "I did not have any pain in my head. Just sick."

"Has that happened before?"

"No." In truth, Muren did not know what to make of it. Mayhap it was a result of her injury and the trauma she had endured combined with worry over Rorie. 'Twas no wonder she had gotten sick.

"You did not wake me," he said.

"So, how did you know I was not in bed with you?"

"I did not know. I did not dream, but somehow I always knew you were near and that we would both heal from these injuries."

"Are you saying you're a seer?" she said with a wide grin. "You must speak of this to no one, Rorie," she said, deepening her voice to try to match his. "I could not bear it if you were to be burned at the stake."

Rorie's eyes grew wide. "Are you making fun of me?"

"No, my lord," she said, laughing when he reached out and pulled her close. "I would not dream of it."

"Good, because I would not want to have to punish you."

Rorie captured her mouth with his and kissed her deeply. She groaned and slipped her arms around his neck and drew him closer. Injury be damned. It had been far too long since they'd shared in their passion. When she shuffled closer, they both winced in pain. Muren smiled at him. They had both gotten this far. Though she'd had no visions for quite some time and she would not wish them back, somehow a peacefulness had settled over her. As though the immediate danger had passed. God, she hoped that was true.

CHAPTER TWENTY-TWO

*R*orie was just rolling onto his back when Ewen entered his chamber. He grinned when Muren ducked her head under the covers.

"Well, it's about time you woke up. I was beginning to think you'd sleep forever," he said with a grin.

Rorie sat up with great care, so as not to irritate his wounds. His shoulder was not so bad, but his gut burned. He could kick himself for bringing that vile woman into his home. By God, she would pay.

"Aye, but no more. Where are Ada and Bane?"

Ewen's brows knit when he saw the lump under the covers move. "They are secure, Rorie. Awaiting your judgement."

Rorie lifted the covers a little and grinned at Muren. "Do you wish to be elsewhere?" he asked her, thinking she might be uncomfortable in her state of undress with Ewen present. Rorie could care less and was perfectly comfortable walking around naked. 'Twas natural, as far as he was concerned.

"Aye," she said in a quiet voice.

"Nay, do not worry yourself, my lady," Ewen said, smiling.

"I will speak with your husband at length as soon as he is up and about." He then turned and reached for the latch, but hesitated.

"What is it, Ewen?"

Looking over his shoulder, he said, "They meant to kill you, Rorie. You and anyone who got in their way. Remember that when you decide their fate." With that, he left the chamber.

The weight of the issue pressed down on him. He'd passed judgement many times over the years regarding various insignificant squabbles, but nothing like this. Once a clansman had been caught thieving from a neighbour, and his sentence was to receive twenty lashes. Rorie was but eight summers at the time and, as his father made him watch, it was a long time before he could get the image out of his head.

What kind of punishment was befitting a person who plotted his death? The scriptures said an eye for an eye, but since he was merely wounded, Rorie could not very well sentence them to death.

"Is he gone?" Muren asked.

"Aye, love. You can come out now."

He loved how dishevelled she looked when she pulled the blanket down and sat up. He would have to deal with the burden soon enough, but for now, he just wanted to look at her.

Returning his gaze, she frowned. "Rorie, what are you going to do about them?"

He shook his head. "I truly do not know."

"You cannot have them hanged. It just would not be right. They have not killed anyone."

He was surprised to hear his thoughts coming from her lips. When he was plotting to confront the king, she'd surprised him with her strategic mind. Just how far did that extend? He would be more than happy to be able to talk with her about such matters.

"What would you suggest?"

She cocked her head to one side, her brows drawn in tight. "You want my opinion?"

"Aye, of course."

She blinked at him a couple of times then smiled. Lord, he could get lost in that smile. "Very well, then. I think they should be made to answer for their crimes."

"But they have already admitted to them, and given a reason for their actions. You think they should be permitted to speak again?"

She looked beyond him for a moment and then nodded. "Aye, I think they should be permitted to speak again."

"To what end?"

"To be sure there are no others involved."

"And why would you think that?"

"Because it does not add up. You dismiss her on the road, and you ignore her, so she then plots to kill you but waits until you seek her aid in order to launch her plan to have you murdered by her son? And then kidnap and hold me for ransom? Really, Rorie, it does not make sense. No one carries that much of a grudge over a slight from a nobleman. There's something more at play here."

God's bones, she was right. Rorie had not had enough time to think on it, but Muren clearly had. Put that way, there was definitely something amiss. Despite his discomfort, he was energized by their conversation. Far more so than by any strategic conversation he'd ever had with Ewen.

"What do you propose? How do we catch her in a lie?"

Muren shook her head. "That's the part I do not know. Can you recall anything of note from the day you visited her at her cottage?"

"Aye! She does not need her cane. She wears a thick pad

underneath her cloak to make her look frail, and that day she showed me. But why would she show me her deception and still plot my demise? Really, Muren, it's making my head hurt."

"Hey, I am the one with the headaches remember?"

He did remember; he also just realized it had been quite a while since her last one. "How do you feel?"

"I am well, except for my side. How do you feel?"

"Best when you are here beside me."

It was true. Though they'd had their differences, there was no doubt in his mind that she was the other half of him. He could endure being laird of the clan with her by his side. When they were together, he was whole.

She placed her hand on his face. "I do love you, Rorie MacKenzie. Even when you are bull-headed."

"Me? 'Tis you who wanted to find yourself, even when danger was at our doorstep." She frowned, and he feared he might have gone too far. "Muren, I jest. I do not blame you for our troubles. They were always ours to bear together." He took her hand in his. "Whatever comes our way in the future, we shall share in it together—the good and the bad."

He held his breath as she regarded him. Opening her mouth a couple of times and then closing it again, she finally said, "We *are* on this journey together. And together we will find the right way forward. After all this time, I realize that I do not need to stand on my own two feet, rather I need them beside yours."

Rorie's heart soared. Mayhap it took almost losing one another for them to realize that, instead of working against one another, they were stronger by working together.

"I wish I was healed already," he said.

"I wish that, too," she said and leaned forward to brush her lips across his.

Lyn entered the chamber then and clucked her tongue at

them. "My lady, if you are well then mayhap we can get you dressed and let the laird rest. I fear he will not be on his feet as quickly as you."

"Aye, but she has only one wound, I have two."

"Aww, wee lamb," Muren said and scrambled down to the edge of the bed when he made to grab her.

"I will be up and about very soon, my lady. And when I am, you will eat those words."

"Come now, my lady," Lyn said and placed a throw over her shoulders. "Let us get you to the inner chamber to clean you up."

Rorie smiled as Muren grinned at him from over her shoulder when Lyn whisked her away. He lay back on the pillows and regarded the wound through his gut. At least it was clean. God's breath, but he was a lucky man to have come through the last few months with his and Muren's heads still firmly planted on their shoulders.

She was right, though. In order to determine the severity of punishment for Ada and Bane, he must first fully understand the scope to which their crimes extended.

~

*M*uren eased into her gown with Lyn's assistance. She was still a little sore, but was surprisingly well, considering what she'd been through. More importantly, Rorie was awake and appeared none the worse for wear. He would surely heal, and mayhap they could finally put the past few months behind them. They had indeed endured so much sorrow and heartache, they were due some happiness.

When Lyn made to cinch the bodice of her gown, Muren's breath caught. Not from her side, rather from her breasts.

"They are tender, my lady?"

Muren placed her hands over them and nodded. When had that started? She had not fallen nor bumped into anything, yet her breasts were suddenly heavy and tender to the touch.

Lyn smiled. "You'll be pleasing his lairdship with this news then?"

Muren blinked at her a few times, and then her earlier sickness dawned on her.

Could she really be with child so soon? She could have danced for joy! What a wondrous gift to help her to focus on the future. "How can I be sure?"

"When was the last time you bled?"

Muren couldn't say. So much had gone on over the past two months it was difficult to determine when, but she had certainly still been at Dunrobin Castle. With all the travelling and turmoil, she'd not even realized she was late. But now she was acutely aware of it. She and Rorie had first made love on Rona, and that was more than a month ago. She smiled and rubbed her belly. Could it really be?

"You will have to take extra care in your healing now, my lady. That bairn needs your body strong, so we must ensure your wound is kept clean at all times."

"Aye, Lyn, and thank you. I shall take extra care, I promise. Will you please tell no one of this? I want Rorie to hear it from my lips first."

"You have my word, my lady. Now, let us get you some exercise, shall we? Mayhap a brief turn about the courtyard and then back to your chamber to rest."

Muren's belly fluttered at the thought to how Rorie would handle the news. He would be as overjoyed as she, of that there could be no doubt.

Walking outside in the cool fall air, she leaned against the stone wall curtain and breathed in, taking all the healing goodness of this place's essence into her body and soul. There was something very special about this place, a connection she could not explain, as though her roots had already penetrated the soil and had found anchor.

And, as before, she was more at home here in this much smaller castle than she had ever been at Dunrobin. Here, she had sisters with whom to bond, ships on which to sail, and her Rorie, with whom she would share her heart and grow old. Aye, she was more at home here than anywhere else she'd ever lived. Taking a deep breath, she turned to enter the castle but instead bumped into Ewen.

"My apologies, Ewen, I did not see you there."

"It is I who should apologize to you, my lady. I fear I owe you that much."

Muren cocked her head to the side. "For what?"

"For urging Rorie to give up on you," he said with a frown she had never seen on him before. "I was wrong, Muren. You were worth all Rorie risked."

She didn't know what to say. Part of her was angered because of Ewen's interference, but another part of her gloried in knowing Rorie had not listened to him and had been true to her every step of the way.

"Thank you, Ewen. I trust now that you would not feel the need to advise him so again?"

He smiled then. "No. In me, you have a loyal ally from now on. I will never doubt your loyalties again, Muren. You have my word."

"Then I forgive you, Ewen. You need not think on it again."

When he made to embrace her, she put her hands up. She could barely manage the pressure of her gown on her breasts. There was no way she could handle an embrace and certainly not with Ewen. He would surely discover her secret, and she was determined that Rorie find out about it first.

"Please, I beg you, my side is still quite tender."

His brow furrowed. "Then I shall escort you to your chamber at once so that you may rest," he said and offered his arm.

Ewen's demeanour was quiet, contemplative. "Is all well, Ewen?"

He drew in a deep breath. "It has been a trying time, my lady, and I just want to see things set right. I have been quite direct in my approach with my brother and what he should and should not do. I suppose, in truth, I felt mayhap I should have been chief since Rorie tends to think first then act. I see now that he was right in his approach all along, in wanting to resolve the danger you were in versus dealing with issues at the castle."

"You think he placed my welfare above those here at Eilean Donan?"

"No, that's what I'm trying to say. In resolving the threat against you, he resolved it for everyone else."

Muren felt sick. She really had put so many in danger. Rorie had tried to tell her, but she'd been too wrapped up in her own head to see anything else. Heat flamed her cheeks. She was ashamed now of the selfishness she'd displayed.

"I am sorry to have caused such turmoil."

"What? No, Muren," he said. "You misunderstand. I said Rorie was correct in his assessment of the situation. You are worth protecting. You have added much joy to his life, and I feel it in my heart that you belong here. I nearly lost you both—"

A lump formed in Muren's throat as Ewen's voice cracked. The only home she'd ever felt connected to was her mother's cottage at Strathnaver. But after her brother had been taken to live with his father at Dunrobin, it had never been the same.

"I thank you for that, Ewen. You cannot possibly know how much that means to me," she said and squeezed his hand.

They walked the remainder of the way to her and Rorie's chamber in silence. A new-found peace settled over her. She was home at last.

CHAPTER TWENTY-THREE

$\mathcal{R}$orie sat at the head of the table in the great hall and waited for his prisoners. Fraser, Grant, and MacLeod had heard about the attempt on his life and insisted on attending. They sat near the end of the table and waited.

He had pondered much over the last fortnight while he healed about how to deal with them. Sometimes he wanted to dig a hole in the ground and leave them there; other times he wanted to give them an opportunity to atone. Neither option sat well with him, especially since all attempts to flesh out a greater explanation had failed.

The easy route for him would be banishment, but that would only lead them to someone else's doorstep. No, he had a better idea in mind for these two.

"Are you certain you wish to be here, Muren?"

"Aye, Rorie. I would not miss this. And you are certain this is the right punishment for them?"

"I am."

"Then you have my full support."

Rorie turned to her. They had shared many quiet moments of late, but he sensed there was something on her mind, as he would catch her staring off at times. Her headaches had ceased completely, and he prayed they were gone for good, though considering her history, he doubted it.

"I am very happy to have it, my love," he said and reached for her hand.

The prisoners were brought forward then. Their clothes were soiled and their eyes squinting at the light. He'd instructed Ewen to keep them in the cells, with as little light, food, and water as needed to keep them alive. The sight of them confirmed his orders had been carried out.

"My lord, I beg your mercy," Ada said and fell to her knees. "I am an old woman and cannot endure a cold, hard cell for the rest of my days."

"You wish me to hang you right now?" Rorie asked. The woman was clever. No doubt she had some kind of escape plan in mind. He'd play along for now.

Ada glanced at Bane and then stared hard at Rorie. "Nay, I'd be lying if I said I wanted to die. Mayhap my son and I can serve you for the rest of our lives."

"Serve me?" Rorie laughed, as did others in the hall. "And exactly why would I let two people who tried to kill me walk about freely in my midst?"

"I never said we would be free, my lord. You could let us out in the daytime to toil for you and then lock us up again at night."

For a minor infraction, the proposal was something he might consider, but these two were dangerous, and he had no intention of risking anyone's life in order to save theirs.

"Tell me why I should not slit your throat where you stand."

"Because the bairn your wife carries will need help when the time comes. Help only I can provide. I have seen it."

The hair on the back of Rorie's neck stood up on end. He looked at Muren. Her eyes were wide, and her mouth was turned down into a frown. Ada had never mentioned anything about being a seer; never mind the fact that Muren had not mentioned anything about carrying a child.

"Are you with child?" he asked and held his breath. He could not see her withholding that kind of information from him. They'd spent much time in one another's company while he healed, so she'd had ample opportunity to tell him.

"I am," she whispered. "Rorie, I was waiting for the right time to tell you—"

"My lord, her child will need help coming into this world. I told her so on Rona, and I tell you now."

Rorie's guts burned. He did not think he could bear more talk of visions. "Is it true? Did she tell you this on Rona?"

"Aye," Muren said quietly.

"Is it just she who is supposed to help you?"

"Aye."

"Take him," Rorie said to Ewen.

"Aye, Rorie."

"Where are you taking him?" Ada screeched in anguish.

"Since you are the only one who is supposed to help us, then we have no use for your son."

"It was all her idea," Bane said. "I had no choice but to go along with it."

"You would abandon your own mother to save your own neck?" she said to Bane. "I'll see you in the next life," she said and spat at him.

"It will be a long time before you see him," Rorie said.

"You will let us labour for you?" Ada asked.

"Not you. Him."

"And what is to be my job?" he asked.

"Fuller," Rorie said and smiled as the colour ran from Bane's cheeks. It was a dirty, nasty job, whereby the worker walked on the wool to soften and cure it. And for it to be cured properly, it needed to be soaked in piss.

"My lord, I am very strong, I am sure there is some way you can find use for me here."

"No. I think you will be just about the best fuller we've ever had. Unless you have changed your mind and now do not want a job? Otherwise, I can certainly send you to the executioner."

"No, my lord. Thank you, my lord."

"And me?" Ada asked.

"You will be handed over to my Lord Hamish here, who will deliver you for examination."

"Examination for what?" Ada asked, and looked over her shoulder at Hamish.

Rorie smiled. The man was by far the tallest in the hall, with legs like tree trunks and a face like a boiled boot.

"For witchcraft. You have admitted to all hands here that you foresaw harm coming to my wife and our unborn child. For that, you must be examined properly."

"No! My lord, you cannot do that to me!"

"Can I not? I believe it was you who admitted to spreading the rumours about my wife. Oh, I believe I am well within my rights to pass any judgement I deem fitting against you for your crimes. Take her out of my sight."

After his men left with both Ada and Bane, Rorie turned to Muren. Her head was bent low and her hands clasped in her lap. She looked miserable.

"Muren, love, what is it? Why did you not want to tell me about the bairn?"

She glanced around, and his gaze followed her around the hall. The other chiefs nodded and left the hall, but there were still lots of people milling about. Perhaps she would prefer to discuss it in private.

"Would you like to go to our chamber?"

"Aye, please," she said and got up to leave.

Trepidation filled Rorie's gut. Her belly did not show a

bump yet, so she couldn't have known for very long; certainly not long enough to know if something was wrong. Rorie followed her to their chamber in silence. He was resigned to the fact that whatever they had to face from now on, they would face it together.

~

*M*uren entered the chamber and walked directly to the stairs leading to the tower. Up there, everything always seemed to make more sense. She had held onto the information while Rorie was healing because she wanted to reconcile what Ada had told her all those weeks ago. And reconcile it she had. She just hoped Rorie would agree with her conclusions.

"Muren, love. Why did you not tell me about the bairn?"

"Are you vexed with me?"

Rorie wrapped his strong arms around her and kissed the top of her head. "No, love, I am not vexed with you. I just want to understand."

Drawing in a deep breath, she said, "I think she is lying."

Rorie pulled back and gazed into her eyes, his brow knit. "About what?"

"All of it. I think she is clever enough to piece things together, and then draws logical conclusions to make it seem like she can see into the future."

"Exactly what did she say to you on Rona?"

"That I would be with child from our first joining, and that the child would need her help coming into the world. She claimed she had seen it in a dream the day before you came for her, and that she had been expecting you. All of these things could easily be made up and, considering I was in a state of confusion over my own visions at the time, I was easy prey."

Rorie pulled her back into her embrace. "You do not believe the child is in danger?"

"No, I do not."

"Muren, you could have talked this through with me. I knew something was on your mind this past fortnight, but I had no idea what."

Muren pulled back from the embrace to gaze up at him. By God, he was the most wonderful man she'd ever known. "Are you ready to be a father?" she whispered.

She squealed when he picked her up and swung her around in response. "Aye, lass. We have many children to produce, so I am very pleased we are not wasting any time."

"Me, too, Rorie. I love you so much." Leaning down, she brushed her lips across his.

Rorie placed his hand on the back of her neck and slipped his tongue into her mouth to dance with hers. How long they stood there nuzzling, kissing, and touching, she could not say, but before long, Rorie swept her up in his arms and retreated down the stairs to their chamber.

He placed her on the bed and joined her there.

"In the afternoon, Rorie? How wicked do you think I am?"

"Very wicked, my lady. And for that I am very grateful," he said and bent low to claim her lips once again.

Muren lifted her leg to allow him better access as he stroked the soft skin from her calf to her inner thigh. Her body tingled with delight. They would have to be careful, for he was not yet fully healed, but all she wanted to do was straddle him and take him deep within her.

"Be careful of your wound," she said when he stripped his belt and tunic off and tossed it on the floor. His erection sprang free, sending shivers of excitement across her flesh in anticipation.

"You need not worry about my wound, my lady," he said in a husky voice.

"Oh, and what should I worry about?"

Rorie tossed her skirts up so that her lower half was completely bare, and slipped his hands underneath her bottom. His hot breath fanned her most private area. She would surely go mad if he did not make contact soon.

"Rorie, please," she said.

She reached for her pillow and gripped it when he flicked his tongue the full length of her. God, how she desperately wanted him to thrust himself hard within her. But he did not, rather he slowly licked and sucked her hot flesh until she was a quivering mess. One hard press on her bud and she would explode, she was sure of it. When she reached down to do just that, he captured her hands and held them to the side. Oh God, he was going to torture her. Surely, she could not survive this, but what a sweet way to go.

Rorie reached up and released the ties at the sides of her gown. Tugging them free, he slipped her gown up and over her head along with her shift, until she was naked beneath him. He grazed his teeth across her nipple at the same time as he slipped two fingers inside her and hooked forward. Muren's hips rose off the bed.

She wanted more, so much more, and he was holding it all back from her. Twisting her body, she whimpered and pushed at his hand.

"Oh love, do you want more?"

"Aye!"

"How much more?"

"I want everything you have."

"Tell me, Muren, tell me what you want."

"I want you inside me, now, Rorie!"

Thankfully, he waited no longer. He grabbed her hips and flipped her over so that she was on her hands and knees.

Holding onto her hips, he placed the tip of his erection just inside and pushed in and out just a little. When she tried to push back to take more of him, he gripped her hips tighter so that she could not move at all. On and on he tortured her. So much so that when he slipped inside a little bit more, she orgasmed around him—and he not fully inside!

Muren gasped as her body pulsed around his hardened tip, her back arching as the waves of her climax ripped through her.

"Christ, you are perfect," Rorie said and slammed fully into her.

Muren's orgasm was barely over before the next one built. He was so deep within her, stroking her very core, that she heightened quickly and, before she could catch her breath, climaxed again.

Tossing her hair back over her shoulder, Muren let out a cry as he reached his peak and exploded within her. Holding her hips, he rocked them back and forth as his own passion spewed forth. How long they stayed like that she did not know, but she could surely stay joined with him forever.

She awoke a time later when the light in the room had darkened. Rorie was snoring lightly beside her, and a fire had been lit. Did that mean someone had come in whilst they were sleeping? A little mortified, she pulled a quilt over them both and curled her body around his. Even in his sleep, his dimples were visible. Rorie's arm came around her, and he mumbled something inaudible. She kissed his forehead and settled down.

Never in her life had she ever been so protected, loved, or content. For all they'd been through and all her attempts to find herself, she was truly whole. And that was in part because of the man lying beside her. Without him, she would surely have been wed to someone else by now.

As she drifted toward sweet sleep, her thoughts turned to

Ronan. Accepting part responsibility for his death was something she would have to reconcile, but she did not have to do so alone. Rorie would be there with her every step of the way.

And she would give him sons and daughters aplenty. She smiled, and the last image that floated across her mind before falling asleep was that of a few small children running around their father in the great hall, trying to get his attention to play. It was the best dream she'd ever had, and she prayed it was the only one she had from now on.

CHAPTER TWENTY-FOUR

*W*ind whipping at his face, Hugh Fraser rode hard to Beaufort Castle, his home.

This business with the king had grossly unsettled him. While his clan had always been mostly supportive of the crown, this Stewart had displayed erratic behaviour of late, and Hugh had a foreboding feeling about what that meant for Scotland. While he believed in unity—especially the value in banding together against common enemies—he could not condone the king's actions concerning Sutherland and MacKenzie.

As he approached the castle, a carriage came into view. His two sisters were not expected at the moment, and his mother rarely travelled anymore, so he was at a loss to think who the owner could be.

Trotting alongside the carriage, he noted the heavy tapestries flung over the back entrance. Stitched into them was an oak trunk. Bissett. But what were they doing here? And in such lavish accommodations? Though their clans had merged a century ago, he'd not visited with William more than twice in his life.

Hugh secured his horse in the stable and went in search of his steward. He would prefer to have a sense of what the visit was about prior to any meeting.

Locating him, Hugh could tell right away something was not right. "We have a visitor," he said to Neville.

"Aye, an unexpected one at that. William Bissett is here to see you on an urgent matter, he says."

"Indeed," Hugh said. "I've not seen the man in several years. Did he give any indication as to this urgent matter?"

"No, but he asked to speak with your mother first and then you."

Hugh tensed. His mother had been frail these last few months, leaving her often confused. He was not comfortable with her keeping an audience with anyone alone. Hugh marched toward the great hall and swung the heavy doors hard enough that they slammed against the stone walls on either side of the entrance. His mother and William Bissett sat by the hearth with a table topped with a trencher filled with food and a tankard and goblets. He was holding her hands and laughing at something she'd said. The image was far too intimate for Hugh's liking.

Hugh drew in a deep breath and strode toward them. Placing a hand on his mother's shoulder, he said, "Mother, are you well?"

She placed her hand over his and looked up with a smile. "I am very well, my love. I've been having the most wonderful time with Sir William."

Her eyes had the spark back in them he'd not seen for quite some time. In fact, she looked better than she had in more than a year. It was enough for him to let the man have his say at least.

"To what do we owe this pleasure, Bissett?" He was not entirely sure why the man's presence irritated him so he could not help the edge in his voice.

Bissett stood and bowed to Hugh. At least the man had not forgotten who was laird. "My lord, I come seeking your aid."

"Aye, so I'm told. In what matter?"

Bissett drew a deep breath. "'Tis the matter of some trouble concerning my daughter, my lord."

Hugh had not even been aware the man had a daughter, much less think of her needing any sort of protection. As chief, he was responsible for all of them and, though there was something odd about the way he was reacting to Bissett, he would not see an innocent lass come to harm for his prejudice against her father.

"Go on," Hugh said.

"Sit down, my love," his mother said. "The matter is delicate, and you're making me nervous standing about with your arms crossed as though you're heading into battle."

His mother's gentle words tugged at him. Nothing had been the same since his wife had passed the year prior, and it had been a very long time since he'd considered accepting any kindness. For his mother's sake, he pulled a chair close to her and sat.

It all seemed very civil; the three of them sitting around the hearth. To an outside observer, it may look that way, but the tension in the air was thick enough to sever with a broadsword. Bissett fidgeted with the hem of his doublet, and Hugh's mother smoothed the side of her skirt.

"Go on, Sir William," his mother said. "Tell him what you told me."

"It seems the king is arranging marriages between his lords in the south with Highland ladies. Have you heard of this?"

That he had. The whole mess with MacKenzie and Sutherland's sister had nearly brought the country to its knees. To his knowledge, the Douglas had returned to

Lancashire empty-handed, but that didn't mean the king wouldn't be back again to target some other unsuspecting lass.

"Aye, I have. You have my assurance your daughters and any other lass under my protection will not come to any harm."

"I thank you for your commitment, my lord, but I am looking for something more tangible than a promise."

Hugh leaned forward and cocked a brow. "Those are bold words for a man asking a boon."

"Oh, 'tis more than a boon I ask, my lord."

Hugh didn't understand and looked at his mother when she placed her hand on his arm. "'Tis been more than a year, my love. You are still young, and you need to find love again."

The words ran through his skull like a bolt of lightning. He jumped up, toppling the chair in the process. "You want me to marry one of your daughters?"

"Not just any one, my lord. My oldest. She is quite accomplished and quite lovely. She will make you a good wife."

"I will not marry again," Hugh said. Christ, this felt like an ambush. No wonder Bissett had wanted to speak with his mother first. "Very underhanded of you, Bissett, to get my frail mother on-side and then get her to convince me of your plot. Know this. I have no intention of taking a wife now or ever again. My word holds true, I will do everything in my power to protect those loyal to this seat, but I will not be coerced into a marriage in order to do so."

"Sit down, Hugh," his mother said. "You act as though I just asked you to gouge out your own eyes."

At that point, he wasn't sure which would be worse.

Her voice had taken on a confidence he'd not heard in a very long time. "Sir William, will you please excuse us?"

"Do you wish me to leave, Lady Fraser?"

"No, Sir William. You and your daughter shall join us for the evening meal. Anderson will show you to the guest chambers."

With that, Bissett left, and Anderson closed the doors behind them.

"Sit down, Hugh," his mother said again.

Hugh picked up the chair and placed it back in line with the others at the table, then took the seat across from her.

"He brought the lass here? Do you not think that odd?"

"No, I do not since they are here on my invitation. I have been meeting with Sir William over these past few weeks and, once I learned of his plight, I plotted to make this arrangement. So, if you want to be vexed with someone, be vexed with me."

"Mother, you know what losing Alice and the bairn did to me—to all of us," he said, praying she would not persist in this madness. He was not capable of going down that road again. Images of his wife in her last moments flashed through his mind and brought on a new wave of aching in his chest. "It would not be fair to her or to me."

His mother reached out and took his hand. "You have become cold and hard in this last year, Hugh. I never see you smile anymore and I never see you laugh. You are still young, and you deserve happiness. I miss Alice, too, but she would not have wanted this for you. My heart aches every single day to see how her death has twisted you. Please, Hugh, please consider this marriage."

"You know I would do anything for you, but this is one matter where I must resist. I do not have the capability anymore to be a husband. Alice's death and the death of my son took that from me. I will remain chief of this clan and protect all those within it with my life, but do not ask me to share a heart that no longer beats."

"And who will continue our line? If you do not marry,

you cannot produce an heir, and you cannot be chief—. 'Tis as plain as that."

"Is that a threat?" He had grossly underestimated her frailty. This was the mother he'd known all his life, the one who was strong enough to take on anything.

"Call it what you like, Hugh, but you cannot hold the chief's title if you cannot continue our line."

"So, you would give it to Connor?" His younger brother was more than capable and more than worthy, but Hugh was the rightful chief, and he would not let anyone take that from him or force him into a marriage he did not want.

"I want you to remain chief of this clan, as you have been since the day your father passed when you were but seventeen summers. Many doubted your capability, but I knew you were strong and noble. This tragedy has left a sickness within you that eats at your soul, and the only cure is that lass upstairs."

"I have never even met her. How can you know she will cure me as you say?"

"Because I have met her, my love."

Hugh's heart pounded in his chest, and sweat broke out on his brow. He simply could not go through with it. "Mother, I cannot—"

"Aye, you can, love. All I am asking you to do today is meet her. That's it. If you truly do not like her, then we will find someone you do like, but I cannot sit by and watch you harden to stone more and more each day. There's love in you still, and I will not let you give up on life."

Hugh stood and regarded his mother. She was a force to be reckoned with when she set her mind to something, and this was no doubt one of those times. But he was not ready and doubted he ever would be again.

"Forgive me, Mother. But in this matter, I must defy you."

With that, he left the hall. Striding toward the stable,

something caught his eye at the top of the keep's tower. Something thick and golden flapped in the wind. Hugh placed his hand over his brow so he could block the sun and get a better view. Once he did, he saw that a pair of hands braced the tower wall and a golden-haired head turned in his direction.

For several heartbeats, he just stood there staring. Unable to see her eyes or expression, Hugh could not tell much about her, but he was certain who she was. His stomach coiled into a knot. His horse whinnied, drawing him back to the present. Hugh turned away from the tower and the lass, mounted his horse, then tore off across the bailey and onward toward the road leading to Inverness. Whether or not he would return, he truly did not know at that point.

CHAPTER TWENTY-FIVE

*R*orie drummed his fingers on the table. His sisters had insisted on a proper wedding feast now that all the danger had passed and he and Muren were healed. They'd been preparing for weeks, and insisted neither he nor Muren lift a finger in preparation. Now the day was here and he'd not been permitted to see her since yesterday.

"You're wearing a hole in the table," Ewen said.

Rorie glanced down at his hand and then stretched his fingers before resting his hand into a loose fist. "Where is she?"

"Lena said they would be here shortly." Ewen chuckled. "You are anxious to see her, aren't you? I never took you for the romantic sort. I thought that was my job."

"I just do not see why there is a delay."

Ewen made some other jest Rorie barely registered. He had found that he did not like being away from Muren for even a few hours, so passing the night in his bed alone had left him tired and cranky.

Movement from the corner of the room caught his eye. His sisters entered, carrying what looked like a crimson silk scarf high above their heads. It wasn't until they were almost to him that he could see Muren following behind. His two younger sisters carried the other two corners so that Muren was in the middle of the procession.

His gaze fell over her body. Her curves were much accentuated by the babe growing in her belly, and the cut of her gown only made her breasts look fuller; he could not wait to get her alone.

Lena cleared her throat, which brought Rorie's gaze to lock with Muren's. Her face was flushed. Had everyone witnessed his appraisal of his wife? Be damned with them all, she was his, and he cared not who knew the effect she had on him.

Rorie stood and outstretched his hand to her. She took it and sat beside him at the table. Normally, only one chair was seated at the head of the table, but he'd insisted an additional one be placed there for her, too.

Squeezing her hand, he smiled at her. "You are so lovely, Muren. You steal my breath as surely as you have stolen my heart."

"I do hope you like my gown as much as your eyes told me just then."

"Oh aye, love. You will see just how much I like that gown when we are alone." He loved the way her gaze dropped to his mouth. "I would take you away to our chamber now, though I believe my sisters may protest for all the fussing they have done to prepare this feast."

Muren smiled and leaned in close to kiss his cheek. "I have a wee surprise for you later," she said.

"What kind of surprise?"

"The kind that will please you very much, my lord."

Rorie swallowed hard as his loins tightened. The way her voice sounded husky was enough to make him want to clear the hall and straddle her across his lap. He intended to have her in as many different ways as he could think of this evening.

"My lords and ladies, welcome to this wonderful marriage celebration of our chief and his lady." Ewen's voice carried easily over the chatter in the hall. "This day, we shall share food and drink and music, and join in wishing them a long and happy life together, with dozens and dozens of MacKenzies to keep them busy."

Rorie smiled. Ewen had always been gifted with words. He was much easier with people than Rorie ever was. There was no doubt in Rorie's mind that he meant every word. Ewen raised his goblet to Rorie and Muren, and the rest of the hall followed suit.

"And now we feast!"

With that, the kitchen servants entered with trenchers of roasted fowl, rabbit, wild boar, salmon, and deer. This was followed by steaming bowls of broth, mounds of crusty bread, and barrels of ale. This was just the first course. The feasting would go on for three days, and his larder would have taken quite the beating by the end of it, had it not been for the karts of provisions that had arrived the day before.

MacDonald, it seemed, was not as opposed to Rorie's actions against the king as he'd first thought. With the gifts, there had been a simple note stating they should meet before the first snow fall to discuss *common challenges*, as he'd phrased it. Rorie would hear him out, but he would not go alone. Trust was a hard thing to regain once broken, and Rorie would be cautious from here on out.

"Something concerns you?"

Her voice could draw him back from anywhere, he was certain. He smiled at her. "Just thinking about the road ahead and how many more challenges we shall face concerning the king."

"Is there nothing closer that can tempt your thoughts?"

He squeezed her hand again as a trencher was placed before them with the best cuts of all the meat. Rorie tore off a piece and offered it to her. He had never liked seeing his mother being fed by his father and hoped she would not object to taking it with her own fingers. Somehow, he suspected she would prefer it.

Muren took the piece of meat and popped it into her mouth, curling her tongue around the meat just before closing her mouth and chewing. Rorie had to shift in his chair at the seductive manner in which she went about accepting each piece he offered. He prayed he would not have to stand at that moment, for if he did, he would surely give all the ladies present quite the show.

"How long must we stay here?" Muren asked after he ate his fill.

"We should stay until everyone has eaten and the music has begun to die down, but what is the point of being chief if you cannot bend your own rules? Wouldn't you agree?"

"Aye, my lord. I very much agree."

Rorie stood then and curled her hand in the crook of his arm.

~

*M*uren was still grinning at the shocked looked of those present, as Rorie bid them all a fine evening. She noted Agatha's furrowed brow and could not look Lena in the eye as they walked by. She would make it up to them by attending early the following morning and attending all day. For now, all she wanted was to be held in Rorie's arms and loved until she could stand it no more.

Lena and Agatha had given her some advice the night before about a certain act which men supposedly loved. She'd never imagined it before and was quite sceptical, so she prayed Rorie would enjoy it as much as the sisters claimed their husbands did.

Now at their chamber, Muren was a little wary of being so bold…until Rorie picked her up and walked through the chamber door, then kicked it closed behind them. He walked with her to their bed and gently placed her on the coverlet. For a moment, he just stood there staring at her. His gaze flicked across her breasts, making her nipples tighten.

When he did not move, she decided to take matters into her own hands, so to speak. Muren pulled the edge of her gown down to expose more of her breasts as she knelt up on the bed. Sliding one shoulder free, she squeezed her breasts together and loved the way his mouth opened in response.

"Are you trying to drive me mad?" he asked.

"No, my lord, merely showing you what you now own."

Rorie sat on the bed and leaned back against the thick post to watch as Muren undid the ties at her sides and loosened her gown. She let the other shoulder slip free, and the gown slid down her front until it was only held on by her hard nipples.

"Christ, you are the most desirable woman I have ever seen," he said through gritted teeth.

Muren let the gown drop then and slid her hands up his legs until his thick, hard erection was exposed. She had not really examined him before and wondered how she was to do what the sisters had told her.

Flicking his tunic all the way back and fully exposing him, she grasped him in her hand and stroked, all the while leaning forward so he could enjoy the view of her exposed breasts.

"Oh God, Muren, what are you doing to me?" His voice was a hoarse whisper.

She leaned forward and took the tip of him into her mouth and sucked hard. His hips came up off the bed in response, and his deep, guttural groan told her everything she needed to know about how he felt about her attentions.

Deeper and deeper she took him into her mouth until she felt him thicken and harden more than she ever thought possible. When he started to shudder, he lifted her from him and then pulled her gown away.

Rorie lifted her legs so they hung over his shoulders and entered her with one hard thrust. Her body shook in response. The act of licking and sucking him had made her wetter than she had ever been before, so much so that his first thrust brought him to the hilt.

Muren's body pulsed around him as he pounded harder and harder into her. The sound of his skin slapping against hers brought her even higher, and when he stiffened inside her and growled, she climaxed so hard stars formed in her eyes.

Holding onto his forearms, Muren moved her hips to keep the sensations flowing through her body until the last wave subsided.

Rorie slipped out of her and lay by her side, playing with her nipple. "I hope you rested well last night," he said.

Smiling, with her eyes still closed, she replied, "I did not rest well because I did not have my husband sleeping beside me."

"Well then, you will have two sleepless nights under your belt."

"But it is still day time," she said.

"Aye, and you will get no sleep this day either."

Muren rolled over on her side and peeked at him. On his side, he was staring at her breasts again, and she noted his erection growing once more. She could not resist thrusting them forward until he cupped one in his large hand and squeezed.

"You are ready again?" she asked. "So soon?" She shuffled

closer to him, thrilling at the thought of him taking her again so quickly.

"Aye, I think I have always been ready for you," he said and brushed his lips across hers.

"And I you, Rorie. I do love you," she said.

"And I you, Muren. You are the heart that beats in my chest, the life that flows through my veins, and the sole reason for joy in my life."

Tears burned her eyes. How many people could claim to share the bond they had forged? Sure, there were couples who had managed to build a marriage, but how many were truly matched with the other half of their soul? Muren reached for him and kissed him soundly on the lips. "You are my heart, my life, and my joy, Rorie MacKenzie."

He kissed her then, slow and deep, as though no kiss had ever come before and no kiss would come after. No matter what challenges lay ahead, they would have one another to help find a way through it. Two bodies with one heart, beating until the end of time.

ACKNOWLEDGMENTS

As I embark on publishing these under my own title, I reflect and re-acknowledge the people who were important in getting this book off the ground in the first place. Below was written in 2017 and still holds true.

Thank-you to my many beta readers, Tina, Vanessa, Kellie, April, on this book who, as always, steer me in the right direction. Thank you to my crew, Melanie, Vicki, and Libby, who tolerated me during my moment of creative crisis while writing this book.

You'll know the moment when you get to it.

Thank you to my amazing editor, Christine, who helps ensure the continuity of this story and makes it fit to read. Thank you to my publisher, Tirgearr, who is always available to respond to my many questions and needs.

Thank you to my street team who support me no matter what. I love you all and am so grateful for your feedback!

Thank you to my readers. I thoroughly enjoy your emails and messages and hope you enjoy Heart of the Highlander. It's the darkest of the series by far and was difficult to write in places, but the story needed to be told nonetheless.

Mostly, thank you to my amazing sons who put up with a lot from their mudder in order for me to pursue this crazy craft. You are the reason I work hard every day. I love you both with all my heart—all except the bit that's left for Fergus.

ALSO BY KATE ROBBINS

Look for these 2nd editions releasing in the coming weeks.

Bound to the Highlander

Aileana Chattan suffers a devastating loss, then discovers she is to wed neighboring chief and baron, James MacIntosh -- a man she despises and whose loyalty deprived her of the father she loved. Despite him and his traitorous clan, Aileana will do her duty, but she doesn't have to like it or him. But when the MacIntosh awakens something inside her so absolute and consuming, she is forced to question everything.

James MacIntosh is a nobleman torn between tradition and progress. He must make a sacrifice if he is to help Scotland move forward as a unified country. Forced to sign a marriage contract years earlier binding Lady Aileana to him, James must find a way to break it, or risk losing all—including his heart.

From the wild and rugged Highlands near Inverness to the dungeons of Edinburgh Castle, James and Aileana's preconceptions of honor, duty and love are challenged at every adventurous turn.

Promised to the Highlander: Highland Chiefs Book 2

Nessia Stephenson's world was safe until a threat from a neighbouring clan forces her to accept a betrothal to a man whose family can offer her the protection she needs. The real threat lies in her intense attraction to the man who arranged the match—the clan's chief and her intended's brother, Fergus MacKay.

When powerful warlord Fergus MacKay arranges a marriage for his younger brother, William, he has no idea the price will be his own heart. Fergus is captivated by the wildly beautiful Nessia, a woman he can never have.

When the feud between the MacKay and Sutherland clans escalates,

Nessia, William, and Fergus all must make sacrifices for their future. Longing and loss, honour and duty. How can love triumph under such desperate circumstances?

~

Enemy of the Highlander: Highland Chiefs Book 3

Two years ago Freya MacKay walked away from the only man she would ever love, her family's bitter enemy, knowing her clan would never accept their love. A fragile alliance has been forged and now he has returned to warn of a terrible threat. Freya MacKay is torn between the familiar surge of passion he evokes and her promise to wed another man.

Ronan Sutherland has lost everything to a cruel uncle who will lay the entire north Highlands to waste if he is not stopped. There is only one who can help—but seeking alliance with his former enemy, Fergus MacKay, means encountering the woman who left him two years ago, breaking his heart.

A bitter feud keeps their clans at one another's throats and it seems nothing will stop one from destroying the other. Will Ronan ever forgive Freya for leaving him? Can he trust her again? Or will the decades of hatred and deceit between their families prevail?

~

Prisoner of the Highlander: Highland Chiefs Book 4

Annabella Beaufort, cousin to the Queen Consort of Scotland, visits court in Edinburgh upon the queen's urging. She has little interest in this wild and rugged land and is pleasantly surprised to find Linlithgow Palace and King James' court quite refined. An attack on Edinburgh Castle by a savage Highlander results in her capture. This flaxen haired giant is like nothing she's encountered before, but her fear of him quickly turns to lust and she prays he will not also claim her heart.

Son of the great Alexander MacDonald, beloved Lord of the Isles, Angus MacDonald refuses to bend to King James' tyrannical rule.

After his father is imprisoned, he becomes acting chief. Unlike his father and his schemes, Angus will attack and bring this king to his knees. His attempt to release his father is thwarted and instead he abducts the Queen's cousin. His desire for her is intense and immediate, despite her flawed Sassenach ways. But he must keep her at arm's length regardless of the raging passion she evokes in him. She is his pawn—his prisoner—and he must always remember that.

Though they fight on opposite sides of the battle for power over Scotland, Angus and Annabella discover a fire that will not be ignored or denied. Will their loyalties to their families tear them apart? If he sets her free, will she return to him? Or will she in turn imprison his heart for all eternity?

≈

Highlander Bewitched: A Highland Chiefs Novella

Stripped of her title and wealth at a young age, Gwendolyn MacGregor was put into service for the chief of the Chattan Clan. Determined to embrace her new life, she shed her noble expectations and even her religion. As a pagan wise woman, she developed a gift for channelling nature's energy and became a contented free spirit in every way—until she meets Calum MacIntosh.

Brother of the great MacIntosh chief, Calum MacIntosh believes virtue is the most important gift a husband and wife can bring to a marriage. He is prepared to join his name with another noble lady when the time is right, until his path crosses with the enchanting lady's maid, Gwendolyn. Despite his efforts to forget her, he is drawn to her as though an invisible tether connects them.

Caught between longing and duty, Gwen and Calum discover a powerful bond that will not be defined by social expectations or status—and will not be denied.

≈

From Tirgearr Publishing

One Knight in Stirling

Sir William MacPherson is honoured by the queen mother's invitation to protect her from her enemies. The only catch: he must reside at Stirling Castle where he will encounter Coira MacLaren; the one woman who can bring him to his knees and keep him there. Her refusal of his marriage proposal a year ago hit him hard and he has not seen her since. Can he harden himself against her, or will their insatiable lust for one another burn them to cinders this time?

Other books published by Kate Robbins

Christmas Crackers: A Short and Spicy Smalltown Romance

Travelling home to spend Christmas with her parents, Caroline finds herself the victim of a nasty patch of black ice and an ill-placed snowbank. Her saviour is none other than the all-grown-up version of her many teenage fantasies, Kirk Drodge. Meeting him again stirs old feelings she thought were in the distant past. Not so much, apparently. This Christmas, maybe she's not the only one with a surprise in store.

The Serpent: Spirits of the Norse, Book One

Oceans of blood have stained Scotland's shores for a century. Forging peace between the Vikings and Scots seems an impossible task, but Giric MacDomnail is resolute. Giric meets with Gunnar, chieftain of Clan Haraldson on Islay, with a proposal to end the carnage. But there's more at stake than peace when he meets Gunnar's sister.

Saga is a shield-maiden who fights her clan's enemies with abandon —backing down from no one. This Scot, come to play them with his pretty words, deserves an axe in his chest. Instead, his reason and his words penetrate her defences.

Giric and Saga must mend the hatred and prejudice between two fiercely proud cultures. Can love be the binding ingredient for a peaceful future?

∾

The Raven: Spirits of the Norse, Book Two

Tides of change crash hard against those who resist. Magnus Haraldson has to work twice as hard to prove he is as much a Viking as his older brother and chieftain, Gunnar. When the latter gets it in his head to arrange a marriage for Magnus, he refuses. After all, there's too much of the world he's yet to see. A chance journey to Dublin changes his path and his mind.

Elspeth MacAlpin follows her brother to Dublin for adventure, but she is not prepared for the new life that is mapped out for her once she meets the mysterious and unforgettable Magnus.

Apart, they are tethered by an invisible and undeniable bond. Together, their passion burns bright enough to disintegrate everything in its path.

∾

Coming 2023

The Wildcat: Spirits of the Norse, Book Three

Only survivors can speak of the storm. Gunnar Haraldson is chieftain of his clan and proud of his lands on Islay. Sustaining a peaceful existence on an island off the coast of mainland Alba is not easy considering his ancestry is Norse. Like his fathers before him, he will do everything in his power to preserve the Viking way. Those are his thoughts every morning—and then reality finds a way to intervene. Most notably in the name of the village healer, Freydis.

Freydis has understood her place between the worlds of the gods and men her whole life. She can see into their hearts and the future, but she cannot see why Odin placed her on the same path as the most infuriating man ever spawned from Loki. So why does she not take up permanent residence on the mainland where she could live out a happy life free from the man her heart won't release?

Gunnar and Freydis will have to look past more than their stubborn nature to combat the uncertain times ahead. What must they sacrifice to secure their future?

ABOUT THE AUTHOR

Amazon internationally bestselling author of the award-winning Highland Chiefs series, Kate Robbins writes historical romance out of pure escapism and a love for all things Scottish. She thoroughly enjoys the research process and delving into secondary sources in order to blend authentic historical fact into her stories.

Ranging a thousand years, Kate's novels are filled with passion, adventure, and political intrigue.

Kate is the pen name of Debbie Robbins who lives in St. John's, Newfoundland and Labrador, Canada.

Stay up to date with new release information by joining my Facebook Group, Into the Highland Mist with Kate Robbins.

www.ingramcontent.com/pod-product-compliance
Lightning Source LLC
Chambersburg PA
CBHW020316200626
46814CB00006BA/2269